HIGHLAND QUEEN

THE CELTIC BLOOD SERIES, BOOK 4

MELANIE KARSAK

CLOCKPUNK PRESS

Highland Queen

The Celtic Blood Series, Book 4

Published by Clockpunk Press
Cover art by Damonza
Editing by Becky Stephens Editing
Editing by Contagious Edits
Proofreading by Siren Editing

❀ Created with Vellum

In loving memory of Suzanne Stewart

CHAPTER ONE

I shuddered. All at once, my conscious mind rushed back. My heartbeat was wild, my breath heavy, and my hands trembled. Knees weak, I pitched sideways, only catching myself the moment before I tumbled to the ground. Blood ran down my arms, dripping from my fingers.

I looked down at the corpse at my feet. The empty shell that had been Duncan lay with his mouth open wide. His eyes bulged as he stared into the night's sky.

Slowly, I became conscious of the splatters of blood all over me. I smelled death. Lifting my hands, I stared at them. They were deep ruby red, covered in chunks of pulp, shredded armor, and blood.

I gazed at Duncan once more.

It was over.

It was done.

The dark presence which had guided my steps receded. My rage settled. Once again, the world around me came into focus. I could smell the mud and the mist. Bodies littered the ground. In the distance, I heard the sounds of men.

"Banquo," I whispered, peering into the fog.

Pausing to grab Gillacoemgain's helmet, I retraced my steps toward the field, following the sounds of the dying battle. Ahead of me, I spotted a small band of men standing perfectly still. When I neared them, they turned and looked at me.

It was the Moray men I had woken from their eternal slumber. Their eyes had taken on the white glaze of death, and they held their broken bodies at weird angles. They turned to face me as if awaiting further instructions.

Andraste, what wizardry have you taught me?

"Thank you, my brothers," I told the men. "Thank you. The deed is done."

I raised a blood-covered finger, pointed it upward, drawing magic from the air.

Blue light crackled around my blood-soaked digit.

"Sleep," I told them, leveling my finger on them. In the air, I made the arcane rune that Andraste had taught me. "Sleep," I said again, releasing the magic back into the ground.

The men tumbled down like rag dolls.

"Cerridwen? Cerridwen!" Banquo called from a distance. "Cerridwen, where are you?"

A moment later, Thora appeared, her nose to the ground. When she spotted me, she turned and barked. Jogging through the mist, Banquo raced to join her. When he saw me, he stopped and stared.

"Cerridwen," he whispered. "Are you... Are you hurt?"

No, not anymore.

"No," I replied.

"It's just... It's so much blood."

I shrugged. "Who knew the young man would have so much blood in him."

Banquo's brow furrowed. He looked toward the field behind me. "Duncan?"

I nodded.

"We need to get you off the battlefield. The day is done, and we are victorious. But no one must see you."

I nodded then pulled on Gillacoemgain's helmet once more.

"Where is Kelpie?" Banquo asked.

I shook my head. "I don't know. Alive, I hope."

Banquo nodded then turned to Thora. "Thora, we need horses. Quickly."

Thora sniffed the wind then turned and raced across the field. Banquo and I followed quickly behind her.

So many bodies littered the field. Men from the south. Men from the north. They lay atop one another. So many lives lost.

There was glory in battle, but so much loss. Too much. For what? So one king could topple another? So one disgusting madman could rule in another's place? No. No more. I would put an end to it.

Thora soon found a small herd of horses prancing nervously near the forest. Two of them bolted when we drew near. Sheathing his sword, Banquo lifted his hands and began whispering in a low tone. My eyes, still lit up with the raven's magic, saw green light glimmer all around Banquo. A moment later, the horses calmed. Moving slowly, Banquo grabbed the reins of two of the mounts. The horses came along behind him.

He handed one of the leads to me then took the other horse. Both of us mounted.

Fog still covered the battlefield. It was hard to even see where we were.

"Thora, you must lead us until the mist clears," I told her.

She turned, put her nose to the ground, then began running.

"Handy to have a magical dog," Banquo said, giving me a slight smile.

We rode into the night. As we did so, we spied men in the shadows, retreating through the woods. We let them pass and rode on.

As we rode, my mind cleared.

I would need to send dispatches. Macbeth and Thorfinn... What had happened on their fronts?

Macbeth and I would need to move south to settle the matter of the crown before England got ideas. And we would need to deal with the southern lords. Thorfinn and Magnus had their own issues in the north. And then there was Duncan's legacy—his wife, his sons. Something must be done, and quickly.

Luckily for me, the horse under me was as sure-footed as Kelpie. The young stallion, blood bay in color with a black mane and tail, raced behind Thora as we made our way back to Cawdor.

*T*he sun had started to rise, the fog clearing when the spires of the castle finally came into view. The grounds around the castle were encamped.

"Lord Banquo! Lord Banquo," the men called in excited cheer when Banquo passed by.

I kept my head low and rode on.

The castle gates were open, and many of the Moray chieftains were inside waiting.

"Lord Banquo," they called when they saw him.

Banquo and I rode to a stop.

"I'll go inside," I told Banquo. "I'll return as soon as I can."

I turned to dismount only to find Standish there, his hand outstretched to help me down. Our eyes met through the visor. He knew.

"I'd know that helmet anywhere," he whispered. "Are you unharmed?"

"I'm all right."

"I almost turned the castle inside out looking for you. But then I saw..."

"Saw what?"

Standish shifted nervously then eyed the ramparts. "The Red Lady," he said in a whisper. "I told the maids not to worry, but you best go inside and let them tend to you before anyone else realizes."

"Thank you, Standish."

"And if I ever see you try to sneak off like that again, my lady, I'll tan your hide—Red Lady or no. My poor heart can't take it."

I smiled softly. "I'm sorry," I said, and I honestly was. I had hoped he wouldn't realize I was gone.

He nodded then turned to the blood bay. "Where is Kelpie?"

I shook my head and forced back my tears. "I don't know. Let's pray he finds his way home."

Standish sighed. "He's a strong horse and a smart one. He'll find his way. In the meantime, I'll take this young man off your hands. What a bloody brute he is," he said, glancing at the bay whose coat sparkled red in the morning sunlight.

I patted the horse on the nose, nodded to Standish, then headed into the castle.

Trying to go unseen, I moved quickly through the crowd and headed to my chambers. Inside, I heard Tira and Rhona arguing.

When I opened the door, both women stopped.

Tira scowled. "Get away, you. Lady Gruoch is not within, and you have no business here."

Rhona's eyes widened. "Tira. Look. The sword," she said, pointing to Uald's Gift. She grabbed my arm and pulled me inside, shutting and bolting the door behind me.

I slipped off Gillacoemgain's helmet.

"My lady!" Tira exclaimed. "Oh, by the Great Mother, look at you. Are you hurt?"

"No, but I need to get cleaned up. There is much to do."

Rhona shook her head. I couldn't help but notice her cheeks

had turned red. "Part of me wants to slap you, my lady. I'm doing my best to hold myself back."

"I wouldn't risk it," Tira warned her companion. "From the looks of our lady, she just murdered the entire southern army on her own."

"Not the whole army, just the king."

Tira tittered nervously, but Rhona met my eyes.

I inclined my head to her.

She returned the gesture.

Tira blew air through her lips, tossed her hands in the air, then turned and pulled out the washbasin. "No sense arguing about it. It's done now. We need to get her cleaned up before anyone else realizes our lady is mad enough to ride out onto the battlefield like she's Boudicca."

"Ah, but there you're wrong," I told her.

"Wrong?"

"Boudicca did not survive. I have won the day."

CHAPTER TWO

*T*ira and Rhona helped me bathe, washing the blood and bits off. Neither said a word, but I knew what they were thinking. I was sorry that they had to see this. I couldn't imagine any other lady's maids suffering through as much as they did.

"All those inches," Rhona said as she rinsed the last of the soap out of my hair, fingering my chin-length locks.

"They'll grow back," I said absently. My eyes closed, I relished the feel of the warm water. Every part of me hurt. The muscles in my arms and legs felt like they were made of stone. And my head felt dizzy. Nausea, from the heat of the water or the exhaustion—I wasn't sure which—crept over me.

"Not in time for the crowning. What will Lady Madelaine say? And look at you, covered in bruises. You'll need a long-sleeved gown. And there's no hiding the bruise on your cheek," Rhona chided.

"It doesn't matter."

Rhona clicked her tongue, a sound I'd heard her make a thousand times at Fleance and Lulach, but said nothing.

There was a soft knock on the door. Tira went to answer. She spoke in low tones, and a moment later, Morag entered.

"Well, here is the shield-maiden returned from the battle," she said then sat down on my bed.

"Have you come to scold me too?" I asked.

"No, I'm just jealous. I had half a mind to slip out myself."

I chuckled.

"Don't encourage her," Rhona said.

"Oh, that one doesn't need encouragement," Morag said with a laugh.

Tira huffed heavily. "Let me lay out a dress."

Rhona handed me a towel and helped me out of the basin. I sat down on a stool in front of the fire while Rhona set about tossing out the wash water. The girls had done their best to clean me up, but when I looked at my hands, I was surprised to see there were still spots of blood on them. I picked up a washing cloth and began to work at the stains. They wouldn't budge. I poured a bit of oil on the fabric and rubbed more. The effort turned the back of my hands red, but still, the splattered spots of blood remained.

"Rhona, do we have any stronger soap?" I asked.

She looked back at me. "My lady?"

"These spots of blood won't come out," I said, working the rag on my hands.

"My lady, you're rubbing yourself raw. Here, let me have a look," Tira said. She laid the dress she was holding on my bed then crossed the room and took my hands. She turned them over, took my washing cloth, then worked on my fingernails a bit. "There, that's better," she said then handed the cloth back to me.

"But...but here," I said, motioning to the splatters of blood I saw on the back and palms of my hands. "And here."

Tira looked at my hands. "Just shadows from the fire, my lady. There's nothing there. Stop scrubbing. You're making your skin red."

My brow furrowed, I looked at my hands. The spots were plain as day. I turned to call Tira back, but my eyes met Morag's.

She shook her head.

Frowning, I looked back at my hands once more. Scarlet marred my palms, fingers, and the backs of my hands. This was no trick of the light. I rose and went to the window, catching the sunlight on my hands. They were there. Everywhere.

"Don't you see?" I asked, showing my hands to Rhona.

Rhona glanced briefly at me. "No, my lady. There is nothing there."

"You're just tired, my lady. No doubt your eyes are swimming. Come along now and get dressed. I am sure there are a hundred dispatches and just as many men waiting on you below," Tira said.

I turned to Morag.

"It will pass," she told me.

It will pass. The girls were right. I was tired, and my eyes were playing tricks on me.

I crossed the room and let Tira redress me. She'd pulled a dark blue gown from the wardrobe. It was a pretty velvet dress with silver trim on the collar. I put my torcs and amulet back on. Lifting my belt, I re-sheathed Scáthach then lifted the dagger with the raven on the hilt, the dagger I had taken from Duncan, my father's blade. I turned it over in my hand, remembering Uald describing it. But I remembered more. I remembered it on my father's belt. The memory had been lost, but with the blade in my possession, it returned once more. I remembered hugging my father when I was just a girl. The beak of the raven had scraped my cheek.

"Now, Macha," my father had said, scolding the dagger. "Be kind to my daughter."

"Macha?" I'd asked.

My father had nodded. "The raven goddess. I keep her here at my side," he'd said with a wide grin.

I clutched the dagger. How strange it was that some memories lay buried, unleashed by the smallest things. My father had carried a raven with him. The irony wasn't lost on me. I went to my trunk and found a spare sheath for the blade. It wasn't a perfect fit, but it would have to do for now. When I returned to the coven, I would ask Uald to make me another. I added the blade to my belt alongside Scáthach.

"Thank you. I'll go down now."

"My lady," Morag said, rising slowly. "Lulach and Fleance…"

She let the question hang unasked in the air.

"They are safe, but hidden, and will remain so until things are quiet."

"Let's hope that day comes."

She was right about that. I inclined my head to her. "Then I had best get to work to see that it does."

I slipped down the steps and headed to my council chamber. The place was packed with people. Banquo was at the head of the table talking to some of the other Thanes. Both the younger and elder Ross were in attendance.

"Lady Gruoch," someone called when I entered.

The men cheered, banging their ale horns and weapons.

I nodded to them. "Gentlemen, my greetings and congratulations on this victory."

The men cheered.

As I crossed the room, I heard whispers in the crowd.

"Look at the Lady Gruoch's hair," someone said.

"A battle sacrifice?"

"No. There is talk amongst the men. They say she was on the field."

"No. It cannot be."

"No? Look at her face. The bruise."

"Some say they saw Gillacoemgain's ghost amongst the men."

"Strange omens."

Ignoring the talk, I went to Banquo who handed me the first of many scrolls in his hand.

Shaking my head, I took Banquo aside. "Malcolm and Donaldbane. What did Macbeth arrange?"

"As far as I know, nothing."

"Then he's let two adders free who can return to strike us."

Banquo nodded.

"Malcolm was with his father at court. Perhaps he retreated with Suthen. We need to find out for certain. Many will try to use those boys, to set them against Macbeth and me. I will see them safely fostered in friendly hands," I said.

"Away from Earl Siward."

I nodded. "They are as much my kin as his. I must have them fostered by those who would not teach them to seek vengeance now...or later." Unless I acted now, it would be Lulach who would have to deal with his unruly cousins backed by a Northumbrian army. I needed to do what I could to stop the bad blood from boiling.

Banquo inclined his head to me. "I will send spies south to track Malcolm down. There was a rumor that the younger son, Donaldbane, had been sent to Iona."

I frowned. "Macbeth didn't send anyone to retrieve him?"

Banquo shook his head. "No. I will see to it. We were so worried about Lulach and Fleance..."

I nodded. He was right. We should have thought of it before. "We'll do what we can now. Thank you."

Banquo nodded then handed the same scroll toward me once more. "Macbeth is victorious."

I took the parchment and read over the dispatch. Macbeth had played his part. Very well.

"And Thorfinn?"

"He and Magnus have also had their victory."

"Thank the Great Mother," I said with an exhausted sigh then sat down.

"Are you all right?" Banquo asked.

"Yes...just weary."

Banquo chuckled. "That is battle weariness. When you can, you will sleep for days. But for now..." he said then motioned to the stack of scrolls waiting.

"Thane," someone called, waving to Banquo.

Another messenger had arrived.

Banquo motioned to the man to stay a moment.

"Go on," I said tiredly. "You have much work to do. I'll be here."

"Rest, if you can, Gruoch," Banquo said, his eyes lingering on mine. I could see there was more he wanted to say, wanted to do, but he could not with everyone's eyes on us. Already everyone thought we were lovers. But in the presence of all our people, it didn't do to show our feelings openly.

Banquo set his hand gently on my shoulder then turned to see to the messenger.

I lifted the first of the scrolls and began going through the reports. By all accounts, Earl Siward had survived. He'd left Duncan in the field and retreated with a large portion of his army. We had spies on him. In the future, I would have to pay for more eyes and ears at his court and would have to protect my own from such infiltration. But for now, Macbeth and I needed to move toward Scone. Only once we had the kingdom safely in our palms with crowns on our heads could we begin to think about what would happen next.

I spent the next several hours going through reports and receiving messengers. We'd had our own losses, but they were not as great as we feared. Still, it was too many men. Too much of a price to pay.

I was staring at yet another scroll, my eyes going misty from exhaustion, when someone called my name.

"Lady Gruoch?"

I looked up to find Standish there.

"Standish? What is it?" I could see from the expression on his face that everything was not well.

"Can you come with me a moment?"

I rose. Every muscle in my body protested, and my head swam. No matter the work, I needed to sleep soon.

I crossed the hall to join Standish. "What's happened?"

He motioned for me to follow him. We made our way out of the castle and back across the yard—which was still bustling with people—toward the stables.

"Thora, your bonnie lass, disappeared out the gate and into the fields right after you returned. She just came back…leading that one," Standish said, pointing.

I followed his gaze to see a groom guiding Kelpie, who was limping badly, to the water trough.

"Kelpie," I called, rushing to him.

At the sound of his name, the old stallion turned and nickered at me.

I rushed to him. But even from a distance, I could see the terrible wound on his leg.

"He's taken a bad injury, my lady. Looks like something caught his leg. A sword, maybe. I'm going to clean and dress his wound now. He… There is a lot of damage, my lady."

I stroked Kelpie's ear. "I'm going to have a look now," I told him.

Kelpie had lifted his hoof, holding his leg up. There was damage to the ligament. He would recover from the injury, that was evident, but he could never be ridden again.

The groom caught my eye. The expression on his face told me he'd already come to the same assessment.

"Treat it as best you can. We must keep the wound clean, let it heal as best it will. Do you need medicines?"

"No, my lady, we are well stocked to deal with such wounds. But some say that when a horse's leg is too badly—"

I raised my hand to stop him. "No. He will be lame, I understand. I'll not reward him for a lifetime of service and friendship in that manner. Oats and pasture. That will be his future."

The groom breathed a sigh of relief. "I hoped you'd say as much."

I pressed my head against Kelpie's neck, wrapping my arms around him. "I'm sorry, old friend."

Kelpie neighed softly at me.

I patted Kelpie once more then turned to look at Thora who was sitting nearby. I bent to take her face into my hands, ruffling her ears. "My good girl. What would I ever do without you? Why don't you head to the kitchen and see what scraps you can win. You've earned them."

Thora thumped her tail, licked my face, then turned and trotted off to the kitchens.

Willful, magical, and wonderful dog.

"Rest and heal, old friend," I told Kelpie. I patted his neck once more then nodded to the groom who took Kelpie by the lead and coaxed him toward the stable.

Watching them go, I sighed. I then turned my attention to the yard. A tent had been erected along the east wall. There, the wounded men were receiving care for their injuries. Even from this distance, I could hear their groans.

We had won, but it had come at a cost.

Now, we had to make good on everyone's sacrifice.

Rather than heading back inside, I climbed the rampart and looked out over the army encamped there. Dusk had come once more. As far as I looked, I saw the light of campfires. Like fireflies in a summer field, the soldiers' fires illuminated the landscape.

I closed my eyes.

Everything the Morrigu predicted had come to pass.

Duncan was dead.

Macbeth would become king.

I would be queen alongside him.

I should have felt happy, excited.

Instead, I felt terrible loathing and dread.

Maybe I had won the day, but I didn't really want it. I didn't really want to be queen. I wanted Duncan to die, to pay for what he did. The rest? No. Once upon a time, I'd dreamt of a life that was of my own imagining, a life not willed by the gods, or memories of past lives, or led by anyone or anything but myself. I'd dreamt of a peaceful life at Cawdor. A life with my children and a man who loved me.

A soft hand settled on my shoulder.

In that moment, I felt frustrated with Banquo for breaking apart my memory.

I opened my eyes to see the shade of Gillacoemgain standing there. He was looking down at me, a soft, sad smile on his face. He reached out and touched the bruise on my cheek.

The caress felt so real.

I lifted my hand to lay it on his.

When I did so, the expression on Gillacoemgain's face changed. A look of terror crossed his features.

I followed his gaze to my hand, which was dripping with blood.

Suppressing a scream, I pitched sideways, black dots appearing before my eyes.

"Lady Gruoch," one of the watchmen called.

I reached out to grab the stones before I tumbled.

A moment later, strong hands steadied me.

"Get Standish. Lady Gruoch is unwell."

"No," I said, regaining my footing. "No. I'm all right. Just tired," I said, righting myself.

My heart pounded in my chest. With terror racing through me, I looked at my hands. The blood stains were still there, but the wet, dripping blood was gone. I scanned around, looking for Gillacoemgain's shade, but he was gone.

"My lady, you should go back inside," the guard told me. "Please, allow someone to accompany you."

"I'm all right now. Thank you. You have your work here. I'm sorry to give you a fright."

"Please, my lady, think nothing of it. You must have a care for yourself and take rest," he said then lowered his voice to a whisper and added, "All warriors must rest after battle."

So, the rumor the other men had spoken was a common one.

I gave the man a soft smile but said nothing. I took a deep breath, righted myself, then headed back into the castle. As I walked, I tried to shake off the image of Gillacoemgain's expression. But no matter what, it wouldn't leave me, and his terror from beyond the grave shook me to the core.

CHAPTER THREE

*I*n the hours that followed, news came in from all around the country. The north was solidly aligned behind Macbeth and me. The south, however, was another matter. While not all the southern lords had followed Duncan into battle willingly—as was the case with Fife—enough of them had done so that it presented problems. Macbeth and I needed to move quickly. With everything so unsettled, it was a relief when news arrived that Macbeth was at Inverness. He sent a rider, requesting Banquo and me to join him there.

I read the scroll then handed the dispatch to Banquo.

Banquo frowned. "Now things become complicated."

"One bastard cousin dead. Now I'll place a crown on the head of the second."

Banquo eyed me but said nothing. He never asked why I had sought out Duncan that night. Part of me suspected that Banquo had some feeling, some intuition on the matter. But he hadn't probed that tender wound. One day, I would tell him the truth.

"I should go," Banquo said. "Thorfinn and Magnus are there."

I nodded. As one of Macbeth's chief generals, Banquo's presence was necessary.

Was mine?

"I will not come. When it's time to go south, I will go. But not yet."

Banquo folded his arms across his chest, nodded, but remained silent.

What was there to say?

Macbeth could be as angry or disturbed as he pleased, but he would also understand the wall I had built between him and me. After all, he had laid its foundation. What more was there to do? I felt nothing for him but contempt.

"My lady," a page called, entering the conference room. "A rider with a message from Echmarcach of the Isles."

I took the scroll and read over the dispatch. I felt the blood drain from my face as I considered what I found there.

"What is it?" Banquo asked.

"Donaldbane. He has been abducted by Ímar mac Arailt. The Irish king's troops besieged the monastery on Iona and took him hostage."

Banquo frowned. "Bold but wise move."

I shook my head. "Echmarcach promises to do what it takes to secure the boy, provided we support him in his moves to retake Dublin."

"Too soon. The blood in Scotland has not yet cooled," Banquo said.

"I will write to Ímar mac Arailt. Perhaps, for once, my Ui Neill blood will make some difference," I said then went to grab a piece of parchment.

"Ui Neill?" Banquo asked, staring at me.

"Yes. My mother's line. The blood of two great dynasties runs in my veins. Remind me again why Macbeth will be crowned monarch?" I said, a waspish feeling washing over my heart. I lifted a piece of parchment from the box only to pause. Once more, I was taken aback by the appearance of the red spots on my hands. This time, the blood looked as fresh as the night Duncan had died.

I closed my eyes.

It wasn't really there. I was just overtired.

I inhaled deeply then let out a slow breath.

"I never knew," Banquo said, bringing me back to myself.

"My mother died young, one of many daughters, and was easily forgotten. But who knows if it will mean anything to the Irish king. Let's hope it is enough to get him to talk."

I willed myself not to pay attention to my hands.

Banquo sighed, went across the room, and poured himself an ale. He returned to sit beside me, staring in quiet contemplation at the fire.

I drafted the letter for the Irish king then set it aside. Though I had carefully chosen my words, I would need to consider the matter from all points. Turning to Banquo, I found his eyes had taken on a dreamy, faraway look.

He was lost to a vision.

Turning, I stared into the flames, hoping to make out what he saw there.

I saw only fire.

The hearth popped, the flames danced, but no visions came to me.

A few moments later, Banquo shook his head then lifted his tankard.

"Banquo?" I whispered.

"All is well," he said, taking my hand. "All is well. Our boys... They are safe and happy."

"Then it is best they remain where they are, for now."

"When it is quiet, I will properly cast to Balor."

"When it is quiet."

Banquo frowned. "I have no wish to see you ride off to Scone."

"Nor do I have any wish to go. I will not stay there long."

"You do not mean to rule?"

"I do. But not from Scone. Let Macbeth go south and play politician."

Banquo frowned. "Without you there, his position is weakened. He is vulnerable. All we have worked for is put at risk."

"My place is in Moray."

"Your place *was* in Moray. Now, you are Queen of Scotland."

"Not yet."

"Soon. And if Scotland is to be ruled well, she needs you."

"But what about you? About us?"

Banquo looked back toward the fire. "I am a druid," he said stoically. "I serve the land and the gods before myself. Just like you."

I stared at him. All along, I had intended to help Macbeth to his victory but had no intention of staying by his side. Not now. Never again. But Banquo was right. If Macbeth was unsteady, I could not leave him alone. He would inevitably fall victim to deceit, come unglued and act against the good of the country, or be murdered. If Macbeth died, I had the right to rule without him. I could be queen alone, Lulach my royal heir. But if Macbeth was murdered, his enemies would come for Lulach and me next.

"Are we never meant to have a moment?" I whispered.

"Yes," Banquo said quietly. "But just moments. We are the tools of the gods," Banquo said then slugged back his ale. "And this tool must get ready to ride to Inverness."

"When?"

"I should go tonight."

"Should. Would it matter much if it waits until morning?" I asked, taking his hand into mine.

Banquo turned and looked at me. He smiled, his chestnut-colored eyes shimmering softly. "No."

"Then go in the morning," I whispered.

He nodded. "I'll go in the morning."

I placed the draft of my letter in a chest and locked it. Banquo and I exited the hall, leaving my armed guards at the door, then went to my chamber where we spent the night relishing just one more moment.

CHAPTER FOUR

*T*he next morning, Banquo rode to Inverness, and I made plans to go to Scone. I was busy with my preparations when Tavis appeared.

"Corbie," he said, smiling nicely at me, but I could see he'd come with something on his mind.

"Good morning," I said with a smile. "Now, tell me your news."

He chuckled. "I'm anxious to return south, but I didn't want to leave you alone here. And Lulach…"

"Lulach is safe."

Tavis nodded. "You'll say no more as to where he is? Not even to me?"

"I'll say… Uald would approve of Lulach's whereabouts."

"Ahh," Tavis mused. "Very well. But what about you, my little raven?"

I grinned at Tavis. "These days, I am hardly anyone's little anything."

Tavis grinned at me, and in that smile, I saw a proud, fatherly expression on his face. "You will always be Madelaine's little raven…which makes you mine as well."

Rising, I left my work and took Tavis's hand. "I'm sorry to see you go."

Tavis nodded then took me gently by the shoulders and kissed my forehead. "You will be an excellent queen, little raven."

Would I? I hoped so. Since the battle, I'd had no visions, no omens. The Otherworld had gone strangely quiet.

"If it pleases the gods."

Tavis nodded. "It does. Don't you see? I should go make ready."

"Stay safe," I told him. "There may still be mercenaries in the hills."

"I will. The hornet nest is stirred up, Little Corbie. You, too, must be watchful."

"Always."

Tavis smiled at me then let me go.

Sighing, I sat back down and got to work. All things promised had come to pass. Now, I just had to ride the wave forward toward my destiny.

*L*ater that day, a rider came from Inverness with word from Macbeth. We would ride south the next morning—him and me—and our army. He instructed me to be ready and to bring Lulach.

I stared at the letter.

No.

I would not bring Lulach. I would keep my boy away, keep him safe until it was all settled. That included keeping him away from Macbeth. If he was as unsteady as Banquo had said, then it would be a very long time before Macbeth would see my boy again. At this point, Lulach had already forgotten Macbeth. Growing up at Cawdor, he knew Gillacoemgain's shade, knew

Gillacoemgain as his father. Macbeth had never taken root in Lulach's heart. And I was glad.

Drafting a quick note, I headed out to the yard to deliver it to the rider. There was nothing to say. I would hear no apologies, no pretty words. I neither wanted nor expected any. I wrote only, *"Come. I am ready."*

I sent the rider away and stood in the middle of the yard taking in the sights and sounds of Cawdor.

Overhead, a falcon called.

I looked up, the sunlight making me wince. There, high in the sky over the castle, Gillacoemgain's bird flew. I caught the sound of Standish's voice. He was on the other side of the yard talking with the grooms. I went to meet him.

"My lady—no, my queen," he said with a smile.

"Not yet," I said with a grin. "But I will ride south tomorrow. When I'm gone, I want the castle closed and garrisoned."

"Is there anything to be worried about, my lady? Any news?"

"No. No threats this far north. But I will keep Moray protected like a precious gem. When I am gone, you will watch it with your sword drawn. I don't know how long I will stay south. Only as long as I must. I would also ask that you assemble a personal guard for me. A dozen trusted men. Can you do so?"

"Of course, my lady."

"Thank you, Standish. And if you have any worries, please send someone to me right away. Do not hesitate."

"Of course, Lady Gruoch. We'll keep the castle warm and ready for you and Lord Lulach's return."

"Thank you, Standish. I don't know what I'd do without you."

"Lady Gruoch," he said, smiling softly. "You're dear to all of us here."

"As you are to me."

"Ah, speaking of dear ones, your grumpy old stallion was out for a bit of exercise this morning. Limping but healing."

"I'll see to him. The blood bay I rode in on. Is he still here?"

"He is, my lady. Fine horse, that one."

"That he is and sure of foot. I'll ride him south. Can you see to it?"

"Very well."

I headed through the stables to the field where Kelpie lingered not far away from the stable door. He'd lifted his leg, resting it. His ears drooped as he watched the other horses. My heart broke for him. "Are you pouting?" I called to him.

He nickered at me, but he didn't budge.

The battle had taken a lot out of all of us. Even Thora had slept most of the time since we'd returned. I joined Kelpie, patting him on his nose, then bent to look at his leg. The wound was still covered, and I saw no signs of blood.

Sighing, I stroked Kelpie's ear. "It is a bad wound, but you will recover. It's time to rest, old friend. I'll go south, and you will stay here and ogle the pretty mares."

He nickered again then nosed my chin.

"Dear one," I said, setting my cheek on his neck. "I'll see you again soon."

Feeling deep sorrow in my heart, I headed back inside. I needed to get Tira and Rhona ready. Soon we would be on the road to Scone where I would be crowned queen, a prospect, which, despite everything that had led up to it, didn't matter to me at all.

CHAPTER FIVE

$\mathcal{I}$ stood in the window of my chamber and watched as a massive army rode toward Cawdor. At the front of it, I spotted Banquo and Macbeth. A cool breeze swept across the field, ruffling my shoulder-length hair. I closed my eyes and attempted to breathe in Cawdor, breathe in the smell of the stones, mortar, wood, and the lingering scent of Gillacoemgain I imagined in every corner. When I closed my eyes and dreamed, I smelled lavender and fresh mint, tasted strawberries and felt sunlight.

But that was just a dream.

The reality was far sparser.

"So, now it begins," Morag, who was standing beside me, said stoically.

"Are you sure you won't ride to Scone with us?"

"No. I will wait here. The boys… They will be back?"

"Yes. Eventually."

"Very well. I will wait here, if I may. Or I could return to Lochaber if you prefer."

"Cawdor is your home now too," I said. In the years that had passed since Merna's death, Morag had become a permanent fixture in my household. But time had advanced upon her. While she had watched over Lulach and Fleance like they were her own blood, her croning days were upon her.

"Thank you, Lady Gruoch. In truth, I'm too old to ride around the country like some wild thing, and the wine in Cawdor is better than in Lochaber."

I chuckled. "You're welcome to it."

Morag laughed. "Now, let's get this on you," she said then turned to the trunk at the foot of my bed. I had dressed carefully, selecting a dark blue riding gown and trousers. I looked the part of a queen in that respect, but with things still so unsettled in Scotland, there was no telling what assassins might line the roads. It didn't pay to be over-bold. I'd cleaned Gillacoemgain's chainmail and would put it to use once more. Morag lifted the chainmail shirt. I stooped while she lowered it over my head. Once it was on, I adjusted my belt, so my father's dagger and my sword were close at hand. I had hidden Gillacoemgain's dagger safely in my boot.

Morag helped me lace the ties on my cloak.

"The helmet is on the bed," Morag told me.

"Very good," I said then went to grab it. When I did so, I was taken aback once more by the scarlet-colored stains on my hands. Stains that no one but me seemed to see.

"Morag, did you set out gloves?"

"No, my lady, but there is a pair here," she said, pulling a pair of kidskin gloves from the trunk. She handed them to me.

I pulled them on, trying to ignore the spots on my hands.

"I'll go downstairs and make sure Tira and Rhona are ready," Morag said.

"Thank you, Morag."

She nodded then headed out.

I went back to the window. I eyed Macbeth at the front of the army.

Just because I was riding south with Macbeth didn't mean I had to tolerate a single word from him. He was nothing to me. No one. I would rule this land and rule it well, with or without him.

Out of the corner of my eye, I saw a shadow beside me.

I cast a sidelong glance to see the shape of Gillacoemgain there.

"Now I will go to Scone. I will become queen. But if I'd had a choice, I'd rather have stayed here all my life, content to be your lady and your wife," I whispered.

While I loved Banquo, my words were true. I missed Gillacoemgain desperately. That beautiful dream Gillacoemgain and I had shared was rare, precious, and fragile... And it had been, in the end, just a dream.

I turned my head to look at him, catching only a glimpse of him before he disappeared back into the aether once more. But at that moment, I caught the soft, regretful look on his face.

One day I would be with him again.

One day.

But not today.

Adjusting my belt, I headed downstairs. Everywhere I looked, people were making ready. I passed through the hall, spotting Thora dozing sleepily by the fire. I went to her, bending to pet her.

"Lazy girl. What, you don't want to become Queen of Scotland's dog?"

Thora lifted her head and thumped her tail. Thora had never been one to miss an adventure, but the war had taken some of the spirit out of her. Both she and Kelpie had returned broken. It wasn't like Thora to let me go without a disagreement. But this time, she didn't seem interested. In a way, I didn't blame her. I wasn't excited to go either.

I patted her gently. "Be good. Keep an eye on my castle."

Thora licked my hand then lay her head back down, closing

her eyes to sleep once more. A nervous apprehension flickered in my stomach. What would I ever do without her?

"My lady," Tira called from the door. "We have everything ready."

Rising, I crossed the room and met Tira.

"Rhona is waiting outside with the Moray men. Standish has the horses ready."

We exited the castle and crossed the courtyard. As we went, I pulled on Gillacoemgain's helmet. In the courtyard, Standish waited with the blood bay stallion.

"My lady," he said, helping me up.

"Thank you, Standish."

"Lady Gruoch, this is Killian," he said, motioning to a dark-haired man I had seen often about the castle. Killian had a serious, hawkish expression. I remembered him from amongst Gillacoemgain's men. He was the second son of one of the clan leaders. "He has agreed to go south with you. He will organize your guard."

I nodded to the man. "Killian. My many thanks to you and the others," I said, motioning to the men assembled there, faces I knew.

"You are safe with us, Lady Gruoch," Killian assured me.

"Safe travels, *Queen* Gruoch. Don't worry about Cawdor. She will be held as you requested," Standish told me.

"I've no worries," I said, smiling gently at him. Gathering up my reins, I nodded to the others then we rode out.

The bay trotted gingerly across the field. I could feel the energy coursing through his veins. It took all the restraint he could muster not to sprint.

"Don't worry," I told the horse. "You'll get your chance."

The stallion turned his ears back to listen to me.

"Wild thing. Swift as an arrow, aren't you?"

The horse neighed softly in reply.

My stomach turned as I approached Macbeth.

The years had done little to change him. His skin was still as pale as milk, his dark hair flecked with just a bit of silver at the temples. He was looking everywhere but at me.

I rode to him, stopping in front of him.

"How now, Macbeth?"

Finally, finally, he turned and looked at me. I saw his light-colored eyes take in my armor. The muscles around his mouth twitched. He inhaled deeply, slowly blowing out his breath.

"Where is Lulach?" he asked.

"Not here."

"Not here? Then, where?"

"Not here, and not coming. Shall we?" I said, motioning to the field.

"But Lulach must come. He *must* ride south with us."

I turned the blood bay and moved my horse alongside Macbeth. The bay snorted and stepped high, making the steed Macbeth rode shy sideways. Macbeth tightened his reins, controlling his nervous animal. I leaned toward Macbeth. "Lulach is not here, and he is not coming. You will not ask about my son again. Ride south, Macbeth."

"Gruoch," Macbeth whispered.

Tapping the bay, I rode to the front of the army, the men of Moray behind me.

Banquo, who had organized the line, called for the army to advance.

Whatever Macbeth thought was going to come next, he was very, very wrong.

CHAPTER SIX

*W*e rode throughout the day without incident. Bonfires lit the fields as we made our way south, a signal to us that the north was on our side. They were lighting our way to glory. From sunup to sunset, we rode southward. That night, the men of Moray prepared my tent. Across the field, I could see Macbeth amongst his own men. We hadn't spoken since the sparse words we had exchanged that morning. It was for the best. I wouldn't waste my breath on him. Once the tent was settled, I went inside to rest.

"Tira and I will find us something to eat, my lady," Rhona said. "There are guards here to keep watch. I can smell that the soldiers are cooking. Let's see what they've made."

"May the Great Mother protect us," Tira said with a laugh, exiting behind Rhona.

I chuckled then began pulling off my armor. My whole body ached.

"My lord," one of the soldiers outside my tent said.

"My lord," the second echoed.

I scowled. The last thing I wanted was to see or talk to Macbeth. I was relieved when Banquo called my name.

"Gruoch?"

"Come."

He entered the tent, closing the drape behind him. "I can't stay long. I just wanted to make sure you're all right."

"Road-weary but well enough. How are the men?"

"Good. Eager to get to Scone."

I nodded. "Are there any reports from our scouts?"

Banquo nodded. "The way south is clear, for the most part. There are mercenaries hiding in the woods, but our soldiers are making quick work of them. We have captured some of Northumbria's spies. Otherwise, most of the lords who allied with Duncan have remained within their keeps, their armies disbanded. I suspect they will seek to broker peace."

Outside my tent, one of my soldiers said, "Sir," a hard tone in his voice.

"Sir. My lady is engaged," Killian said. His shadow reflected on the tent, he moved protectively toward the tent opening. Another second soldier joined him, blocking the path.

Banquo and I both turned.

"Gruoch, perhaps you should remind the men of Moray that I'm about to be crowned king," Macbeth called.

Still, the Moray soldiers didn't move.

I met Banquo's eye. A thousand unspoken words passed between us. I shook my head then pushed the heavy fabric of the tent door aside.

"You should applaud them for their loyalty to your wife and queen. It's good to know that Moray will always see that I am safe. Did you need something?"

Macbeth frowned hard. "I understand Banquo is here. I would like to discuss the reports from the south."

I glared at him, unable to hide my disgust. "Let him pass," I told Killian. "This time only," I added under my breath.

"Yes, my lady," Killian replied, meeting my eyes.

I stepped back inside.

This was only the beginning. Somehow, I was going to have to find a way to live with this man, rule alongside him. I was going to have to find a way to co-exist with someone I utterly loathed. How does a person do that without losing their mind?

"Banquo," Macbeth said, giving him a nervous smile.

Banquo inclined his head to Macbeth. "I was telling Gruoch that our scouts indicate that the way south is mostly clear. There are a few small bands, paid men, in the hills. I have sent men to route them already. Siward has spies out, but the Northumbrian army has withdrawn all the way back to their own lands. The southern lords have gone home, their armies dispersed."

"What resistance Siward tried to rally has come to nothing," Macbeth said.

"Once Duncan fell, there was no support. Even the southern lords will not back the Earl of Northumbria," Banquo said.

"What about Crinian and Bethoc?" I asked.

"Still in Edinburgh," Macbeth replied. "We believe that Suthen and Malcolm fled south when the fighting began."

"How deep?" I asked.

Macbeth shook his head. "I don't know yet."

Banquo turned to me. "From what we were able to extract from Siward's spies, I believe they have withdrawn to the court of Harthacnut."

Harthacnut was the son of King Cnut who passed during the struggles. Cnut's timing was certainly excellent, but by all accounts, Harthacnut was worse than his father. Hated by the people of England, inept and cruel, he didn't strike me as long for the throne. He'd already lost Norway to Magnus and Thorfinn. But sending Malcolm and Suthen to Harthacnut was a wise play on Siward's part. One day, they would return to take what Macbeth and I had stolen.

"A smart play," Banquo said.

I nodded.

Macbeth turned to me. "I understand that Donaldbane was taken prisoner by the Irish king and that you've sent word."

"Yes."

"We must try to ransom him," Macbeth said.

"The cost will be very high," Banquo warned. "He will want the isles from Echmarcach."

Macbeth nodded, considering. "That will brew another war. We should finish this one first. We'll find another way."

I raised an eyebrow at Macbeth. That was the first sensible thing I had heard Macbeth say in years.

"Agreed," Banquo said.

At that, Macbeth smiled softly then turned to me. "And you? Are you in agreement?"

I gave him a steely gaze. What game was he playing? Or was he, too, trying to find a path forward. "Yes. For now."

Macbeth nodded. "Thorfinn and Magnus have taken the fleet north, Magnus for his throne, Thorfinn for Ingibjorg."

At that, Banquo chuckled.

"Do they expect any resistance?" I asked.

Macbeth smiled. "Only from Ingibjorg's father. It will be easier to subdue Norway."

At that, Banquo laughed. I could not help but grin, feeling glad for Thorfinn that he would finally be with the woman he so adored.

I cast a glance at Banquo who smiled gently at me. I returned the gesture.

Out of the corner of my eye, I saw Macbeth stiffen. "Well then. We'll ride in the morning. I'll see to the men now," Macbeth said.

Banquo turned back to Macbeth. "Very good. I'll inform you if any further news comes through from the field."

"Thank you, Banquo," Macbeth said then went to the tent flap. He paused. "Goodnight, Gruoch."

"Goodnight," I replied.

The tent flapped in Macbeth's wake. I exhaled a deep sigh of relief.

"Let me get us some wine," Banquo said as he rummaged through the supplies that had come from Moray. Digging into the trunk, he pulled out two goblets and a decanter, pouring a drink for us both. He handed one to me.

I moved to pull off my glove but paused.

No.

It would be better if I left them on.

I took the goblet.

"Are your hands cold?" Banquo asked.

"Yes," I lied.

Banquo raised an eyebrow but said nothing. I hated that he knew when I wasn't telling the truth. Sighing, Banquo drank. "Well, there is one bit of good news. Macbeth seemed steadier that I have seen him in years."

"Seeming is not being."

"True."

"And what do your druid's eyes tell you?" I asked.

"When it comes to Macbeth, my vision is like muddy water. Seeing him a madman lets me keep him at a distance. It keeps you away from him. It keeps you with me. Seeing him well makes me pity him. If he is well, he can be your husband again, which my heart will not permit. But a steady Macbeth means a steady Scotland. We need him to be steady, not for us, but for the country."

"I agree that he needs to be well for the good of the country, but you are wrong on one count. It doesn't matter if he recovers his wits. I will never permit that man near my heart again."

Banquo raised his goblet. "Praised be the gods."

I lifted mine as well. "Yes, praised may they be," I said.

Chuckling, Banquo drank. But I froze. I stared at my hand. The fabric of my glove was marred by red spots. The blood had seeped through.

"Praised may they be," I whispered again then drank the wine knowing that what I was seeing was not possible. And even though it was not possible, the spots of blood remained.

CHAPTER SEVEN

*T*he next day, we rose at sunrise and set off on the road once more. Unlike Duncan, we would not call all the lords and ladies from far and wide to come and lick our boots. They could come or not. It was up to them. Macbeth would be crowned, I alongside him, because we had won the battle. The rest would be settled one of three ways: by words, coin, or steel.

I had expected Scone to be silent as we rode toward the abbey. What met us, however, was far different.

The first sound was that of the pipers. The music caught me off guard. The blood bay twitched his ears, straining to listen. First, I heard the pipes, then drums, then horns. As we rode over a rise, a crowd greeted us. The joyful sound of the bagpipes filled the air. The people lined the streets to welcome us. Cheering, they threw flowers in our path and called our names.

"Lady Gruoch…Lord Macbeth…Look, there's the Lady of Moray…Lord Banquo…Queen Gruoch…King Macbeth."

King Macbeth.

Queen Gruoch.

Duncan had not been a popular ruler. He hadn't shown much interest in his people other than collecting taxes from them and sending them to war when it pleased him. Duncan's costly and unsuccessful wars against his cousins in the north had hurt the southern provinces. Perhaps I had underestimated how much.

Leaving the army encamped around the city, we rode on with a large contingent to the abbey. There, we were met by the sentinel who spoke to Banquo at length.

Macbeth reined his horse in beside me but did not speak.

After a few moments, Banquo joined us. "You were expected. They're ready for you and whatever lords and ladies will be in attendance. There are people waiting to see you both already."

Macbeth turned to me. "We must arrange a workroom."

"Arrange yourself as you will," I said then dismounted. I patted the blood bay's neck then passed his reins to a waiting groom.

"My lady, we have prepared chambers for you, your maids, and Lord Lulach," a footman told me, straining to look, presumably, for Lulach.

"Tira, Rhona, please see to the chambers, and get some rest," I told my maids.

"Yes, my lady," Rhona said.

"Yes, my lady," Tira agreed.

I turned back to the attendant. "I need my own, private meeting space. I'll need to have an audience with any messengers who've come to see me."

"Oh. Yes, my lady," the man said, looking surprised. He turned to a page beside him. He said something in a low tone to the boy who sprinted off like his trousers were on fire.

"My lord," another attendant said, motioning for Macbeth to follow him. "If you will come with me, I will show you to your council chambers."

Macbeth signaled to the man to wait a moment. Dismounting, he stepped toward me as if he wanted to say something in private. I recoiled at the thought of having him so close to me. Involuntarily, I stepped back.

Noticing the gesture, Macbeth froze. I saw him master whatever emotion briefly crossed his face, and then he said, "It will be better if we share a counsel chamber."

"When necessary," I replied. "Only when necessary."

Macbeth clenched his jaw. "Fine," he spat. His temper making his cheeks turn red, he turned and stalked away.

I caught Banquo's eye. He frowned. "Lady Gruoch, I must see to the men. Do you need anything else here?" Banquo asked.

"No, Thane. I seem to be in good hands."

Banquo smiled at me. "Then I will see to you soon. The Moray guard will stay with you."

I nodded to Banquo who mounted his horse.

I turned back to the attendant.

"Lady Gruoch, if you will come this way," the man said, gesturing.

Motioning to the Moray men, I turned and followed the man back into the abbey.

*I*t was strange to walk the same halls I traversed when I'd come to see Duncan crowned. Everything had been about pageantry. Beautiful lords and ladies roamed the halls looking like walking decorations. The place had been adorned with flowers, garland, and silks. Now, everywhere I looked, I saw steel. Macbeth and I had won through bloodshed.

But the difference was a good thing.

I had no use for frills and false faces and endless discussions on the weather.

England was unsettled.

The southern Scottish lords were unsettled.

Our people were poor and uneducated.

The country was weak in commerce.

Duncan had made no allies abroad save England.

There was much work to be done.

The attendant led me to a chamber where servants were busy shifting tables, building up the fire, or washing down furniture.

"Will this suit you, Lady Gruoch?" the man asked.

I eyed the place. There were two doors, one that entered by the main hallway and another at the back of the room.

"Where does that door go?" I asked. I motioned for one of the Moray men to investigate.

"To the hallway on the west side of the abbey," the attendant said.

"You said I had messages? Riders?"

"Yes, my lady," he said then turned and motioned to two boys who carried satchels full of scrolls.

"Anything from Fife?" I asked.

"No, my lady, but there is a special envoy waiting for you—in particular."

"An envoy?"

"From Que—Lady Suthen."

"Bring them in," I said.

"But, my lady, you've just come in from the road. Surely, they can wait until you've taken some refreshment, some rest…"

"I said bring them in," I repeated, my voice sharp.

The man nodded. "I'll go get them now."

I turned to the Moray men. "Killian, check everyone for weapons. No one comes in without being disarmed."

"Yes, my lady."

A table had been set at the front of the room. A maid busily washed it down while the others finished setting up the space. I went to the girl.

"Lass, I know you're busy, but will you see to it some refreshment is brought for my men. Some ale and bread. Whatever there is to be had."

The girl paused mid-wipe and looked up at me, her eyes wide. "Ye-yes, my lady. Of course."

"Thank you," I told her.

The girl quickly mopped the water off the table then turned and ran off.

I turned and looked around the room. The chamber, which only a few moments ago had been a hodgepodge of chairs and tables, had already started to look like a formal meeting hall. I went to the hearth. There was a bright, cheery glow in the fire. I grabbed a chair and slid it toward the fireplace.

"Lady Gruoch," one of the servants called, rushing to my side. He grabbed the chair. "Please, allow me."

"I was just moving it closer to the fire. I still have some chill from the road," I told the lad who stared at me.

"Of course. But let me. You shouldn't be lifting chairs, my lady," the boy said, gently taking the chair from my hands and setting it before the fireplace.

The two maids who'd been working on the fire quickly tidied up the kindling then rose, scrambling to get out of the way.

"My lady," the boy said, adjusting the chair for me.

I looked from him to the maids. A half-laugh bubbled from my lips.

"My lady?" the boy whispered. "Is there anything wrong?"

The two maids looked at one another, worry in their eyes.

I shook my head. "No. Nothing at all. It's only...my gods...do they really not move their own chairs? How absurd. No wonder my father was never at court. Thank you all for your quick and hard work. The room looks wonderful, and the hearth is warm. Thank you all so much."

The servants looked at one another, seeming unsure what to say.

"My lady," the first maid said, bobbing a curtsey which the second maid awkwardly mirrored. The pair rushed from the room.

I smiled at the boy who'd helped me with my seat.

"My lady. I'm not sure if I should offer to help with anything else or not," he said with a smile.

"I'm well. Thank you. What is your name, lad?"

"Gordon, my lady."

"Thank you, Gordon. You moved the chair most excellently."

The Moray guard chuckled lightly.

I lowered myself into the seat and looked at the fire. Madelaine. Madelaine needed to come soon because there was no way I was going to be able to navigate this alone. I closed my eyes, feeling the warmth of the fire on my face. My back ached. It felt good to sit.

I would be queen.

This was how queens were treated.

This was how other queens were treated. Not me.

"My lady," the attendant called.

I opened my eyes to see a group of three well-dressed men at the door. They frowned, their expressions sour, as Killian disarmed them.

The attendant crossed the room, the two pages following along behind him. "These boys will run messages, errands as needed. I will send a secretary as soon as I can find one."

I shook my head. "No need. These boys will do for now."

"Oh. Well. Very good. I will go see to Lord Macbeth now."

"Is his council chamber close by?"

The attendant nodded. "Down the hall, two rights, then on the left. But he is not there at the moment. He's retired to his chamber to take some rest."

Of course. "I see."

"The envoy," the man said, motioning to Suthen's men.

I nodded. "Thank you."

At that, the attendant left.

Rising, I went to the men.

"Gentlemen, please come and take a seat by the fire," I said.

At that, Gordon, who'd been standing nearby, still uncertain about what he should be doing, leaped into action. Working quickly, he moved other seats near the hearth. When he caught my eye, he smiled.

"Lady Gruoch, it is good of you to see us. I am Wattles, special counselor to Que—Lady Suthen. My companions, Sir Lamont and Lord Billingsly," he said, motioning to the others.

"Please, gentlemen, take your rest. I apologize for the delay, we've only just arrived."

"Yes, my lady," Sir Lamont said. I heard the tone of annoyance in his voice. He eyed me over, glancing at my armor with disgust on his face.

I set my hand on the hilt of Uald's Gift.

The move caught the man's attention.

Sir Lamont, who was undoubtedly part of Lord Siward's entourage, met my gaze. I held his glance until he looked away.

"Kind of you, so kind of you," Lord Billingsly said as he took his seat.

I motioned for the others to sit. I also took my seat near the fire. Killian and three other guards took positions not far from me. I cast a glance around the room. Both doors were now guarded, and the rest of the men were stationed around the hall. No matter how Sir Lamont felt about me, he undoubtedly would not tempt steel.

"My lady," Wattles began, "Lady Suthen implored us to come to Scone to appeal to you directly. War is fought between men. Mothers cherish something quite different. Young Malcolm is with his mother, but Donaldbane..." he said then paused, waiting to see what I already knew.

"He's not with his mother as well?" I asked, the lie making my mouth feel dry.

"No, my lady. Perhaps you don't know. Young Donaldbane showed an interest in godly things. He was in Iona studying with the holy brothers. He was abducted from Iona by the Irish king. Lady Suthen has sent us to ask for your help in getting her son back."

I raised an eyebrow then turned to the fire. "And why doesn't Earl Siward send an envoy? Perhaps Harthacnut can be of help."

Sir Lamont exhaled heavily but said nothing.

"The Irish king has no interest in what Suthen has to offer. And Earl Siward…. To be frank, my lady, Earl Siward is not presently in a position to be of use to the Irish king. Whereas, you…." Lord Billingsly opened his hands wide to indicate the matter was obvious.

"Lady Suthen spoke highly of you, Lady Gruoch," Wattles said. "She asked me to send her personal pleas, one mother to another, with a soft reminder that Donaldbane is your second cousin."

I nodded then considered their words. I had no doubt that Suthen worried for her son, but there were other cards being played here. If I delivered Donaldbane to Suthen, I might as well cut Lulach's throat. But if I rescued him and fostered the boy myself, then Suthen's son would be raised as an ally to Lulach. Suthen wanted her son safe, but there were many different kinds of safety. One way or another, she would see one of her two boys close to the throne. Suthen knew that if I fostered Donaldbane, he would still have a chance even if Siward never managed to topple Macbeth and me.

"Please assure Lady Suthen that I will do my best to see to Donaldbane's safe return. I understand her well and will do what I can. Tell Lady Suthen that I will send word as soon as I have news of her son."

"I wish all troubles could be handled with such ease and grace," Wattles said.

Lord Billingsly nodded vigorously in agreement.

Sir Lamont continued to look dour.

"Well, perhaps if we had more queens ruling, they would be," I said. "My men will see you out."

At that, Wattles and Lord Billingsly rose, both of them bowing to me. Sir Lamont gave the briefest of nods then turned to go. The Moray men escorted them back to the door. I stood and watched as the gentlemen were escorted down the hall and away from the meeting room.

The door at the back of the hall opened and three maids carrying trays heaped with food—cheese, bread, and meat—and tankards of ale entered. My stomach growled hungrily.

"Come, Moray," I called to the men. "It was a long ride to hear news on an empty stomach."

"Aye, let's see if the ale tastes any different under a new king," one of the soldiers said.

"Under a new queen," another corrected.

"Sirs," one of the maids said, passing the drinks around. "Help yourselves. There's plenty more."

"Suppose they'd try to poison us?" one of the soldiers asked, sniffing the drink.

I looked at the maid who had gone absolutely pale at the suggestion. "No. Of course not. I poured it with my own hand and...and had a drink myself to steady my nerves."

I chuckled. "And she looks quite well. I think we're safe." I lifted one of the tankards. "What shall we toast?" I asked the others.

"You, my lady," Killian said, taking a tankard. "To our new queen, who will be a fair and just ruler."

I inclined my head to him.

"To Queen Gruoch," Killian called.

"To Queen Gruoch," the men answered.

I lifted the tankard and took a sip. When I did so, I felt eyes on me. I lifted my gaze for just a moment to see Killian studying me, his dark blue eyes resting on my face. He smiled softly, raised his cup in toast, and took a drink.

Surprising even myself, my stomach twinged with girlish softness in response to his heavy gaze. He was handsome, but I was married three times over. It hardly mattered how attractive he was.

My cheeks flushed red.

Really, Gruoch. How absurd, I chided myself.

But the thought lingered nonetheless.

CHAPTER EIGHT

*I*n the days that followed, we settled in and began our preparations for the crowning. With the place bustling with news and people—most of whom I did not know and did not trust—I was relieved when the first of two very welcomed visitors arrived.

There was a knock on the door followed by the call, "Corbie?"

A moment later, Madelaine pushed opened the door and rushed into the room, an excited smile on her face.

Outside my door, I caught sight of Killian who gave me a knowing wink then closed the door behind her.

"Lady Madelaine," Tira said, then curtsied.

Rhona, who had been in the adjoining room, joined us. "My lady."

"What a welcome sight you all are," Madelaine said as she wrapped her arms around me, pulling me into a tight squeeze. "Corbie! Your hair," she said when she pulled back. She touched my short locks. "What happened?"

"For the Morrigu."

"I won't begrudge the dark lady her sacrifice, but now we'll have to work some magic of our own for the coronation. Oh, my little raven. Now, where is Lulach?" Madelaine asked, looking around, a confused expression on her face.

"My lady, shall Tira and I bring you and Lady Madelaine some refreshment?" Rhona asked, motioning to Tira. Clearly, Rhona understood I needed to speak privately with Madelaine.

I nodded. "Yes. Please."

Tira looked a bit confused, but Rhona dragged her out the door behind her.

I went to the window and looked out. The yard was busy. As much as I had hoped that the crowning would end quickly, and I could return to Cawdor—with Banquo—it was beginning to look like the politics of the country were sloshing their way toward me. I was surrounded by news and need. Every day, visitors arrived to meet with Macbeth or me. There was struggle, hunger, and strife in every corner of Scotland. Dealing with all of it was exhausting. What Duncan had been doing all these years, I had no idea. But he had not been ruling. At least, not well.

"Lulach isn't here," I told Madelaine.

"Where is he?"

"I sent him to Balor. Lulach and Fleance will stay amongst the druids until things are settled."

"Hmm," Madelaine mused.

I turned and looked at her. "Was it the wrong decision?"

She shook her head. "No. Keep him hidden. Boite disappeared for a time as a boy as well. Our mother saw to that. But Kenneth would not let Malcolm go. The men they later became is evidence of their upbringing. This is good for Lulach. Besides, you will have enough to manage without tending to Lulach and Fleance as well."

I nodded. "Duncan's ineptitude reveals itself each day."

"What he learned at Malcolm's foot and what you learned in Moray are, no doubt, very different."

"Gillacoemgain was a good ruler, that is true, and I learned much from him. But it is you and Epona I credit," I said with a soft smile. "I learned how to manage things from watching the two of you."

"Corbie," she said with a dismissive wave.

"It's true. You must care about what happens. If you don't—"

"You end up with Malcolm...and Duncan."

I nodded.

"Very well. All right, my Corbie, you've hidden Lulach from me. I can accept your reasoning on that, but I think you've had my man long enough. Where have you stashed Tavis?"

A knot hardened in my stomach. "Tavis?"

Madelaine caught the confused sound in my voice. She'd been blustering about the room, fingering the dresses hanging in my wardrobe. She turned and looked at me. "Yes. Tavis."

"Tavis rode south just after the war. He...he's not in Fife?"

The color drained from Madelaine's face. "No. He's not here? He didn't ride with you?"

"No," I said, a terrible feeling of dread washing over me.

Madelaine covered her mouth with her hands. "Corbie, he never returned," she whispered.

I went to the door.

"My lady," Killian said, coming to attention the moment I opened the door.

"I need to speak to the Thane of Lochaber at once."

"I will see to it, my lady," Killian said. He signaled another guard to take his place then headed down the hallway, moving quickly.

I shut the door behind me then turned and looked at Madelaine.

"Oh, Great Mother, what if something's happened?" she whispered, tears welling in her eyes.

"Don't think like that. Surely, you would have felt it. Banquo will come. He will be able to see. We will ask him to search for Tavis the old way."

Madelaine sat down on the corner of my bed. All the mirth that had surrounded her had deflated.

"Maybe he found some good hunting. Or perhaps he missed you and Fife and is on his way now," I said, but even as I spoke the words, I knew they weren't true. I could feel Tavis, just on the edge of my awareness, and all was not well.

"I hope so," Madelaine whispered. "Oh, Corbie."

I sat beside her, wrapping my arms around her. "We'll pray to the Goddess for his safe return."

"May she listen well to our words."

*B*anquo arrived within the hour, a worried expression on his face.

"Gruoch? What is it? I was in the field with the men when one your guards came," he said then paused, looking toward Madelaine. "Lady Madelaine," he said, giving her a short bow.

"Tavis did not return to Fife," I told Banquo.

I could see him turning my words around in his mind then he nodded. He pulled his dagger from his belt.

"Lady Madelaine," he said, turning to her. "I need a lock of your hair."

Madelaine took the dagger from Banquo's hand then cut a red curl, which she handed to Banquo.

Banquo nodded to me then went before the fire. Kneeling, he poured some water into the cauldron. He then dug into his vest and pulled out a small pouch. From within, he withdrew some herbs and berries. He dropped them into the water as he whispered quiet words. He pulled other herbs from a pouch hanging on his belt. He tossed these onto the flame. The room filled with heady sage and the sweet scent of herbs. Madelaine and I stood behind him, watching him as he worked.

I could feel the energy around me shift and move. The light streaming through the window bent oddly, scattering at strange angles, the shadows twisting. When I narrowed my gaze and looked at Banquo with my ravens's eyes, I saw the green glow that often surrounded him.

Banquo whispered under his breath then tossed Madelaine's hair onto the fire.

The scent of burnt hair filled the room. I felt dizzy. I reached out for Madelaine, so I wouldn't swoon.

Banquo stilled and looked into the water.

After a moment, he winced and clutched his side.

Madelaine moved to go to him, but I held her back.

Banquo shuddered then lifted his hands, covering his eyes. I could hear him whispering but couldn't make out his words.

A moment later, he sat back on his heels.

"I know where he is," he said, his voice soft.

"And?" Madelaine asked. "Is he…"

"He is injured, Lady Madelaine," he said, gently touching his side once more. "I…I just hope we can reach him in time." Banquo rose and turned to me. "I'll send riders at once. He is not far from your old keep," he told Madelaine. "There are some soldiers amongst my men who follow the old path. They will understand," he said, touching the tattoo on his forehead. "I will go to them now."

"Thank you, Banquo," Madelaine said, tears trickling down her face.

Banquo passed me a look. I could read the words behind his eyes. It might already be too late. With a nod, Banquo left.

Exhaling deeply, I closed the door behind him.

"Oh, Corbie. Whatever would I do without Tavis?"

I shook my head. Having been separated from Banquo, I knew

well the pain. But I could not imagine Banquo dying. If Banquo died, I would lose my mind. It would be the very end of me.

"Don't think like that," I whispered. "Have faith, not fear."

Madelaine nodded mutely but said nothing more. In the face of uncertainty, fear is a monster that's impossible to slay.

CHAPTER NINE

*I*n the days that followed, I did my best to keep Madelaine preoccupied. We expected to hear word any time now. The waiting, the worry, was difficult to bear. To keep her busy, I asked Madelaine to manage the ladies who'd come for the crowning while I attended to other work. I was in my meeting hall reading over some dispatches when I heard a trumpet herald.

Then another.

Then another.

I set the scroll down.

Someone of great importance had come. I rose.

A moment later, Macbeth appeared in the doorway. All smiles, he entered the hall to fetch me. But as he drew near, he remembered the ice between us. He stopped.

"Gruoch, will you please escort me to the square?" he asked.

"Who has come?"

"Thorfinn."

"Here? He's come here?"

Macbeth nodded. "By ship," he said then came closer. My temper rose as he took each step. How dare he come so close to me? I imagined pulling my dagger from my belt and stabbing him to death. What would happen if I were to do such a thing?

They would think me a mad woman.

I cast a quick glance at my hands. There, I saw the bloody spots.

Maybe I was.

"He wanted to surprise everyone, to present a united force. He wants them all to know that to tempt me is to tempt him."

"Us."

"Sorry?"

"There is no *me*. There is *us*. *We* will be the rulers of this land, Macbeth. Not you alone."

Macbeth stared at me. "Yes. You're right. He went north to fetch Injibjorg. If all went well, she is here with him. Will you come?"

I turned to one of the pages. "Please find Lady Madelaine and ask her to meet us in the square."

"Yes, my lady," the boy said then ran off.

I nodded to Macbeth. "Very well."

Signaling to my guards, I joined him. Two of my Moray men followed along behind me. Macbeth cast a glance back at them.

"You are quite safe, Gruoch."

"Who says I don't feel safe?"

Macbeth frowned. "Have it your way. I have been thinking about our next steps. There is a small castle not far from here, Glamis. It isn't a large estate, but it is well fortified and comfortable. I went hunting there when I was young with—well, before the troubles. Between here and there is the ancient hilltop fortress at Dunsinane. I have sent a party to inspect the fortress. It is in need of repair, but I'd hoped to keep my—*our*—seat there."

"At Dunsinane Fortress?"

"Yes."

I cast a sidelong glance at Macbeth. In the very least, the plans he was making were wise. As much as I wanted to return to Moray, we needed to stay south and get the country in some sort of order. Macbeth and I needed our own place, somewhere from which we could control both north and south. Dunsinane would work well.

"Very well."

"We will leave Scone immediately after the crowning. I've sent people ahead to ready Glamis. Perhaps Lulach will join us at the fortress when it is completed."

I said nothing. If Macbeth believed he had any right to know anything about my son, he was sadly mistaken.

Macbeth exhaled heavily. "Must you be so difficult?" he said coldly.

We turned the corner to the yard. There, I spotted Banquo alongside Thorfinn's party. I stopped, blocking Macbeth's path. I turned and looked at him. "If you are so eager to have a child underfoot, perhaps Elspeth can send your son, Findelach."

Macbeth stared at me, his eyes widening in surprise.

It took everything inside me not to bash his face in.

Saying nothing, I turned back toward the square. Lifting my hand, I waved. "Thorfinn! Thorfinn, many welcomes," I called then crossed the space between us, leaving Macbeth behind.

*A*s I approached Thorfinn, I couldn't help but notice the strikingly beautiful woman on a pale horse alongside him. Thorfinn dismounted then went to help her down. Hand in hand, he led the woman toward me.

"Lady Gruoch," Thorfinn called.

Banquo followed behind the pair, chatting merrily with the Northmen who'd come with Thorfinn. The morning sunlight shined on Banquo's chestnut-colored hair, which was now sprinkled with flecks of silver. How handsome he was. Even still, my heart was moved at the mere sight of him. Banquo caught my eye then smiled softly at me.

I returned the gesture, not caring in the slightest if Macbeth was watching. I then turned my attention back to the newcomers.

"Jarl Thorfinn…and is this the much-renowned Injibjorg?" I asked.

"My lady," the girl said, inclining her head to me.

Thorfinn's report of Injibjorg's beauty hadn't been a boast. She had beautiful, straw-colored hair, which she'd swept into a braid that nearly reached her knees. And she was, as Thorfinn had suggested, a curvy girl. She would, no doubt, produce many sons for the jarl.

"Welcome to Scotland," I told her, taking her hand.

"By Odin's beard, what a place," Thorfinn said, glancing around at the mix of southern lords and ladies and priests who filled the square. They all stood still as statues, staring in wonderment at Thorfinn and his men. The Northmen who'd arrived with Thorfinn where a rough-looking crowd with long, braided hair, tattoos, and enough weapons to slaughter pretty much anyone they wanted. No wonder everyone looked nervous. Suddenly, I was delighted Thorfinn and his men had come.

Macbeth smiled awkwardly, casting reassuring and calming glances at the gathered nobles. "Yes, well, customs are a bit different this far south. Come, old friend. Let me see you and Injibjorg inside. Banquo, can you see to Thorfinn's men?"

Banquo inclined his head to Macbeth. At every turn, Macbeth found one reason or another to keep Banquo and me separated. I didn't blame him for trying to minimize the rumors. But I hardly gave a damn. After all, it was Macbeth who had failed our marriage, not me. If Macbeth had stayed steady, had been a good and decent person, all would have been well.

"No need," Thorfinn objected. "These men have traveled long and far to see you, Macbeth. We will feast together. And I want

Banquo to tell me about the battle. So, Lochaber, did you see Duncan lose his head?"

Banquo laughed. "Unfortunately, no. I did see his blood. There was a lot of it."

Thorfinn laughed. "Too bad you didn't get that head on a pike. He could have ridden with Macbeth to Scone.

Macbeth laughed nervously then clapped Thorfinn on the shoulder. "You will scandalize the ladies," he said, motioning to Injibjorg and me. But it was evident that it was more the southern lords and ladies within earshot whom Macbeth was worried about, not us.

Injibjorg chuckled. "Have you not heard of shield-maidens, King Macbeth? My mother was a shield-maiden of great renown. Talk of battle doesn't frighten me."

"Well… It's just… Never mind. Let's go within and feast," Macbeth said then nodded to Banquo.

I frowned. Who did Macbeth think he was to order Banquo in such a manner?

A king.

He thought he was king.

And he was…or soon would be.

At my doing.

I looked down at my hands, then took a deep, shuddering breath. A slick of red covered my fingers. Droplets of blood dripped from my hands onto the stones below. Pausing a moment, I closed my eyes and took a deep breath, pushing the image away.

"Queen Gruoch?" Injibjorg said, reaching out to take my arm. "Are you all right?"

I exhaled slowly then opened my eyes. Queen? Queen? "Yes. Thank you. Sorry."

She laughed lightly. "Not at all. All women swoon so when

they are with child. One day soon, I hope to swoon too. If I can get Thorfinn off his ship."

"With child? Me?" My hand drifted toward my stomach, but I froze just short of touching my stomach for fear that I would leave bloody marks on my clothes. I clenched my jaw then forced myself to look. There was nothing there.

"I am very good at noticing such things. Some people call me a völva. You see, I can tell the moment a woman conceives. And I can even guess the gender, and I am always right. For instance, you are carrying a princess for this land."

I stared at her.

She laughed again then took my hand. "Don't look so startled. It seems I've given you the news before the gods. I hope they don't mind my presumption. In my mind's eye, I see you large and round with child. And I sense a sweet girl within you. Odin sends you happy tidings. I am delighted to be the first to give you such glad news."

"I… Thank you. But please, say nothing to anyone else," I whispered.

"No? There is no need to doubt. I know some ladies do not wish to excite their men with the news too soon. But I assure you, I am never wrong."

"I have no doubt in the wisdom of the old gods…and those to whom they lend their voice on this earthly plain. But, please. Say nothing."

"As you wish."

"Injibjorg, where have you gone?" Thorfinn called to his wife.

"Here," she called. She squeezed my hand then let me go. She went to her husband who gave her ass a hard squeeze as we made our way to the feasting hall.

A small band of priests passed us. They crossed themselves at the sight of Thorfinn and his men.

Banquo fell into step with me. "What is it?" he asked, his eyes searching my face. "Something Injibjorg said upset you."

"Nothing."

He chuckled lightly. "You can't lie to me, Gruoch."

"It's nothing. Please don't worry yourself."

"Cerridwen," Banquo whispered silently so others couldn't hear.

I took Banquo's hand, forcing myself not to look when I did so for fear the vision would return. "Later."

Banquo looked at me, his eyes meeting mine. "All right."

Was it possible? Was it really possible that I was carrying the child of the man I loved? As we passed into the abbey once more, a raven alighted on the archway.

Its sharp cry shattered my happy thoughts.

I looked up at the bird.

Banquo followed my gaze. He lifted his hand and touched the mark of the stag on his brow.

The bird cawed loudly once more then turned and flew off.

My hand drifted to my stomach.

And where I should have been filled with a deep sense of joy, a terrible feeling of dread washed over me.

CHAPTER TEN

*H*aving Thorfinn at court changed the tone of everything. Scone had felt stifling. Coupled with the gloom of not knowing what had happened to Tavis, I was glad Thorfinn had come. Madelaine smiled and treated all the visiting lords and ladies with utter kindness, but her eyes remained haunted. Add to that Injibjorg's startling proclamation had my world feeling like it was spinning off its axis.

That night, the Northmen brought joy and laughter to the feasting hall. While I worried for Tavis and prayed to the Goddess for his safe return, I couldn't help but be moved by the Northmen's merriment. Was I really with child? Banquo's child? It was almost too much to hope.

"I dare say," Fife, who had been seated next to me, said, "that Jarl Thorfinn is a man much maligned by his own reputation. He's quite the jolly chap."

As kind as Fife's words were, he too eyed the Northmen warily.

"So he is. Though I suspect he's as fierce in battle as he is determined in mirth."

"Which makes him all the more dangerous," Fife said with a

chuckle. His eyes drifted to Madelaine who was talking with Lady Lennox. Madelaine smiled, but her stare was vacant. "Has there been any word?" Fife whispered to me.

I shook my head. "We expect news at any time."

"She paced all night long, half awake, half asleep. I am an old man, but I am not a blind man. Tavis has been a loyal companion to her. Do you think... Should I take her back to Fife?"

I shook my head. "She won't go. I've already suggested it. She will stay here until there is news."

Fife sighed. "I love your aunt dearly. I hate to see her in such a state."

"That is very generous of you, sir. All things considered."

Fife laughed then patted his over-round belly. "She has been very generous, all things considered. A fine woman, your aunt. She has told me, somewhat, of her life with Allister," he said then coughed uncomfortably. "Malcolm should have taken better care of his sister."

"Malcolm was not one to concern himself with the well-being of his siblings. Ask my father."

Fife huffed a laugh. "No truer words spoken, Lady Gruoch," he said then clinked his glass against mine.

"Fife, will you join us for hunting?" the Mormaer of Lennox called to him, taking his attention away.

I looked around the table. Macbeth was deep in conversation with Thorfinn and Injibjorg, the Northmen laughing and talking amongst themselves. I turned to Banquo who was sitting diagonally from me. His hand rested on his mouth, and he was studying me carefully. He had a thoughtful expression on his face.

I laughed lightly. "You look far too serious. Should I call for someone to refill your cup?"

He shook his head, his expression softening. "No."

"Something troubling you?"

"Trouble is an interesting word."

"You riddle, druid."

"Yes," he replied with a wink. He lifted his cup and took a drink.

"Banquo," Thorfinn called to him. "You must sail back with me. We will go to Norway and help Magnus prepare to make war against Denmark. The Macbeths will keep Scotland quiet."

"It's been too long since I was in Lochaber," Banquo said. "I shall leave the fighting to you."

Thorfinn laughed. "Banquo's bones are weary. You've worn him down, Macbeth."

"Him? Nothing ever wears him down. No matter what, he is persistent in whatever course he chooses, to a fault," Macbeth said, his voice hard.

"Aren't we all," Banquo replied, giving Macbeth a disinterested glance.

"Then bring Fleance in the spring," Thorfinn told Banquo. "And Lady Gruoch will send Lulach. I'll teach those boys the ways of the sea and shield."

At that, Madelaine scoffed. "Do you think I'll let my nephew run wild with you, Jarl Thorfinn?"

"Lady Madelaine," Thorfinn said, eyeing my aunt with great intensity. Thorfinn stroked his long beard as he considered her. "I see that Lady Gruoch's beauty is common in her family line."

Madelaine grinned wickedly. "Not so. My brother Malcolm was quite hideous."

At that, Thorfinn chuckled.

"Lulach will soon join Gruoch and me at court," Macbeth said. "He was sent away for safekeeping until the war was over. But soon, I'll have my son by my side again."

At that, Madelaine stilled. She glanced at me.

I lifted my cup and drank, not daring to look at Macbeth. I wouldn't fall for whatever traps he sought to set for me. He didn't know where Lulach was, and he would not know. Not now. Not until I willed it.

The conversation around us faltered as everyone sensed the tension in the air.

For once, I had to thank the Lord, because it was at that moment that Bishop Lawrence cleared his throat to say, "My king, the processional is planned for eleven in the morning. Everything is ready, if that pleases you."

"It does," Macbeth said. He lifted his cup and reached down the table to clink it against that of the bishop. "It pleases me to no end. And you, Lady Gruoch," Macbeth called. "Does it please you as well?"

I turned and looked at him.

Macbeth's blue eyes were wide, a wild gleam therein. He grinned, and I could see the muscles under his eyes twitching.

"Of course she is pleased," Thorfinn interjected on my behalf. "Who would not be pleased to be queen of this great land? A toast, to King Macbeth and Queen Gruoch," Thorfinn called loudly, lifting his tankard.

"To King Macbeth and Queen Gruoch," the crowd echoed.

"Long may they reign," Thorfinn added then drank. But when he did so, his eyes met mine over the top of his tankard. He, too, had seen the mad sheen. Thorfinn's eyes held a warning.

*T*he dinner seemed to stretch on forever. While the Northmen, Thorfinn, and Macbeth were still celebrating, the rest of the company had disbanded. Banquo walked me back to my chamber.

"So, what had you looking so worried?" I asked Banquo.

He shook his head. "These days, I see visions, this time and the future overlapped. It's hard to make meaning of it all."

"Maybe I can help. What are you trying to make meaning of?"

Banquo smiled lightly. "Who can say for sure?"

"You remind me of someone."

"Who?"

"An ancient thing who riddles like yourself."

"The Wyrds."

I nodded.

He shrugged. "Everything is too muddled. If I understood, I wouldn't hesitate to tell you."

What had he seen? Did he have an inkling of what Injibjorg told me? I wanted so desperately to tell him, but now was not the time. I wanted to tell Banquo when and where the moment could belong to us alone—as it should.

"Speaking of news. Anything about Tavis?" I asked.

Banquo shook his head. "No. No one's returned yet."

"And do you sense anything?"

"Not anything good."

"As I feared. Tavis is like a father to me."

"And dear to your aunt. I can only hope the gods, too, care for him." Banquo flicked an eye behind us where my guard followed a safe distance away. "I like how dedicated your men are to your safety, but I can't even steal a kiss with them around."

I chuckled. "I'm sorry."

"I believe that dark-haired guard of yours is in love with you," he said, motioning with his chin to Killian who was standing just outside my chamber door.

"Are you jealous?"

"Of course."

"Good."

Banquo chuckled. "I won't see you in the morning. Not until Moot Hill."

I nodded.

"Cerridwen," he said in a whisper. "I am so proud of you."

I took his hand and squeezed it. "Thank you."

He returned the gesture. "I will see you tomorrow, *Queen* Gruoch."

"Goodnight."

"Goodnight."

*S*ighing, I let Banquo go. Emotions washed over me— from frustration to joy to worry—but I was too tired to master any of them. More than anything else, I wanted to sleep.

Once I was in the chamber, Tira and Rhona helped me redress into my nightclothes. I was just settling in when there was a knock on the outer door.

"I'll go see," Rhona said.

A moment later, she returned with Madelaine.

"Rhona, Tira, will you give us a moment?" Madelaine asked.

The maids nodded then left us alone.

I moved to get up, but Madelaine motioned for me to stay in bed. "Rest. You look very weary, Gruoch."

"That I am."

"Gruoch, you must not let Lulach come into Macbeth's reach again. At dinner, he said—"

"He lied. He doesn't know where Lulach is. He will never come close to my boy again."

"Thank the Great Mother. I saw that odd spark behind his eyes."

"He is unwell, mad in fits and starts. He can't be trusted."

"Oh, my Corbie. What will you do?"

"When the coronation is done, I will return with you and Fife. I will see Crearwy and speak to Epona. Some things are not clear to me. I need her advice."

"And then?"

"And then, I will see. I may have to join Macbeth in Glamis. I don't know." The truth was, if what Injibjorg said was true, then much was in upheaval.

"What about Banquo? Will he really return to Lochaber?"

"I don't know."

"All is uncertainty. There is no news on Tavis?"

"No. I'm sorry."

Madelaine wrung her hands together. "I can't stand it," she whispered.

"If there is no news by the time the coronation is done, we will all ride to your keep together."

She nodded. "I'm sure he's fine," she said, putting on a brave face, but I saw her chin tremor. "Now, you must rest, my dear. Tomorrow, we will see you crowned queen."

"As the goddess wills."

Madelaine rose, kissed my cheek, and then set a loving hand on my head, stroking my hair. "As the goddess wills. Goodnight, little raven."

"Goodnight."

She kissed my cheek once more then left me alone.

I closed my eyes. Under my blankets, I shifted my hands to my stomach. Was I with child again? I couldn't remember when my courses had last come upon me. They hadn't since Banquo's return that I could remember. Was Injibjorg right?

"Andraste," I whispered into the darkness. "What trouble are you stirring up?"

But there was no reply.

And a moment later, I was lost to dreams.

CHAPTER ELEVEN

The following morning, Madelaine did her best to make me look like a queen. She'd brought with her the most beautiful gown I had ever seen in my life. The dress was scarlet-colored and embroidered with silver thread on the neck and sleeves.

"A gown for a queen," Madelaine said as she tightened the laces. "But, Corbie, I don't know what to do about your hair. A veil, maybe?"

"I've come to rule, not set fashion."

Rhona shook her head. "If it were not for us, I swear you'd go to the stone in an apron and mud-covered field boots."

"And what would be so bad about that? There is work to be done. Perhaps I could herd some sheep on my way."

Tira, Rhona, and Madelaine chuckled in unison.

Madelaine tugged the laces around my waist, making me grunt. My hands drifted down to my waist, and as I felt my stomach, I realized there was a swell that had not been there before. My aunt paused then and let out a soft *hum*. A moment later, she loosened the laces.

I said nothing. It was not the time.

Tira ran a brush through my hair, braiding it to the side. She decorated my short locks with a silver pin and some wildflowers. "That will have to do," she said.

"That works fine," Madelaine said.

Lifting my belt, threaded with my sword and daggers, I started fastening it.

"Oh, Corbie. Must you?" Madelaine asked.

I looked down at my weapons. "Must I what?"

"The gown is so lovely."

"So it is, and it will be just as lovely if Siward decides to ambush us. But with these at my side, I might get a bit farther."

Madelaine sighed but didn't protest.

Turning to her bags, Madelaine produced a length of red fabric that put me in mind of the red robe of the Morrigu.

"What is that?"

"A cloak."

"Oh, how beautiful," Tira gushed.

"Turn," Madelaine said. She attached the cloak to my shoulders with silver broaches made in twisting Celtic knot designs. Once she had adjusted the cloak, she stepped back to assess her handiwork. She nodded. "A queen."

Tira and Rhona wrapped their arms around each other's waists and stood admiring me.

"My Lady of Moray," Tira said, her voice cracking with emotion. "How beautiful you look."

Rhona nodded vehemently. "But Lady of Moray no more. Now she is Queen of Scots."

"I will always be the Lady of Moray."

Both women smiled at me.

There was a knock on the door. Rhona went to answer. On the other side, I could hear Killian.

"They're ready for you, my lady," Rhona told me.

Madelaine kissed me on both cheeks. "I'll go join Fife. I'm so proud of you, Corbie," she said, kissing me once more before turning to Rhona and Tira. "Girls, go on now and get your places so you have a good view."

I nodded to them, indicating that they were free to go. They both bobbed a curtsey then departed, Madelaine following along behind them.

I took a deep breath and closed my eyes. "Be with me, Lady," I whispered, then went to the door.

On the other side, the men of Moray waited.

"My lady," Killian said. They all bowed when they saw me.

"Come, lads. Let's go and stand for Moray."

The bells on the chapel rang as Macbeth and I progressed to Moot Hill where the Stone of Destiny awaited. For Duncan's coronation, the ceremony had taken place within the abbey itself, and the stone had been safely tucked under his throne. Macbeth had asked for the stone to be returned to the mound near the Celtic cross where the ancient kings had received their coronation.

The people of Scone lined the streets, throwing flowers in our path as we made our way to the site. The scene was festive. Bagpipes and trumpets played, the people cheered, and a crowd of noble lords and ladies had come to watch. But I was also keenly aware of the amount of steel I saw everywhere. Not only was this a coronation, but it was a show of strength. There would be spies in the crowd, enemies watching. They would report everything that happened here back to Siward and Harthacnut. The message we were sending was clear: Scotland was strong once more.

But what they didn't know was that the new king was anything but stable.

Just under his practiced smile, a thunderstorm was brewing inside Macbeth.

What would happen when that storm broke loose?

I glanced at Macbeth who rode beside me. He was finely bedecked, his armor glimmering in the sunlight. As he rode, he kept his gaze forward, eyes fixed on the coronation place.

He hadn't spoken to me since dinner the evening before. No doubt, I had frustrated him by failing to play his game.

That was fine.

I had no interest in partaking in his antics. I was here for my people and for Lulach.

And for whatever life was now growing inside me.

A girl.

Another girl.

Banquo's daughter.

If it was true, then I would need to figure out a way to hide her as I had done with Crearwy. If that was what Banquo wanted.

What would Banquo want?

Until I spoke to Epona, nothing was certain.

And Andraste was giving no hint of anything these days.

"Gruoch, Queen Gruoch," the villagers called, waving to me.

I smiled and waved to them.

One day, my son would come to Scone. He would sit on the stone of kings and become ruler of this land. Everything I did, I did for Lulach.

I took a deep breath, smiled, and waved once more.

Macbeth and I finally arrived at the Celtic high cross.

The place had been beautifully bedecked with arches of greens trimmed with ribbons. The audience waited. Thorfinn and Injbjorg, Madelaine and Fife, and Banquo stood at the front. The other royal thanes, mormaers, and lords and ladies stood nearby.

I looked at Banquo.

He had a strained look on his face. On the surface, he looked delighted and proud. But under that, I saw the deep lines of worry. He smiled at me, inclining his head.

I returned the gesture.

A groom took the reins of my horse, and another attendant helped me down. Macbeth and I moved into place, our guard behind us.

The bishop signaled for Macbeth and me to come forward.

Macbeth ever-so-slightly offered me his arm.

Never. Instead, I set my hand on the hilt of my blade.

"Fine," Macbeth hissed under his breath.

We moved forward, coming to a stop before the bishop.

"Who comes to Scone today to take their place on the stone of destiny?" the bishop called.

"Macbeth, son of Findelach and Donalda, heir to the throne by right of blood and combat," Macbeth said in a loud voice.

"And who comes as queen?"

"Gruoch, daughter of Boite and Emir."

"Come, Macbeth, son of Findelach, and Gruoch, daughter of Boite," the bishop said, taking us both by our hands. He led Macbeth to the great stone which had been set upon a sturdy dais. Alongside it was another seat that had been carved with ancient symbols. Behind us, the tall stone cross cast its shadow.

The bishop motioned for us both to sit. He then came behind us and began the service in Latin. I only half listened as I eyed the crowd before me.

Thorfinn, whose arms were crossed on his chest, openly frowned at the bishop, but when his gaze fell on Macbeth, he smiled.

Madelaine was openly weeping. She gave me the softest of smiles.

I turned to Banquo. He stared at me. There was an odd shimmer of the Otherworld all around him. His eyes were wide, nostrils flaring. He was having a vision. And from the looks of it, not a good one.

"Bring them," the bishop said, motioning to one of his attendants.

I turned to look.

Two attendants came forward. They carried pillows on which were set two crowns. The boys stood behind Macbeth and me.

The bishop moved to stand behind me. He lifted the heavy silver crown off the first pillow. The metal was old and thick. I had never seen the crown before. It was not the beautiful diadem Suthen had worn to Duncan's coronation.

"In the name of Lord Jesus Christ, by right of victory and blood, I crown you Queen Gruoch of Scotland," the bishop said as he lowered the crown on my head.

In that same moment, a raven alighted on top of the Celtic cross behind me. It squawked loudly.

An audible gasp rolled through the crowd. Several of the Christians crossed themselves.

I turned to look at the raven.

No one would name me queen in the name of Lord Jesus Christ alone. While I had no quarrel with the White Christ, it was the Red Lady who had brought me here. And she would always have her say.

The bishop looked up at the raven, an annoyed expression on his face.

Over the hum of the whispering crowd, I heard Thorfinn's soft laugh.

The bishop frowned then turned to the other boy holding a crown. On the second pillow sat a solid gold coronet trimmed the blood-red rubies.

"In the name of Lord Jesus Christ, by right of victory and blood, I crown you King Macbeth of Scotland. Upon the sacred stone of destiny, may you take your place in the annals of this mighty kingdom," he said then slowly set the crown on Macbeth's head.

The raven squawked once more then flew off.

"Rise, King Macbeth and Queen Gruoch, and be greeted by your subjects," the bishop said then turned to the crowd. "All hail King Macbeth and Queen Gruoch."

"All hail," the massive crowd called in unison.

Smiling, Macbeth waved to the crowd who cheered loudly.

I joined him in the gesture, but when my eyes rested on Banquo once more, my joy faltered. In the place of the man I loved, I saw a dead man, a corpse, standing there with a dagger in his heart.

CHAPTER TWELVE

The lords and ladies gathered that day in the great hall to celebrate our coronation. As was the custom in older days, the warriors who had gathered hung their shields on the wall, displaying to all which lords, thanes, and clans had come to pledge their fidelity to the new king.

While Duncan's feast had been a lively event—full of proper dinner etiquette and stimulating conversations on the weather— our feast was far different. Pipers played, and lords and ladies danced. The Northmen drank and laughed, and even the more refined in the crowd seemed honestly at ease. Macbeth worked his way through the room, meeting with the southern lords, accepting their congratulations and—it did not escape my notice —introducing himself to all their fair daughters.

Killian had sent some of the men of Moray to work the room as well, but their eyes were looking for something far different from beautiful girls. And he was right to do so. Amongst all the cheer, I could feel the seeds of anger. The southern lords smiled to Macbeth's face, but they exchanged wary glances when his back was turned. More would need to be done to bring them back into the fold. Money, land, or properly placed threats would be needed, not pretty words. Surely Malcolm had taught Macbeth that.

My eyes also scanned the crowd for Banquo. He wasn't there. In fact, I hadn't seen him since having that strange, terrible vision at the coronation. My stomach knotted with worry.

"They will want to send ladies to court once you are settled at Dunsinane," Madelaine said.

I scoffed. "Well, I shall tell them no thank you."

"Corbie, it's tradition," she protested.

"It *was* a tradition. I will not lord over a court of luxury and waste. There is work to be done."

Madelaine sighed. "There are some elements of politics you must come to accept, despite how odious they may seem, including making nice with the ladies."

"We shall see," I said then turned to the bishop who was on his second decanter of wine—speaking of luxury. "Lord Bishop, I have a question for you."

The bishop swallowed the large mouthful of wine he was savoring then coughed lightly. "Yes, Your Majesty?"

"This crown," I said, touching the coronet on my head. "It appears quite old. What can you tell me about it?"

"Ah, you ask an excellent question, Your Majesty. King Macbeth chose the crowns for the coronation. That is the ancient crown of Moray."

"Of Moray? Who wore it?"

"Well, we are not entirely sure. Some say it was passed down from the ancient Pictish kings, saved from loss and ruin by your ancient ancestor, Kenneth. But no one can say for certain. King Macbeth thought it would befit you, the Lady of Moray, to be crowned with the ancient crown of your people."

"And it does," Madelaine said, touching the crown gently.

"That was very thoughtful of His Majesty," I said, casting a glance at Macbeth.

"And King Macbeth's crown?" Madelaine asked.

"Newly made, Lady Fife."

Madelaine nodded but said nothing.

Now, why would Macbeth make a special effort to have me crowned with a piece that would hold meaning for me, a crown that would tie me to the land and people I had come to love? Macbeth didn't care at all for me. So why make such a gesture?

"Thank you, Lord Bishop," I said. The man nodded, but he was already refilling his wine goblet and hardly paid me another thought.

"I don't see the Thane of Lochaber," Madelaine told me as she scanned the room.

I shook my head. "No. I haven't seen him since the coronation."

"So, does he know?" Madelaine asked in a low whisper.

"Know what?"

"That you are with child?"

I turned and looked at her. "How do you—"

"Corbie, I may not have borne you, but I was a mother to you all the same. And I know your shape like my own. The laces on the gown…"

I smiled lightly. "Then you are wiser than I, for it had escaped my notice until Injibjorg said something."

"I wondered," Madelaine said.

I raised an eyebrow at her. "Wondered?"

"I wondered why you would go into battle in such a state. You didn't know."

I shook my head. There was no use in trying to keep anything from Madelaine. "No, I didn't know."

"It is a glad tiding," she said, setting her hand on mine.

When she did so, I followed her gaze only to find my own hands covered in blood once more. Slick red blood covered my fingers. The ruby red liquid marred Madelaine's pale skin.

Gasping, I pulled my hands back and grabbed a cloth. Moving quickly, I turned to clean the filth from Madelaine's hands, but when I did so, I found nothing there. I glanced at my hands again. The marks were there, red splotches staining my skin, but the dripping blood was gone.

"Corbie?" Madelaine said, startled. She took my hand again. "What is it?"

"Nothing."

"Nothing? That was not a nothing."

"I'm plagued by strange visions. Like clouds on a summer's day, they come then go, blocking the sun in the interim. I just need some air."

"Do you want me to come with you?"

I shook my head. "Please, stay and keep the others company. I'll return shortly," I said then rose.

"Very well," Madelaine told me, a confused and worried look on her face.

Killian stepped forward to pull out my chair.

"My Queen?" he said.

"I'll retire for a short while," I told him.

Killian signaled to some other guards.

We turned and headed toward the exit of the hall. As I went, I was greeted with bows and curtsies. I felt like I could barely catch my breath.

We had just reached the doors when the crowd parted to reveal Banquo—but not Banquo—standing there. Once more, I saw my love like a man dead. His face was pale, eyes a milky white, clothing ragged. And again, I saw a dagger hanging from his chest, his clothes marred with blood.

I gasped and stepped back, tripping on Killian.

"Cerr—Gruoch?" the corpse said. But when he opened his mouth to speak, his lips and tongue were black. A swarm of flies flew out, some of them pausing to land on his face.

"No," I stammered.

"My Queen," Killian said, holding my shoulders to keep me upright.

"Who has done this?" I whispered, staring at Banquo, abhorred by the sight. "Who has done this?" I demanded loudly.

"Lady Gruoch?" Killian said again. He then turned to the others and whispered, "Our Queen is not well. Let's get her to her chamber."

"Do you see him there?" I whispered to Killian. I lifted my finger and pointed at Banquo. Blood dripped from my extended digit.

"Lord Banquo? Of course."

"But do you *see*?"

Banquo advanced quickly on me. Closing my eyes, I suppressed a scream.

"Gruoch," Banquo said sharply, grabbing my arm.

"She's taken ill, my lord," Killian said.

"No. She's had a vision. Come, let's take her from this place before the others notice something's wrong. Gruoch, look at me," Banquo said, taking my hand.

I shook my head. "No."

"It was a vision. Look at me."

His hand in mine, I felt the warmth of his flesh.

Great Lady, let the vision pass.

I opened my eyes only to find Banquo standing there, whole and alive.

"Banquo," I whispered.

"What did you see?" he asked.

I shook my head, not wanting to tell him.

"My queen?" Killian said.

"Killian, I'm all right now. Please, let's return to my chamber," I said. Banquo and I departed then, the men of Moray following close behind.

"You were frightened of me," Banquo whispered.

"Not *of* you, *for* you."

"*For* me?"

I nodded.

Banquo frowned. "This day has been full of ominous portents."

"At the crowning, you saw something as well."

Banquo nodded.

"I'll ride with Madelaine when we are done here. Will you come with me?" I asked.

"Yes. I too need…time."

"Banquo, what does it mean, such ill omens?"

"You know as well as I," he said, his voice dark.

Dark times were ahead. On the day I had been crowned queen, I had foreseen the darkest visage I could imagine…the death of my soul mate.

CHAPTER THIRTEEN

*B*anquo stayed with me late into the night. We spoke of everything except our visions. We mocked the courtly southern lords in their fancy silk robes and pondered over the shows of wealth we saw all around us. We spoke of Lulach and Fleance. And we reminisced about Sid. There was no subject under the sun we didn't touch save our visions.

I didn't know what Banquo had seen during the crowning, but I knew him well enough to know that the vision still plagued him.

He was doing his best to hide his worries from me.

But I was hiding more than that from him.

"Thorfinn and Injibjorg will leave soon," Banquo said. "What will you do once they are gone?"

"Madelaine advised me to go to Glamis, but I'm not certain."

Mainly, I was not sure because I was still getting used to the idea that I was with child. I couldn't reconcile the idea. I didn't dare tell Banquo the truth that was tripping over my tongue. I was carrying his child. The idea was a joyous one, but a problem all the same. Macbeth and I had long been finished. I didn't care what he thought, but I did care about what Macbeth might do. The resentment he felt for Lulach, son of an uncle he hated, would be nothing compared to the resentment he would feel for the child I carried.

And if it were a girl…

"You said you want to return to Lochaber. Is that your plan?"

Banquo nodded.

"Why don't I come to Lochaber with you?"

"I would love to show you my home, but there would be talk."

"Not if we keep things quiet. I could go to Moray and travel from there."

Banquo smiled. For the first time, the clouds that covered his face lifted. "Let's consider it more. We'll make a plan," he said then tapped his drink against mine. He drank then eyed me over. "You look very tired, my Cerridwen. It's late. I should leave you now."

"I wish you could stay."

"So do I. Trust me. But I'll see you first thing in the morning," he said then rose.

I followed Banquo to the door. He stopped and took my face into his hands.

"I love you," I whispered.

"And I love you," he replied, leaning in to kiss me. His lips were sweet and warm. I caught the scent of the earthy smell that always perfumed his skin. I was carrying Banquo's child. How impossible it seemed. I was carrying his child.

He pulled away then set a soft kiss on my forehead. "Sleep well."

"And you."

Banquo opened the door.

The guards outside came to attention.

I waved farewell to Banquo, nodded to my men, then went back inside, bolting the door behind me.

I went to the table. Sitting there was a beautifully ornamented box. I opened the lid. Inside was the ancient crown of Moray. I lifted the heavy silver piece and inspected it. There were old engravings that had worn themselves almost invisible along the band. I stroked the metal with my finger. Setting the crown down for a moment, I reached back and undid the braids Tira and Rhona had made and let my short hair fall loose. I lifted the crown and placed it on my head.

I walked over to the fire and gazed into the cauldron hanging there. My reflection wavered on the surface of the liquid. Banquo was right. I did look tired. My skin was pale, and there were dark rings under my eyes. Hardly the picture of a youthful May Queen.

But I was in bloom.

My hands drifted to my stomach.

I closed my eyes.

"Are you there?" I whispered.

At that moment, I felt something. I felt life.

But more, I felt a shift in the world around me.

The air cooled, and I smelled wisteria.

"How now you, midnight messengers?" I whispered, opening my eyes once more.

I was standing on the terrace before the great cauldron, but neither Andraste nor Nimue were there.

The fire crackled, and a soft breeze blew, stirring up the sweet scent of flowers.

Frowning, I looked all around.

I was alone. I walked through the ruins. As I passed by the living quarters, I heard the soft sounds of someone sleeping. I peered into Nimue's room to find her on her bed. Moving further down the hall, I discovered Andraste sleeping as well, snoring like Thorfinn.

Winding down the halls of the ruins of Ynes Verleath, I made my way to the room of the eternal flame. There, I found a robed figure kneeling before the broken statue of the Goddess.

It wasn't the red-robed Morrigu or even the Crone. I had seen this lady only once before. It was silver-haired Scotia.

The Goddess whispered, her incantation nearly inaudible, then rose and walked toward me, her silver cloak billowing all around her. Her eyes twinkled like the stars. She eyed me over then walked in a circle around me, assessing me.

"Avenger. Warrior. Queen. You have come full circle, Cerridwen. Now it is time for you to do my bidding."

"And what is your bidding, Great Lady?"

She reached out and took my crown into her hands. She turned the circle around and around. The movement made my head swim.

"Like a wheel of fortune, with no beginning and no end, you must spin the wheel of fate once more and make something new. A new Scotland. A land reborn. You will fashion it with wisdom, cunning, and faith. Now, you must do my work," she said then set the crown on my head once more. As she did so, she said. "Rule in my name."

"I am your servant."

She straightened my crown, pushed my hair behind my ears, then looked me in the eyes. "And like all servants, you will grunt and sweat under the yoke. The chore will burn and wound you. But in the end, it must be done."

"With your help, all things are possible," I whispered. But there was so much more I wanted to say. I wanted to ask about my child. I wanted to ask about the visions I had seen of Banquo. I wanted to know why there was blood all over my hands. And I wanted to know what to do about Macbeth.

Scotia set two fingers to my brow. When she did so, an image of Macbeth came to mind. He was wearing humble traveler's robes and holding a staff. Alongside him were monks and other holy men. He wore a simple wreath on his head. I watched him walk away from a castle I didn't recognize. And beyond that castle's walls, I saw a very long road threading out into the great unknown. With the eyes of a raven, I watched the road twist and turn until it reached a vast city over which hovered a white dove.

Scotia pulled her fingers away. "Wake now, Cerridwen, and begin." She blew gently on my face, making me wince. When I opened my eyes once more, I was lying on the floor in Scone. I clutched the ancient crown in my hand, but the ornament's sharp edges had pricked my fingers. Droplets of blood dripped down my hand, melding with the stains thereon.

The first hint of morning light peeked in through the window. My body aching, I rose and set the crown back in the box. Lifting a rag, I went to clean the blood from my fingertips only to find my hands covered in slicks of red once more.

I squeezed my eyes shut. "It's not real. There is nothing there."

Opening my eyes again, I went to my bed, lay down, and pulled my blankets up to my neck. Tira and Rhona would be there soon. I needed to get some sleep before the day began again.

When I woke, I had much to consider.

Including the city of the dove…Rome.

CHAPTER FOURTEEN

"My lady," Tira chirped happily. "Lady—no, Queen —Gruoch. Best get out of bed."

"Leave her be a while longer. Get me some kindling for the fire," Rhona said.

"But the other lords and ladies are already at morning meal," Tira protested.

"Let Lady Madelaine entertain them. If our lady is tired, let her sleep. She's worked herself half to death."

"But what will they say if she doesn't come for morning meal?"

"That's she's odd and unfriendly."

"Rhona!"

"I hardly think Lady Gruoch would mind such gossip," Rhona said then added, "since she knows herself it's true."

Both of the maids chuckled lightly.

"But still," Tira protested.

"Lay out her clothes. When she rises, you'll have everything ready."

"By all the gods, who could sleep with such noisome and gossiping maids anyway?" I complained from the bed.

At that, they both laughed.

"Now, see what you've done," Rhona complained to Tira.

"Well, it's time to get up anyway."

"Right, otherwise I'll seem odd and unfriendly," I said.

Both of the maids stilled. For a moment, it seemed they were unsure if I had been offended or not.

I laughed. "I am odd and unfriendly. Rhona is right. There are only a handful of people in this world whose company I enjoy. I suppose that includes the two of you...most of the time."

The maids chuckled.

Rising slowly, I began getting ready for the day. Once I had properly cleaned up, I dressed in the green gown Tira had selected. With a yawn, I headed toward the feasting hall.

As I neared the room, the scents of roasting meat and bread assailed my nostrils. I paused a moment when a wave of nausea swept over me.

"Queen Gruoch?" Magnus, one of my guards, said, offering his arm to steady me.

"I'm all right," I reassured him. Pregnancy was such an odd thing. The kitchen smells made me feel both ill and famished at the same time. "I think I'm still tired."

Magnus, a stout man with a red beard, smiled warmly but made no comment.

I arrived in the feasting hall to see, much to my great relief, that the number of people gathered there had slimmed down to half.

I went to the end of the table and took the empty seat between Madelaine and Macbeth.

"My Queen," Macbeth said politely.

I forced myself not to sneer at him.

"Good morrow to you all," I said. I gave Macbeth a passing glance.

Madelaine wrapped her arm around me and kissed me on the cheek. "My dear."

I smiled at her then turned to Banquo.

He lifted his cup to toast me.

I grinned at him.

"We'll be setting sail this morning," Thorfinn told me. "Much work to be done in the north, and I don't want Injibjorg to get used to southern luxuries," he said, patting his wife on the back of her head.

She laughed. "Southern luxuries?" She glanced down the table at the richly-dressed lords and ladies sitting there. "Some of the men dress like women here."

We all laughed. She was right. But her observation was also an important one. Many of the southern lords were dressed in such a manner to show there was great wealth in their lands. How had they come by it? What trade or deals had they won to earn it? And why hadn't any of that wealth come north? That was something Macbeth and I needed to know.

"I'm sorry I can't go with you," Macbeth told Thorfinn. "But Gruoch and I will depart for Glamis within the week."

"I will go with Fife for a time and join you after," I said absently.

There was a brief, awkward silence.

"Of course," Macbeth chirped. "I meant you'd join me in Glamis afterward. Naturally, since we are in the south, you will spend time with Madelaine. But you will always be welcome at court, Lady Madelaine," Macbeth said. "I suspect Gruoch would appreciate having you there."

"To herd the chattel," Injibjorg said, motioning down the table.

I laughed then turned to Thorfinn. "All these years you bragged of Injibjorg's beauty. You didn't tell us that the gods had cut her tongue to match yours."

"Why do you think I found her so beautiful?" Thorfinn said, laughing merrily.

I raised my cup. "Then a toast. To a perfect match."

The others around me raised their cups.

"To Thorfinn and Injibjorg," I said.

"To Thorfinn and Injibjorg," the others called.

I lifted my cup and drank, fully aware that Macbeth's eyes were on me—as were Banquo's. The sooner I got out of this place, the better.

*T*he Northmen packed their belongings after the morning meal and got ready to return to their ships. We all joined them in the courtyard to wish them farewell.

I kissed Injibjorg on both cheeks. "I wish you safe travels."

"May Freya watch over you and your little one," she told me.

"Thank you." I squeezed her hand then let her go. I then went to Thorfinn. "I am sorry to see you leave so soon, but I understand there is much to be done."

Thorfinn nodded. "Things are not as settled for Magnus as they should be, but I will make sure things stay quiet in the north for you, Queen Gruoch."

I grinned at him. "I expected no less."

He leaned forward, his voice low. "Gruoch, you must be watchful. The paint covering the surface is already beginning to crack. Don't get too far away or we may lose everything we've worked for," he said then passed a glance toward Macbeth who was speaking to another of the Northmen.

"I understand."

Thorfinn nodded.

"Safe travels, all of you," I called then stepped back.

"Brother," Banquo called to Thorfinn. "Fair travels."

"And to you, Thane of Lochaber," Thorfinn said, touching his fingers to his brow.

Banquo mimicked the gesture.

I moved to join Banquo.

"Macbeth has asked me to move some of the men, a standing army, to Glamis. I will begin today and will meet you at the coven as soon as I can," Banquo whispered. "I've already told Macbeth I will go to Lochaber for a time, but he has asked me to return to court as soon as possible."

I nodded. "I shall see you soon. Stay safe."

"And you. Gruoch, are you well? You looked very pale this morning."

I couldn't help but smile. I was dying to tell him the truth. But not now. Not here. "I am very well, Thane."

At that, Banquo smiled. "Good."

"Queen Gruoch," the Thane of Fife called, crossing the yard to meet me. "We will ride this afternoon. You'll be joining us?"

I nodded.

"Very good," he said happily. "Now, let me see about our escort," he said then wandered off.

"I'll send Tira, Rhona, and most of the Moray men to Glamis. Have you been there before?" I asked Banquo.

He shook his head. "No, but the report is it's a small but sturdy castle."

"And the fortress of Dunsinane?"

"Old, by all accounts, but Macbeth has already arranged for workmen to refortify the castle and craftsmen to improve upon it."

I frowned. "Why did he choose such a place?"

Banquo shook his head. "Why does Macbeth do anything?" he said then looked toward Macbeth.

I followed his gaze. Macbeth had taken to horse and was

reining in beside Thorfinn. Apparently, he would ride to the port with the party.

I shook my head. "Who knows? And now he is King of Scots, for better or worse. And we have placed him there. We are the ones who must ensure no harm comes from our doing."

"May the Great Father and Mother give us strength," Banquo said.

"And all the gods watch over us," I said. While Scotia had set me on my path, something told me that I would need to elicit the help of all the gods—even the White Christ—to keep Macbeth in check.

CHAPTER FIFTEEN

*T*hat morning, Tira and Rhona finished packing my things then headed off to get their own belongings ready to take to Glamis. I was in my chamber making the final preparations to depart with Fife when there was a knock on the door.

"My Queen," Killian called.

A moment later, the door opened. Macbeth pushed past Killian.

"A word?" Macbeth said.

"Well, you're already here," I said then motioned to Killian to shut the door.

He did so with a frown.

"I don't like that your guard tried to stop me. I am king," Macbeth said then crossed the room to the table where he poured himself a glass of wine. He sat down and took a long, slow drink as he gazed around the room.

"They are charged with protecting me."

Macbeth set down his goblet with a clatter. "From me? From their king?"

"Of course."

Macbeth blew air through his lips.

"What do you want, Macbeth?"

"When will you come to Glamis?"

"I don't know. But I will come. I am sending my household ahead to join you if you are hunting for reassurance. Though you will not harass any of my people."

"Harass your people? What nonsense."

"Nonsense? Tell that to Ute. You will leave my people alone. That is not a request."

Macbeth turned and poured himself another drink. "And in the meantime, what am I supposed to tell the lords and ladies who want to see you? The ladies who want to come to court to join you?"

"Tell them Queen Gruoch is traveling and that I will invite them when Dunsinane is ready."

"And will you?"

"Perhaps. We shall see…once Dunsinane is ready."

"Why are you going with Fife?"

"Because I wish it."

"There is work to be done."

"So there is. I have already begun my work. Have you?"

Macbeth huffed then ran his fingers through his hair. The action was so rough I thought for a moment he might rip his hair from his scalp. "I know what to do."

"I hope so. The southern lords are rich beyond any reasonable measure. They scowl and talk behind your back. Crinian, who holds all the silver in this land, is noticeably absent. Duncan's son, Donaldbane, is still unaccounted for, and we have no more allies today than we did when the war began."

Macbeth threw his wine goblet across the room, the red liquid splashing the skirt of my dress. The cup hit the door then fell with a clatter.

"I know what to do," Macbeth shouted at me.

I set my hand on the hilt of Uald's Gift. "Then go do it. Besides, I think it's time for you to leave."

Macbeth glared at me. He eyed my blade and then his eyes went to my gown where the red wine marred the pale green fabric of my dress. He furrowed his brow as if he were confused by what he saw. Then a look of realization crossed his face.

"Gruoch, I—"

"It's time for you to leave," I repeated.

Macbeth let out a noise that sounded like a growl then rose roughly, the chair falling in his wake. He stalked to the other side of the room and wrenched the door open.

Outside the door, my guard stood waiting. Their blades were drawn.

I motioned to them, and they stepped aside to let Macbeth pass.

Macbeth thundered down the hall and out of sight.

I took a deep breath, calming the beating wings of the raven that were echoing at the edges of my senses. Pulling on a placid smile, I went to Killian. "Killian, please divide our men. I want most of the Moray guard to go to Glamis to keep an eye on my household while I am gone. You and two other men will ride with me to Fife."

"Yes, my queen. Are you...are you all right?" he asked, glancing down at my hand still resting on the hilt of my blade.

"How can I be anything but well?"

He smirked but said nothing else.

I inclined my head to him then closed the door behind me.

I couldn't wait to leave Scone.

CHAPTER SIXTEEN

That afternoon, as we prepared to leave Scone, a rider—one of Banquo's men—arrived. Banquo, who had already gone to Glamis, wasn't there. I flagged the man down.

"Sir, do you have a message for Lord Banquo?"

The rider nodded. "Yes, my queen. Lord Banquo, he..." he began then paused.

"You may tell me anything you would tell Lord Banquo," I said, reassuring the man. For once, I hoped news of my relationship with Banquo would help soften the situation.

It did.

"Lord Banquo sent some of us out looking for a man."

"Tavis? Did you find him?"

The man lowered his gaze. "Yes, Your Majesty."

For a moment, I felt like my heart stopped beating.

I grabbed the man by his arm. "And?"

"He was close to Lady Madelaine's castle but senseless. He was badly injured. I took him there, left him in the care of that house, then came straight here afterward."

"Bless you, sir," I told him. "Go, get some refreshment. Thank you," I said then turned to go.

"Your Majesty," the man called. "You should hurry."

I swallowed hard then nodded. I rushed across the courtyard to Madelaine and Fife who looked like they were almost ready to depart. I forced myself to stay calm. It wouldn't do for me to show my worry. As it was, Madelaine was going to be in a fit of distress.

"Corbie?" Madelaine called.

"Aunt, we must go to your castle at once. A rider has come. Tavis has been taken to your keep. He is injured."

Madelaine gasped.

Turning, Fife snapped his fingers and called to his men to make ready. "We'll ride together," he told Madelaine. "Now."

Not waiting another moment, I grabbed the reins of the blood bay and mounted. Wheeling the horse around, I trotted over to Killian and the other Moray men. "We need to leave now," I told them.

Working quickly, the men finished readying their horses and supplies then mounted.

I rode back to Madelaine. She was watching Fife's men make ready. Her brow furrowed, and she chewed her lip.

"Thane," I called to Fife who turned and looked at me. "Moray is ready to ride. We shall go ahead."

Fife inclined his head to me.

"Let's go," I told Madelaine.

I nodded to Killian, and our small party set out.

We rode quickly across the land. I wanted to ride harder than I did. I knew that during the battle I had not been careful. But now that I knew I was with child, I hesitated. After all, I had already lost a wee one. I didn't want to risk another, especially Banquo's child.

Regardless, we rode briskly across the land and arrived at the castle in the early evening.

I was surprised when we were met by a familiar face, Ute.

"My lady," she called to Madelaine. She rushed to my aunt and helped her down.

"Where is he?" Madelaine asked, her eyes wild.

"With a healer in his chamber."

Without waiting another moment, Madelaine rushed off.

"Ute," I called lightly, slipping off my horse.

"Gruoch," she said happily. She pulled me into an embrace.

I leaned back and looked at her. "How good to see you," I said. The years in Fife had given Ute time to recover. She'd regained much of the weight she'd lost in the last months she'd been with me. Where her cheeks had once been hollow, they were full and rosy once more. She smiled at me, but there was worry behind her eyes.

"Tavis…how is he?"

Ute shook her head. "Fever. The wound has festered. It's good you're here. You should come now."

I nodded. "Do we know what happened to him? Has he said anything?"

"He's in no state to speak clearly. From what we have been able to glean, he sustained a sword wound on his side. It looks like he tried to treat it, but the wound went bad. He's burning up, and convulsions started an hour ago. He…Gruoch…" she said then shook her head.

Ute led me to a chamber on the second floor of the castle. Even before we got to the room, I could smell sickness.

I entered to find a servant with a blood-covered apron and a healer I didn't know. I cursed myself for not carrying my medicines with me. The room smelled of illness and incense. Madelaine was sitting at Tavis' bedside, his hand in hers.

"Tavis," she whispered. "Tavis, can you hear me?"

"Why is this room closed?" I asked. "Open the casement and freshen the air."

The servant and priest looked up at me, both pausing to stare.

"Oh…Your Majesty," the servant said, dropping a curtsey.

"Your Majesty," the healer repeated.

I waved a hand dismissively. "No time for that. The windows," I said then went to Tavis.

"Corbie," Madelaine whispered, moving aside so I could see.

As she had with me, Ute relayed to Madelaine what had been happening.

"Tavis?" I whispered, setting my hand on his head. He was burning with fever.

I went to the washbasin and cleaned my hands. I then returned to the bed. I pulled back the coverlets to see the wound there. It was neatly dressed, but the scent of rot wafted from the bandages which were tinged yellowish from the liquid that had seeped from the wound.

"Fresh water," I told Ute.

Working gently, I removed the bandages to see the festering wound underneath. Someone had carved into Tavis's side. By now, the wound should have begun to heal, but it hadn't been properly cleaned.

"Tavis?" I said, gently touching his shoulder. "I will try to clean your wound. Can you hear me? It will be painful. I'm so sorry," I said then motioned for Ute to hand me the pitcher of water.

"My queen—" the healer began in protest.

"Send him out."

Madelaine moved quickly to remove the others.

Working carefully, I washed Tavis. Again and again, I cursed myself for not bringing along any of my herbs or medicines.

Frowning, I worked hard at cleaning the wound while Tavis winced and groaned. It soon became evident to me that the infection was severe. Dark, spidery veins had crept across his chest. If the poison was already in his blood, it could kill him at any time. Working as best I could, I cleaned the wound then applied what paltry medicines the healer had brought with him. There were medicines that could help, that could slow the infection, but none were on hand. Wordlessly, I redressed the wound once more.

"Corbie, will he be all right?" Madelaine asked through a mask of tears.

I rose and washed my hands.

"Corbie?"

"I must ride out at once. Either Druanne will come, or I will tie her to a horse and make her come."

"But Corbie…"

"Madelaine, we need Druanne," I said, forcing myself to be strong, but in spite of myself, my voice cracked. The truth of the matter was, Tavis was dying. Unless I got Druanne there in time, he would not live.

Madelaine caught the sound in my voice. A sob escaped her. "All right," she whispered. "Then go. Quickly."

I turned to Ute.

"I'll go get help. Please, watch over them both," I said, motioning to Madelaine and Tavis.

Once more, I turned to Tavis and set my hand on his forehead. "Old friend," I whispered. "Please hold on. Help is coming."

Tavis let out a soft groan but did not open his eyes.

Without another word, I turned and left the chamber.

Moving quickly, I returned to the stables where the blood bay was getting his fill of oats and water. I pulled my saddle from the wall and began readying him to ride once more.

"Queen Gruoch?" a voice called.

I turned to find Killian there.

"Where are you going?" he asked.

"To fetch a healer."

"It's dark," he said in confused alarm. "Can't you send someone?"

"No. I cannot. I must go."

Without another word, Killian fetched his own horse and began saddling him.

"What are you doing?" I asked.

"Coming with you."

"No, you may not."

"Forgive me, my queen, but Standish made me promise that no harm would come to you. I don't intend to falter on my promise."

Frowning, I nudged the bay away from the oats then finished saddling him.

"Then you must learn to keep secrets."

"Secrets? I... Of course, my queen."

"And you need to start calling me Gruoch, or I may lose my patience with you. Come. We must hurry," I said then slid onto my horse.

"As you wish...Gruoch."

We rode off into the night. Part of me wanted to let the bay run the way I knew he could, but the other part of me remembered how fragile my womb was. I had lost Macbeth's child. Banquo's child was more precious to me than anything on Earth save Lulach and Crearwy. Yet Tavis's life was at stake. I had to hurry.

We rode deep into the night, finally reaching the stream where Tavis often camped. When we arrived, I debated what to do. I had never agreed with Madelaine's reluctance to bring Tavis to the coven. He was not a practitioner of our faith, but he knew what the coven was and had even befriended Uald. There would have been no harm in bringing him, yet he never came. I glanced at Killian. He had proven himself loyal, and I knew he worshipped the old ways. He was not the problem. Crearwy was. No one from the outside could ever see my daughter. Not even a man I trusted to protect my life.

"What is it?" Killian asked. "Do you need to rest?"

"No. We are nearly there, it's just…this place I'm going to is special. It is closed to the outside world. I will ride ahead but will return soon with holy women, healers, who must be taken back to the castle at once."

"I should ride with you."

"I assure you, I am safe here. Make camp here. I'll send word or come myself within the hour."

"Gruoch," Killian protested.

"By the Great Mother and Father God, I ask you to trust and obey me," I said, and with a twitch of my fingers, I pulled a bit of magic from the aether, wrapping glamour around me.

Killian flexed his brow then inclined his head. "As you wish. I see there is an old fire pit here. I will camp… for now."

I nodded. "Thank you."

Killian huffed a laugh. "Secrets then, Lady Gruoch?"

"Don't we all have our secrets?"

"I suppose we do. Your secrets are safe with me," he said then bowed. I couldn't help but catch the glimmer in his eyes. Maybe Banquo was right. Perhaps Killian did hold some affection for me. It was a love I could never return, but if he admired me, he would be more inclined to keep my secrets.

"Thank you," I said then turned the horse and rode into the night.

I moved through the dark forest, guided only by the moonlight. An owl shrieked, and animals moved through the woods, unseen. At that moment, I wished I had Thora with me. She had been a constant comfort and protector. I keenly felt her absence.

I pushed through the woods, finally arriving at the coven when the moon was high in the sky. I was surprised to find the place quiet. No one had risen to greet me.

The fire was out in Sid's house. Her windows were dark.

Frowning, I tied the bay then went to Uald's smithy. I crept quietly inside to find her in her sleeping chamber, snoring loudly.

"Uald," I whispered, gently shaking her shoulder.

She woke with a start and sat bolt upright. She grabbed a dagger from her bedside and brandished it in front of her.

I stepped back. "Don't kill me."

"Cerridwen?" Uald asked, her eyes clearing.

"Yes."

"What…when did you arrive?"

"Just now."

"Epona didn't tell us to expect you."

I shook my head. "The entire place is asleep."

Uald frowned hard. It was not like Epona to miss that a visitor was coming.

"Why are you here?" Uald asked.

"Tavis is gravely ill. I must wake Druanne. She must go at once."

"Oh, well, this will be interesting," Uald said with a chuckle then rose.

"That's why I need you. Will you go with her? I need to see Crearwy, but Tavis…"

"No. You stay. I will take Druanne."

"I have a man at the old camp. He will ride with you."

"Corbie has another man. That's not much of a surprise."

"Not that kind of man," I said. I had enough problems to sort out without complicating things further by entertaining a romantic dalliance.

Uald rose and grabbed her things. She nodded to me.

We crossed the coven square to Druanne and Aridmis' house. Uald knocked on the door.

There was a shuffle inside. A moment later, Aridmis, her blanket wrapped around her, opened the door.

"Good evening. Or is it morning?" she said.

"Who is it?" Druanne called.

"It's Uald. And Cerridwen."

"What?" Druanne asked sourly. Her bed creaked, and a moment later, Druanne appeared behind Aridmis. She scowled at me. "What are you doing here?"

"I'm here for you," I said, biting back the hundred or so nasty words that wanted to spew from my mouth. "Tavis is with Madelaine at the keep. He took a sword wound and is gravely ill. The wound has festered. I think it may be in his blood. I have no proper medicines with me, and Fife's healers are unlearned. We need you."

"Where is Epona?" Druanne demanded.

"Asleep," Uald answered, a sharp tone in her voice.

Aridmis looked at Druanne.

"And you want me to go...out there?" Druanne asked.

"I will ride with you," Uald said. "And Cerridwen has an escort for us."

"Oh...wonderful," Druanne said, rolling her eyes so hard it must have hurt.

"Enough, Druanne. Tavis is dying. That man has been true to the secret of this coven and one of its daughters for many years. Please. Please come," I said.

Druanne blew air through her lips then turned and went back into the house. I heard the rattle of boxes, bottles, and tools as she began collecting her things.

"I'll get the horses ready," Uald said then turned and headed back to her smithy.

Aridmis stepped outside, pulling her blanket more tightly around her.

"I wish you many felicitations," Aridmis said. "I saw it there, your crowning," she said, pointing to the heavens. "But wish I had seen it with my own eyes. Queen of Scotland."

I nodded. "May the Goddess guide me."

"Hmm," Aridmis mused with a heavy shrug.

I looked at her. "Aridmis, you're making me nervous."

"What's fair is foul and foul is fair," she said.

"You're not the first to say that to me," I told her, remembering that Andraste had said those very words to me just before my entire life turned upside down.

"I know," Aridmis said with a wink.

A moment later, Druanne reappeared, bags and boxes in hand. "I'm ready."

I nodded to her then the three of us went to join Uald who was leading the horses. I took the reins of Uald's steed, so she could mount.

"My man's name is Killian," I told Uald. "He is a loyal man. Ask him to take you to the keep. Please reassure him that I am safe here."

Uald nodded.

I took Druanne's things, so she could get on. As she settled in, I secured her bags and cases. "Thank you, Druanne."

"Who am I to say no to the Queen of Scotland?" she said then turned her horse and headed toward the coven exit.

Uald shook her head then followed Druanne into the night.

Wordlessly, Aridmis and I watched them go.

I cast a glance around the coven. It was so quiet. It seemed to me some of the buildings had fallen into disrepair. Everything looked run down.

"What do your raven eyes see?" Aridmis whispered.

"I don't know."

"Decay. Decline."

"Yes."

"You must prepare yourself. As do we."

"For what?"

Aridmis took my hand and led me to Epona's house. Moving quietly, we went inside.

The light from the hearth made the place glow a soft orange color. Someone stirred in one of the rooms in the back. And a moment later, a shadow appeared in the eating area—but it wasn't a person.

It was a dog.

A black puppy.

"Thora?"

The dog wagged her tail then walked over to me.

No, this wasn't Thora. This pup had a spot of white just above her eye. I recognized the puppy. She wasn't Thora, but she was one of the pups from Thora's litter. Eochaid had done as I'd asked and delivered the puppy for me.

"Well, grand-dog-daughter, how do you fare?" I whispered, patting the dog on her head.

"She appeared in the coven not long ago. Uald swore she looked just like your dog. But Sid...Sid knew," Aridmis said.

The puppy licked my face then went and lay down in front of the fire.

Aridmis lit a taper, and we headed to the back of the house where Epona slept.

At first, I was confused. In Epona's bed was a woman whose advanced age put me in mind of Andraste. The woman had white hair tinged yellow. Her face was deeply lined and marred by age. She looked old and frail under her heavy blanket.

She sighed in her sleep.

It was then that I realized that the woman *was* Epona.

"Aridmis," I whispered.

She nodded. "Her time is coming to an end."

A soft sigh sounded from the other room. Aridmis shifted the candle, panning the light therein. On a small pallet was a little body lying under a heavy bear fur. A mop of dark hair fell from the bed to the floor.

Crearwy.

There was no denying she was my child, but in her placid face, relaxed with sleep, I saw the mirror of Gillacoemgain's sister.

"That's not possible," I whispered.

"What's not possible?" Aridmis asked.

"She looks like Gillacoemgain's sister. Just like her."

"And why isn't that possible?" Aridmis asked.

"Because..."

Aridmis set her hand on my shoulder. "Goodnight, Cerridwen."

I stared at Crearwy. It didn't make any sense. Certainly, Gillacoemgain's sister did share some looks with me, some small features, but it was almost as if I was starting at the shade herself.

"Aridmis," I said, my heart thudding in my chest.

Aridmis turned and looked back at me. "Cerridwen, why should you be surprised? All children resemble their family," she said then turned and exited Epona's house, leaving me standing there, reeling at her words.

It wasn't possible.

It just wasn't possible.

Both Epona and I had seen a vision the night I was assaulted, a vision that showed us I would have twins. And Andraste had plainly stated that I carried Duncan's children.

But Andraste tells lies.

The words echoed through my head. But whose words were they? My own? The Goddess? The raven?

Setting my candle down on the table beside Crearwy's bed, I

slipped onto the pallet beside her. Covering us both, I wrapped my arms around my daughter and pulled her close to me.

She stirred a little in her sleep then sighed contentedly.

Exhausted from the long night's ride, worried for Tavis, confused about Epona, my mind in a fit of confusion, I lay staring at the wall.

Crearwy took my hand into hers. "Welcome home, Mother," she whispered.

My heart full of joy, I finally relaxed and drifted off into dreams.

CHAPTER SEVENTEEN

I woke the next morning to the feeling of someone playing with my hair. I opened my eyes to find Crearwy sitting up in bed working on a braid.

"Mother, what happened to your hair?"

"I cut it."

"Why?"

"Because I wanted to honor the Morrigu before I went into battle."

"Did you go into battle?"

"Yes."

"And did you kill many people?"

"A fair few."

She nodded. "And did you win?"

"Yes."

"So, now you're Queen of Scotland?"

"I am."

"Does that make me a princess?"

It did if anyone knew she existed. "Yes."

"Well, your hair is too short to braid properly."

I chuckled. "You sound like my maids."

"You have maids?"

"Yes, Tira and Rhona. And there is also Morag, who looks after Lulach and Lord Banquo's son, Fleance."

"How funny. You have women looking after you like you're a child."

"Well..." I began, but then I realized she was right. It was rather ridiculous.

The black puppy, roused by the sound of voices, appeared. She jumped on the bed with us.

Crearwy giggled. "Now, Beauty," she chided the dog. "Behave."

"Beauty? That's what you've named her?"

Crearwy nodded. "She thinks *she's* the one who is a princess."

I patted Beauty on her head. "Well, Thora always did think herself important. No wonder her daughter would be the same."

"Thora? Your dog? Sid told me this puppy was a gift from you, but I wasn't sure if I should believe her."

"Always believe Sid."

Crearwy flexed her brow as she thought about my words. "Druanne looks at Sid like she's a mad woman."

"That's because, for all of Druanne's wisdom, she cannot see the Otherworld. Sid is not mad."

"No. I didn't think so. But I do think she likes to play tricks... for fun."

"Well, that I can believe."

"Crearwy?" Epona called from the other room. "Who are you talking to?"

"My mother."

There was a pause, and I heard the bed creak. A moment later, Epona appeared in the doorway.

"Cerridwen?"

I sat up and looked at Epona. She and Andraste could have been sisters. "Oh, Epona."

She chuckled lightly. "Yes, I'm sure I'm quite the shock. What are you doing here?"

"Madelaine and I were planning to come, but Tavis is gravely ill. Druanne and Uald have gone to Madelaine's keep."

Epona nodded. "Oh. Yes. Well...she will miss him terribly," she said absently then turned and headed back into the main room. "I'll make the breakfast."

I looked at Crearwy who didn't seem a bit disturbed by Epona's odd behavior.

"Let me go help," I said then kissed Crearwy on the forehead.

"All right. I'll go feed the animals since Uald is gone," Crearwy said.

"You know how?"

She laughed as though I'd asked a silly question. "Of course."

"Don't forget to put on your cloak."

"Mother."

I bit the inside of my cheek. They were right. She was every bit as sharp around the edges as they said.

Pushing my hair back, Crearwy's half-braid falling out, I went to the main room and started banking up the fire.

Moving slowly, Epona began setting out the dishes. "Now, there is Crearwy and me, Juno, Tully, Aridmis, Cerridwen, and... and...and Flidas. I will set a place for Sid. She will come back to see Cerridwen," she whispered to herself as she worked.

"And May?" I asked.

"May? No. She left a year or so ago."

"Where did she go?"

"Somewhere west. We had a girl here for a short time, a promising acolyte, daughter of a clan chieftain, but she left. May went with her. Crearwy was grown enough, and May wanted to start a new life."

"She just...left?"

"Not like that. We all supported her."

"But how did Crearwy take it?"

"She cried a bit, but all things change," Epona said.

I frowned. No doubt Crearwy had suffered from the loss. I hated the idea that she'd grieved, and I had not known, had not been here to comfort her.

Once the fire was burning steadily, I opened Epona's cupboard and had a look. The rations were paltry.

"Epona, do you want me to ask Madelaine to send some supplies?"

"Yes. Yes, that would be fine. Ask Madelaine to get some things for us," she said then went to the bin where she used to keep the bread. It was empty. Epona gazed at the empty container as if she was confused.

I pulled out some oats and honey. Digging through Epona's stores, I found a few fresh eggs. I got to work mixing up the batter for breakfast cakes while Epona set out cups.

"Why are you here, Cerridwen?" Epona asked.

"As I said, I came to see Crearwy. But with Tavis ill, I had to fetch Druanne. Unfortunately, that also means I must return very soon. Madelaine will need me.

"And why else?"

I sighed softly. "Epona, I need your guidance."

"About what?"

"A seer told me I am with child."

Epona's gaze narrowed. She looked at my stomach. "And are you with child?"

"I believe so. My courses have not come. And I do feel the quickening in my womb."

"Macbeth's or Banquo's child?"

"Banquo's, of course. What should I do?"

Epona stared at me, her eyes looking misty. She sighed. "I'm sorry, Cerridwen. I cannot say. The sight has left me."

Her words struck me to my core. "But Epona, Crearwy is far

too young to be the leader of this coven. Why have you let go so soon? Crearwy is not ready."

"I was letting go a little at a time. And then one morning, I woke up and my magic was gone," she said, opening her hands.

"Gone?"

"Just like that. No visions. No glamour. No anything. Now there is only my mind and my hands. They will have to be enough to serve me in the days ahead."

"But what will we do?"

"Uald is ready to lead this place until Crearwy is of age. The others know the way."

"I love Uald, but she is not like you. The gods don't speak to her as they speak to you."

Epona laughed. There was bitterness in her voice that I'd never heard before. "The gods don't speak to me anymore. As for your unborn child, I don't know. And I am sorry for it. I never saw you with another child in my visions."

"Epona, I have something else to ask."

"Hmm?"

"The night I came here after...after what happened. You saw that I would bear two children. But did you see, clearly and for certain, that Duncan was their father? Please. Try to remember."

Epona sat down. She tapped her fingers on the table as she looked into the fire. "That night was so strange. Full of omens. Before you returned, the skies raged. Wolves howled. The owls and ravens shrieked. But the vision..." she said, squinting as she looked into the flames. "I saw two children. Clearly. And I knew that your daughter would come here. She had to. I saw Crearwy grow in this place. I saw her make things right for us again. I saw you carrying twins."

"But then? Right then? Was I with child *at that moment*?"

"At that moment..."

"Epona, I did as you advised me. I took Gillacoemgain to bed at once. Crearwy looks so much like Gillacoemgain's sister. And Lulach's smile... Is it possible the visions you had—the visions *I* had—were confused? Deluded? Is it possible that Lulach and Crearwy really are Gillacoemgain's children?"

Epona sat back and sighed. "The gods play games. They move us as they wish, and then leave us blind as they wish. What did Andraste say?"

"That they were Duncan's children."

"And how many hard choices did you make based on her words?"

My life. My whole life had been set into motion based on those words. "Many."

"The gods move us, Cerridwen. Andraste, she has become like them. Perhaps she is a goddess now, I cannot say. The magic she uses is beyond my understanding," she said then shook her head. "But I have never cared for her meddling. Nor for her, to be honest."

"Then it is possible that they are Gillacoemgain's children after all? Is that what you're saying?"

"My visions were no more exact than your own. I cannot say for sure Duncan was the father. I saw children. I saw you round with twins. But the father..."

My knees felt weak. I sat down.

"You must ask Andraste. That secret, black, and midnight hag. You must convince her to tell the truth. After all, it's done."

"What's done?"

"The deed without a name."

I was about to ask Epona what she meant when the door opened to reveal Juno, whom I had met only once before, and two women I did not know.

I rose.

"Cerridwen," Juno said with a smile. "Many welcome returns."

"By all the gods, this is Cerridwen?" the older of the two women asked.

Epona laughed lightly. "Cerridwen, this is Tully."

I smiled at the woman. She had long, pale blonde hair streaked with grey. Like Uald, she wore trousers and a tunic. Her skin was tanned and weathered, a testament to her days on the road.

"I'm so pleased to finally meet you," I said, moving to embrace her. All these years, I had heard tale after tale of the mysterious Tully who wandered the country looking for new recruits, following wherever the Goddess led, traveling to each of her sacred groves.

"Your timing is auspicious. I am about to travel north, now that our new rulers have things quieted down," she said with a wink.

Epona chuckled lightly. "Cerridwen, this is Flidas," she said, introducing a girl with long, brown hair standing behind Tully. At once, I noticed the girl bore a tattoo on her brow that was not unlike Banquo's.

"Sister," I said, inclining my head to her.

"Flidas is called by the nature spirits, creatures of the wood. Her mother is the leader of another coven," Epona explained.

"It's good to meet you, Cerridwen. You are much spoken of here. And well-loved."

I smiled at her, feeling uneasy under the sharpness of her gaze. It was almost as if she was seeing through me to someone or something else. "I'm pleased to meet you as well."

Flidas smiled at me.

"I was about to make breakfast," I said, picking up my bowl once more. Turning to the fire, I lifted the pan and began ladling cakes thereon.

"Epona, let us finish your work," Juno said, taking the water pitcher from Epona's hand.

Epona relinquished her work without complaint then sat on a

stool before the fire. She watched me work. The other women went into the kitchen of the house, chatting busily.

"The other covens," I said to Epona. "I am in a position to do more. To help. It would be helpful to know where—quite literally —I can be of use."

"Balor," Epona said. "Speak with Balor. I do not have the say I once had."

"Perhaps not, but I think you must still have some influence," I said, casting a glance at Flidas.

Epona chuckled. "A raven's eyes miss nothing."

I grinned but said no more.

Aridmis returned not long after, Crearwy along with her.

Once my cakes were made—and I felt rather proud of myself that I had managed not to burn any—everyone sat down to eat. Once more, I sat at the table with my sisters. I hadn't been Queen of Scotland for a week, but in Epona's home, I felt more at ease than I had in some time. But the starkness of the meal wasn't lost on me. While the offerings at the coven had always been humble, they had never been meager. As I looked at the others, I realized Aridmis looked far thinner than I remembered. Worries bubbled up in me.

Crearwy sat beside me, Beauty squeezing into the small space between us. Much like Thora, Beauty waited for scraps, but she was far more elegant in her manner. Lifting her paw, she gently nudged Crearwy. Crearwy fed bits of bread and dried meat to her dog. Beauty ate cleanly, not dropping a bite. If I had not already been sure of her lineage, Beauty's outstanding ability to win bits of food certainly would have convinced me Thora was her dam. Yet Beauty's manner was far more refined than Thora's. Where Thora would chomp and slobber, Beauty waited politely and ate cleanly. Crearwy had picked a good name for her dog.

The others chatted as they ate. I kept quiet, watching Crearwy as she interacted with the women. My sisters treated my daughter well, but Flidas' eyes missed nothing. And I did not miss hers. I sensed no malice in the girl, but there was magic at work within her. When the meal was done, Crearwy took my hand. "Come, Mother. We have work we must attend to. The others will help Epona."

"What work, my love?"

"You'll see," she said.

I looked at Epona who nodded. Crearwy led me out of the house and across the square to Sid's home. We opened the door to find the place dark and dusty.

"You tend the fire. I'll remake the bed," Crearwy told me.

"Is Sid coming?"

"That's what Nadia said."

"Nadia?"

Crearwy nodded. "She came to me when I was feeding the horses. I told her you were here. She left to get Sid."

"So you see her…always?"

"Only when she wants to be seen."

"You were born in this room," I told Crearwy.

"So they tell me. I've seen this room, Epona's house, Aridmis' house—all the little houses—the barn, the smithy, and the forest. My world," she said, a bitter tone in her voice. "They tell me Madelaine has castles. And my mother has a kingdom. I have the coven."

"Crearwy," I said, stopping to look at her. "You must understand…I mean, I am certain Epona has explained…"

"That I'm here for my own safety? Yes, I understand. My brother Lulach will become king, and I will rule the trees."

I stared at her, shocked to hear such a harsh tone in her young voice.

"Things are not easy for women at court. Here, you are free. You can live any life you please. I've given you a free life. You can choose any life you want."

115

"*Any* life?" she asked.

"Well...I mean..."

"Hmm," Crearwy mused then opened the door. Carrying a blanket with her, she went outside and shook out the linen.

I turned back to the fire. Rattled by Crearwy's dark words, I nearly burned my fingers on the flames when I set a log in the hearth. I pulled my hands back only to see the spots of blood thereon once more.

Sitting back, I looked into the fireplace. Flames flickered to life.

Outside, I heard Crearwy snapping dust from the linens. I lifted my hands and looked at them. I had murdered my cousin. I had married the man who killed my husband. I had forsaken my druid for Lulach's sake. I had left my daughter behind, a daughter who appeared to resent my choice. And if she disliked it now, how much she might grow to hate me in the future? I had done all these things because I'd believed Andraste's words.

I stared into the flames.

"Andraste," I called sharply.

The fire crackled.

"Andraste."

The flame flickered, and a moment later, a window opened to Ynes Verleath. There, I found Nimue.

"Where is Andraste?" I asked.

"Hail Queen."

"Nimue, where is Andraste?"

Nimue shook her head.

"She is a coward. Tell her I *will* have the truth from her, one way or another."

Nimue nodded. The expression on her face suggested that she was not in disagreement with my anger.

"Nimue, do you know the truth? Do you know the answer to the question I want to ask?"

"And what is your question?"

"Is Gillacoemgain Lulach and Crearwy's true father?"

"I only know what you know. I see only what you see, Cerridwen."

"And what is it that you see?"

"I see what you see," she said with a soft smile and then the vision faded.

I sat back and ruminated on her words. Did she mean that her vision was blocked the same as mine, or did she mean that she and I saw the same thing—that Andraste had lied? That Gillacoemgain was their father. Was she trying to tell me that what I was realizing was true?

"You riddle, Nimue. Shame on you," I whispered to the flames.

A moment later, Crearwy returned. She lay the blanket on the bed.

"Daughter, please come to me," I whispered.

I could tell from the expression on her face that she was still unsettled, but she came all the same.

I wrapped my arms around her, pressing my head against her soft belly. How sweet she was, soft and warm with skin as smooth as butter. I sighed heavily.

"What is it, Mother?"

"If I have failed you, I am sorry. I did what I thought best for you. I may have been misled."

Crearwy patted my head. "Then don't be misled again. I'll go get some water now." Pulling from my grasp, she snatched two pitchers from the table and headed out the door.

I rose slowly, feeling dizzy as I did so. I set my hand on my stomach.

"Easy," I whispered.

"Cerridwen?" a voice called from the door.

I turned to find Flidas there.

"I'm sorry. I don't mean to disturb you, but I've seen something that confuses me."

"What is it?"

"I've seen you at my mother's grove. In my visions. Have you been there?"

"I...No."

She nodded slowly. "No. You're right. Your hair was different in my vision. I'm sorry. I was hoping you had news of my mother. I haven't seen her in some time."

"I'm sorry, no."

She looked around the room. "I'm very fond of Sid. Will she be here soon?"

"I believe so."

"Good," she said then smiled happily. "It's hard to find such honest souls. Again, I'm sorry to bother you," she said then turned and left.

Flidas' manner unnerved me, but she was right about one thing. I turned and gazed at the flames. Honest souls were in short supply.

CHAPTER EIGHTEEN

I spent the rest of the morning with Crearwy, indulging her whim to ride my horse.

"What do you mean he doesn't have a name?" Crearwy asked as she rode him in circles around the coven square.

"I never thought of one."

"It feels like he wants to jump into the heavens and run. He's very swift."

"How about Swift?"

"Swift," Crearwy said with a laugh. "That's perfect. You should have just called him that from the beginning."

I chuckled.

Horseback riding was followed by hunting the woods for mistletoe, which mostly consisted of Crearwy chasing Beauty through the forest, digging for truffles, unsuccessfully tracking deer, and all manner of other curious but exhausting things. When we returned to the coven, Crearwy decided she wanted to work at weaving.

"I'll take some rest," I told my daughter.

"All right. I have to help Epona with the lunch soon anyway," she said. Jumping up, she gave me a peck on the cheek then ran off.

My heart was filled with joy, but my body felt weary. I returned to Sid's house. The fire was burning nicely. After our work that morning, the house was bright and clean. I lay down on the bed, promising myself I would only close my eyes for a few minutes. But sleep came quickly upon me. I was deep in my dreams when I felt someone sit down on the bed beside me.

"Crearwy? I'm sorry. Is it time to eat?"

"Almost time for supper," a snippy voice replied.

I opened my eyes to find Sid sitting there. She was grinning at me.

"Sid."

"Slept the whole day, did you? That's what they told me. What, crown too heavy?"

"Something's too heavy."

"Oh, yes, Epona was whispering. Finally caught our man's lightning seed, did you?"

I chuckled. "Apparently."

"Well, that won't complicate anything."

I huffed a laugh. "You're right about that, old friend."

After I sat up, Sid handed me a package wrapped in parchment that looked more like leaves than paper.

"What is it?" I asked.

"A gift."

"You brought me a gift?"

"Not I."

"What is it?"

Sid chuckled. "That's not how a gift works. Open it."

I moved aside the brittle wrapping. Within, I found a pair of gloves. "What are these?"

"Gloves, of course."

I chuckled. "I see that. But from whom?"

"The Unseelie Queen."

I looked from Sid to the gloves to Sid again. "What?" While the Seelies were known to be benevolent, the Unseelies were another matter. The Unseelies, at least what I knew of them, disliked humans and often caused harm. While all the fey stayed away from humans, the Unseelies found mankind particularly repugnant.

"That's why I'm late," Sid said. "The Unseelie Queen came to the Seelie court to bring me these to give to you. Everyone was in a titter. Then the Seelies were vexed because they had no gift for you. I told them they needed none, but everyone was upset. And no one understood the gift, not even me, until I saw."

"Saw what?"

"Those rosy fingers of yours. Can't get the blood off?"

"You see it? You see it too?"

"Oh, yes. I'm just glad it stayed on your hands and didn't get all over my bed. Gruesome. You must have had quite the time with your cousin to leave such a mark."

"What is this mark, Sid? Why are these stains there?"

"It's a curse. You've stained your very soul. Don't you see? Such a pity. You always had such lovely hands. But try these on. They're made with cloth found only in the land of the fair ones."

A curse.

I had stained my soul.

I lifted the gloves. They were made of soft black fabric that felt like silk but was sturdier. The hems were trimmed with silver embroidery. There was a pattern in the material itself. It appeared and disappeared as I moved the fabric.

"Are they bespelled?"

"That's what I asked. They are. But the Seelie Queen looked them over and promised they'd bring you no harm. My guess is that the spell quiets the bloody marks."

I slid the gloves on, waiting for the red spots to soak through. But they didn't. My hands stayed covered and clean.

"Did the Unseelie Queen say why she sent these?"

"No. And I didn't have the nerve to ask her."

"No matter what gloves I put on, the spots remained. The blood always soaked through," I told Sid.

"Not now," Sid said, taking my hand.

"Not now. Why would such a creature send something to me?"

"One day you will take your place among the Wyrds. Perhaps she hopes you will remember her kindness then."

I sighed. "We shall see."

"Right. But we shall see later. Now, you need to go."

"Go? Go where?"

"Back to Madelaine."

"But I just got here. And *you* just got here."

"I know, but Nadia says you need to go now. Madelaine needs you."

"Sid! I haven't seen you in years."

"So I complained. But I'm told that it's urgent. So you must go. Kiss me once, like you mean it, and then you can depart."

Not waiting for me, Sid set her hand on my neck and pulled me into a deep kiss. Her mouth was warm and sweet as if she had been eating honey by the spoonful. She slipped onto the bed with me, straddling my lap. With her free hand, she gently stroked my breast.

My mind wanted to resist, but in the end, I fell into her kiss.

I loved Sid.

I loved Sid in ways I didn't understand.

And I loved her kiss.

After a time, Sid pulled back. She sighed heavily. "Now, I have to let you go. What a pain. I'll see you again though," she said then leaned toward my stomach. "And you, wee thing, what are we going to do with you?"

I shook my head, a million emotions flowing through me at once. "Sid."

"Have you met Flidas?"

"Yes."

"And what did you think?"

"I'm not sure."

"I'll take her to bed while you're gone. At least it will help me feel less lonely."

"Sid," I said with a shake of the head.

Sid paused then and took my face into her hands. "I love you, Cerridwen."

"I love you too."

"Now go say goodbye to Crearwy. And come back soon."

"Sid, I think I've made a terrible mistake."

At that, Sid laughed loudly. "We all make mistakes, Cerridwen. Who can see them at the moment they're made? Now, go on."

Sighing, I reluctantly rose. I pulled on my coat and headed outside to find Epona and Crearwy sitting on the bench near the fire. Epona was holding the same counting board she had used to teach me. My heart was warmed by the sight.

"Here she is," Sid called. "And as I told you both, she must go."

Crearwy looked up at me, a stormy expression on her face. She set her own counting board down then stormed off in the direction of the barn.

Leaning on her staff, Epona rose. She watched Crearwy go.

"Sid, are you sure I must leave?" I asked.

Sid nodded. "Yes."

I sighed.

"Tully has saddled your horse," Epona said, motioning to the blood bay—Swift—who stood looking at me. "Please make sure Druanne and Uald return safely."

"Of course," I said then pulled Epona into a hug. She was so frail, so small. I could scarcely believe it. "Banquo may come here if he doesn't stop at the keep first," I told Epona.

She looked at Sid.

"I'll fetch him and put him on a new route. Let's see if he wants to have some fun before I set him free. Would you mind, raven beak?"

I rolled my eyes. "I'll leave that for him to decide. I must see to Crearwy," I said, motioning to the barn.

Epona nodded.

Sid wrapped her arm around Epona's waist and set her head on Epona's shoulder. "Just moments. Always, just moments," Sid whispered.

"That is the way of life. In the end, it was all just a moment."

"End? Not yet, horse lady. Come, let's have a look at Cerridwen's bloody beast."

When I entered the barn, I paused and listened. The horses and goats turned and looked at me, all of them hopeful for something to eat. She wasn't here. I then heard the sound of soft crying coming from the smithy. Crossing the barn, I found her sitting beside Uald's cold forge. She was weeping quietly, her head cradled in her arms.

"Crearwy," I said softly.

"How can you go?" she demanded, turning to me, her face red with fury. "How can you just leave? You just got here. I never see you. It's like you never wanted me, only Lulach. How can you just leave?"

"I don't want to go. Nadia said Madelaine needs me. Tavis—you will not know him, but he was like a father to me—is gravely ill. Madelaine needs me."

"I need you!"

"Crearwy—"

"Take me with you. I want to come. I don't want to be here. I want to be with you."

"You are loved and safe."

"Yes, yes, yes. I know. I'm safe. But safe from what?"

"From terrors you cannot imagine. From pain you cannot imagine. Please believe me, I would never leave you for any other reason."

"But Lulach can go? Lulach can be out there. Lulach can be a prince."

"Lulach is with the druids right now."

At that, Crearwy threw up her hands. "So, he gets to do both? That's fair?"

"It's different for women. Things are not fair, not equal, in the world outside this place. Macbeth is a lunatic. I will not let him have any say over your fate."

"Then don't. Tell him no. I am Gillacoemgain's daughter, not his."

I smiled at her. "You are. Had your father lived, things would have been so different, but—"

"But he didn't live. He died. Your husband killed him. You married the man who killed my father! How could you?"

"Crearwy, it's difficult to explain."

"Don't explain anything to me. Just leave. Just go. You don't want to be here anyway. Go away, and don't come back."

Full of fury, she shoved Uald's tools to the ground then took off in a sprint, leaving me to stand there not knowing what to do. Tears welled in my eyes. Crearwy was right to be angry, and I had no good answers for her. She was too young to know the terrible things that had happened. How could I explain it to her?

A moment later, someone approached me from behind. "I'll go after her," Aridmis said, setting her hand on my shoulder.

I looked at my old friend. "Aridmis, I…"

"She will forgive you in time," Aridmis reassured me. "She will need to forgive all of us, in time. Be well, Cerridwen," she said then headed into the forest after my child.

My heart heavy, I rejoined Sid and Epona. Epona wouldn't meet my eyes.

"Children get angry with their parents. Parents get angry with their children. It is the way of things," Sid said. "For instance, I understand that Eochaid once spent a year in Moray, but he never bothered to tell his mother. Seems a kind lady there looked after him. Have anything to say about that, raven beak?"

"Only that I hope he is well, and I send him my love."

Sid shook her head.

I climbed on my horse and settled in.

Epona reached out and took my hand. "There are too many words, and I cannot find the right ones."

"I will see you again," I told her.

She nodded softly then let me go.

I looked back toward the smithy once more. There was no sign of Crearwy or Aridmis. Feeling miserable and completely unsure what to do, I tapped my horse's reins and rode out of the coven, hoping that Sid was right.

One day, I hoped Crearwy would understand and forgive me.

CHAPTER NINETEEN

I kept my focus on the path forward: nine oak, nine ash, nine thorn. Soon, I made my way to the glen Madelaine, Tavis, and I had visited when the Goddess called me to come to the coven. So much life had passed since then.

The moon was climbing into the sky. It cast a silvery sheen on the water, the stars glowing like gems on the surface of the loch.

Pulling Swift to a stop, I gazed out at the placid surface. I thought about everything that lay in front of me. There was so much to do. So much to consider. But all I really wanted was to turn around and ride back to the coven.

Crearwy was not wrong.

I had a lot to answer for.

I had done my best for her, made the best choices I could based on what I knew. If I had suspected that Gillacoemgain was truly her father, things might have been different. I might have made different decisions, which could have changed both our fates. But I hadn't.

A cold wind swept across the water. I shuddered. As I gazed down the shoreline of the loch, I realized there was a man standing there.

Setting my hand on my blade, I turned Swift and rode toward the figure.

There was something strange about the man. When the wind blew, his wraps twisted in an odd manner.

Swift took a deep breath and snorted as if he didn't like what he saw. He stepped higher, his gait telling me that he was ready to bolt at any moment.

"Easy," I told the horse. "Don't you dare knock me on my ass while I'm with child, or I'll have you roasted for dinner."

At that, he snorted.

The wind blew once more. While the apple tree nearby was vacant of blossoms, I distinctly caught the scent of the spring flowers on the wind.

The figure stepped toward me.

I gasped.

Tavis.

"Tavis?" I called.

He lifted his hand. It was at that moment that I realized I was seeing him and seeing through him all at once.

"Tavis," I whispered, my hand covering my mouth.

He smiled softly. The wind blew once more, carrying with it the smell of apple blossoms, then Tavis disappeared.

"Oh, Great Mother, watch over him. Farewell, friend," I whispered, tears slipping down my cheeks. I tapped Swift's reins and turned him in the direction of Madelaine's castle.

Nadia was right.

I needed to get to Madelaine.

*R*iding as quickly as I dared, I reached the castle late in the night. Ute met me in the hall. Her face looked pale and drawn. There were dark rings under her eyes.

"Ute," I said, rushing quickly across the hall.

She shook her head. "I'm sorry, Gruoch. The lady you brought is a very talented healer, but it was too late."

"Where are they?"

"Upstairs with Madelaine. She's...inconsolable. It's good you came back."

Ute and I went upstairs to Madelaine's chamber. Inside, I heard Uald's voice.

I entered at once.

Madelaine's face was deathly white, her eyes ringed red. She rose when she saw me. "Corbie," she wailed. She rushed to me, wrapping her arms around me. She buried her head in my neck. "He's gone," she whispered. "He's gone."

"Oh, Madelaine," I said, unable to choke back my own tears. "I'm so sorry."

"Whatever will I do?" she whispered.

I hugged her tight but didn't answer. There was no good reply to her question.

Madelaine shuddered and wept miserably.

Eventually, Uald rose and took Madelaine from my grasp. "Come. You'll make yourself sick," she said then helped Madelaine back into her seat. Uald turned to Ute. "Is there any mead about?"

"Yes, my la—I mean, Uald."

"Let's have some. All of us."

"I'll fetch it," Ute said then left the chamber.

I cast a glance at Druanne who, much to my surprise, looked very sorrowful.

"I'm sorry," she told me. "I did everything I could think of. He must have been out there for days. His blood was poisoned. There was no stopping it."

Swallowing hard, I crossed the room and set my hand on Druanne's shoulder. "Thank you, Druanne. Thank you for trying."

She nodded then dabbed a tear from her eye.

Uald sighed then took a drink from her tankard. "There's ale," she told me, pointing to a pitcher.

I shook my head.

"Well, now that Corbie's here, we should return in the morning," Uald told Druanne. "Epona will be worried."

"Take a wagon. You need to take supplies from the kitchen," I said then turned to Madelaine. "They need whatever you can spare."

Madelaine nodded mutely.

"Epona's calculations were…off. And our crops didn't grow as they should have this year," Uald explained.

"Epona's state…there are no words for my shock," I said.

Uald nodded. "We are all in shock."

Druanne shook her head. "After all these years, to see her magic leave her like that. It's…disquieting."

Druanne was right. If the gods would abandon Epona in such a way after she had dedicated her entire life to them, what did it mean for the rest of us?

I sat down next to Madelaine and took her hand.

Tears streamed down her face, but she didn't say anything.

"Tavis will be sent to the gods in the morning," Uald told me. "Ute arranged it."

I nodded.

Madelaine moaned.

"Druanne," I said, turning to her. "Can you fix Madelaine something? Something to help calm her?"

"Of course," Druanne replied. She went to her cases sitting near the bed. She dipped into her box and pulled out a number of pouches. I watched her as she worked, recognizing some of the herbs. She was grinding herbs to help Madelaine sleep and to calm her mind. She wore them down into a fine powder then mixed the concoction in water. She handed the drink to Madelaine. "Drink it all."

Madelaine took the cup and mutely drank.

I passed Druanne a grateful look.

She inclined her head to me then went to clean up her tools.

Ute returned not long after, carrying a tray.

"Lady Gruoch," she said, motioning behind her.

I rose.

Killian stood in the hallway. "Lady Gruoch," he said.

I followed Killian into the hallway, closing the door behind me.

"Killian, thank you for seeing them safely here."

He nodded. "I would have returned to escort you back. I wish you had waited."

"I was safe. But thank you."

"I am sorry about your friend. I remember him from Moray. He was there with Lord Lulach. He seemed to be a good man."

"He was."

"Do you need anything? Is there anything I can do for you… Gruoch?" he said, reaching out to gently take my hand.

I was so surprised by the gesture, I didn't know what to say. "I… No, Killian. Thank you," I said, pulling my hand back. "We will leave in a few days. Take some rest."

He inclined his head. "If there is anything you need or want, please don't hesitate to ask me."

"Thank you."

Leaving him, I returned to the chamber. Uald had poured us all a glass of mead. "Let's toast," Uald said, lifting her glass. "To Tavis, a fine man, companion, a great hunter, and a friend."

Madelaine choked back a sob.

"To Tavis," we said, lifting our drinks.

Mindful of my little one, I sipped just a little in Tavis' honor.

Uald polished off her drink then set her cup down. She turned to Druanne. "Another?"

Druanne shook her head. "No. I need to get some sleep. I confess I'm weary."

"If you're ready, my lady, I can escort you to your chamber," Ute told her.

Druanne rose. She went to Madelaine and wrapped her arms around her, squeezing her tight. Afterward, she departed with Ute.

"What about you?" I asked Uald. "Maybe you should rest as well."

"No. I'll stay here with Madelaine and finish this bottle," she said, lifting the jug of mead.

Madelaine smiled weakly. "You'll be on the floor by morning."

"Your floor looks softer than my bed. I can't remember the last time I was in this castle."

"We were girls. Boite was here."

"Oh, now, *Boite* I remember. The castle was nothing compared to him."

Setting down my cup, I unhooked my belt and slid off the raven-capped dagger. I crossed the room and handed it to Uald.

She rose. "Corbie, where did you get this?" she asked, her voice full of awe.

Madelaine squinted. "Is that…is that the raven dagger?"

I nodded. Uald turned the dagger over in her hand, studying her smith mark. She touched it gently.

"Boite," she whispered.

"Wherever did you find it?" Madelaine asked.

"On Duncan. I took it from him then used it to carve out his heart. He told me it was a gift from Malcolm."

Madelaine stared at me, her eyes wide.

"You took it from him in battle?" Uald asked.

"Yes. And now it has come home to you once more. Keep it."

"No. It should be yours. Lulach's."

"No. You keep it."

Uald wrapped her hand around the sheath and pressed the blade against her chest. "I think we may need another bottle to get through this night. But, Corbie, aren't you drinking," she said, eyeing my still-full cup.

"No," I said with a sigh then sat back down. "I'm pregnant with the Thane of Lochaber's child."

At that, Uald laughed out loud. In spite of herself, Madelaine chuckled.

Uald poured herself another glass then refilled Madelaine's cup.

"Well then," Uald said. "Let us toast once more. To Boite and his grandchild."

Madelaine and I lifted our cups then drank.

I stayed with Madelaine and Uald until Madelaine couldn't keep her eyes open anymore, Druanne's concoction working on her. Uald, on the other hand, drank herself blind and fell asleep—or unconsciousness from drink—on the floor.

"No sleeping on the stones," I told Uald, lifting her off the floor. With a heave, I moved her toward Madelaine's bed.

"Corbie," she whispered, her voice coming out a slur.

"Yes, Uald?"

"I loved your daddy."

"So I figured."

"Never found another man I liked after Boite."

"Just think, you could have been my mother," I said, giving her another shove as I rolled her onto the bed beside Madelaine.

Uald laughed loudly then fell back into a drunken sleep once more.

I covered them then went out to the hall where I found Camden, one of my guards, waiting for me.

"My queen," he said, bowing to me.

"I'm for bed," I told him.

He nodded then escorted me to my chamber. "I'll be here until dawn, Your Majesty. Someone else will come then."

"Thank you," I said then went inside.

Sighing, I lay down to rest. I felt dizzy from exhaustion and too tired to change. Lying down, I studied the gloves that had come from the Unseelie Queen. Closing my eyes, I reached out to the other world. I tried to feel the fey there. Their magic was chaotic and foreign to me, but I could sense their presence.

"Many thanks, Great Lady," I whispered.

What the dark fey wanted from me, I had no idea. Perhaps it was just as Sid said. One day, I would join the Wyrds.

One day.

Maybe.

If I ever had the heart to forgive Andraste.

CHAPTER TWENTY

I rose the next morning to a familiar warble in my bedchamber; Ute was singing. I had missed her companionate presence.

"Good morning, Ute."

"Gruoch. Good morning to you."

Groggily, I rose to see it wasn't long past sunrise.

"Uald and the healer—Druanne—are downstairs getting ready to depart."

"Madelaine?"

Ute sighed. "Still in bed."

"Leave her there."

Ute nodded.

"And how are you, Ute? Tell me how you've been," I said.

"Very well. Honestly, Lady Madelaine looks after herself. I don't have much to do. I've… There is a man in Fife's household. I've formed an attachment."

"Have you?"

"We're not married yet, but we are planning. It's a happy life. And now you are queen."

"Yes," I said with a sigh.

Ute nodded but said nothing. What could she say? Like me, she hated Macbeth, and I didn't blame her for it. I understood her hatred very well.

I rose slowly and went to the basin to wash my face. I then prepared myself for the day, dressing in the gown Ute had set out for me.

"Do you need anything else?" Ute asked.

I shook my head. "No. Thank you. It's good to see you doing so well, Ute. It makes my heart happy."

She smiled softly at me. "Thank you, Gruoch. That means so much coming from you. I'll go check on Madelaine now," she said then left.

I pulled on my boots and headed downstairs. Uald and Druanne were talking to Madelaine's staff. Servants were hauling bags of barley, oats, and flour out the front of the castle and loading them into the wagon.

"Will it be enough?" I asked Uald, watching as the footmen passed.

She nodded. "That should get us through. Hunting is still good."

"Don't hesitate to ask Madelaine for help. I didn't like to see things so thin," I said.

"Epona is not herself," Druanne said. "The rest of us will step forward to guide things in the future."

Uald set her hand on my shoulder. "And look after Crearwy."

I nodded. "Thank you both. Are you leaving now? Should I wake Madelaine?"

Uald shook her head. "No. But thank her for us."

I nodded then embraced Uald. "I'd offer to send a guard to travel with you, but I know you won't accept."

"You're right," Uald said with a wink. She then turned to Druanne. "Ready?"

Druanne nodded.

"Thank you, Druanne."

She sighed. "There is little to thank me for."

"You comforted him in the end," Uald said.

Druanne frowned. "It was too little too late."

"Thank you all the same," I told her.

To my surprise, she gave me a half smile. She and Uald then climbed into the wagon. Their horses were tied to the back of the cart. I was relieved to see the wagon was fully loaded with goods. One less thing to worry about.

"Tell Madelaine we're keeping the wagon and horses," Uald said with a grin.

I grinned then waved to her.

Uald chuckled, raised her hand in farewell, then rode off into the misty morning.

I stayed and watched until they were out of sight. I turned then and walked out onto the field surrounding the castle. Allister had been dead for many years, but I still could not escape the memories that haunted the place. Everywhere I looked, I saw something that put me in mind of my life here. I climbed the nearby hill then walked toward the valley where the stream flowed lazily past the castle. How many days had I spent here, hiding from Allister and his men?

I sat down by the water. It was still cold, the ground below me not yet thawed. Spring, it seemed, did not want to come. I gazed into the water. It was here that Gillacoemgain had found me the morning after I'd made love to him. He had come with words of love on his lips. I entwined my gloved fingers and pressed them against my mouth. For so many years, I had believed Duncan to be Crearwy and Lulach's father. But every time I spoke of their father to them, every time I had declared Lulach to be the son of Gillacoemgain, it had felt like the truth. Perhaps, because it was. Perhaps, after all the loss and pain, I had finally won something back. If they were indeed his children, then Gillacoemgain wasn't really lost. He would live on in them.

I set my hand on my stomach.

"You, on the other hand, present a very big problem."

"Gruoch?" a voice called.

For a moment, I stilled. Remembering this place and this moment with Gillacoemgain, I rose, half expecting to find his shade there.

Instead, I found Banquo.

"Banquo?"

He grinned.

I rose and crossed the field to greet him.

He cast a glance around. Once he was sure we were alone, he planted a kiss on my lips. "I was met on the road by a fey thing. She told me what happened and that I should come here."

"It's good you've come. We need to perform rites for Tavis today. Will you…"

Banquo nodded. "Of course. How is Madelaine?"

"As expected. It breaks my heart to see her like this. But you must tell me, how was Sid? Did she delay you overlong?" I asked, arching a playful eyebrow at Banquo.

He coughed uncomfortably. "She tried."

"And did she succeed?"

"Not in full. I like that woman, but my heart belongs elsewhere."

Somehow, it felt unfair that Banquo and I loved one another so much—without Sid. Echoes of past lives wanted to impose themselves on me. I reminded myself that I was not obligated to choices I made in another time and space. I loved Sid well, but this life was mine. And so was Banquo.

"This is where you grew up," Banquo said, looking back at the castle.

"Alas."

Banquo raised an eyebrow at me.

"Madelaine's first husband, Allister, was a very cruel man. It was not an easy upbringing," I explained.

"I'm surprised he would dare be anything but kind to the sister and niece of the king."

"Perhaps it was different while my father was alive. Afterward…"

Banquo frowned. "I'm sorry for you both."

I nodded but said nothing more on the matter. It was rare for Banquo and me to find moments alone. I didn't know how long Banquo would be able to stay, and we would have little chance to talk away from the prying eyes of others. While the timing was not ideal, there may not be another chance.

"Banquo," I whispered. "I must tell you something."

Banquo stilled. "Is something wrong? I know you've seen some visions you have not shared with me."

For a fleeting moment, I remembered the image of Banquo with the dagger in his chest. I pressed the memory from my thoughts. "No…" I said then took his hand. "For once, it's something good, actually." I set Banquo's hand on my stomach. "Something unexpected, but good."

Banquo looked down at his hand then back up at me. "Cerridwen?" he gasped.

"I am with child."

Banquo stroked his hand across my stomach then stepped back. He shook his head over and over again, his eyes going wide.

"Banquo?" I stepped toward him.

"No, no, no," he whispered.

"Banquo?" There was strange energy all around him. He seemed to waver in and out of this plane of reality. "Banquo, stop." I grabbed his arm. "Banquo."

He gasped loudly then shuddered. "Cerridwen."

"What happened? What did you see?"

"Oh, Cerridwen," he said then pulled me into an embrace. He was shaking.

"Our child? Did you see our child?"

"Such strange and prophetic things. Dark omens. Cerridwen… a child."

"Yes. A child. Tell me what you saw. Was it something about our child? Tell me."

"No…just dark signs. I don't know what lies ahead, but there is trouble in our path."

I nodded. "We will make a plan. We will keep our child safe. I must return to Glamis for a time, only to set some matters of state in order, then I will return to Moray. We will find a way to hide her, protect her."

"Her?"

I nodded. "Injibjorg. She saw a daughter for us."

Banquo stepped back then stroked my cheek. "A daughter. You're going to give me a daughter?"

I smiled softly at him. "Yes," I whispered.

"Then may all the gods protect her," Banquo said, touching my stomach gently once more. "May all the gods protect her."

That night, a funeral pyre was laid out for Tavis. We placed trinkets, food, drink, and items Tavis had loved, alongside him. Madelaine clung to me as we watched Banquo perform the funeral rites.

Dressed in his druid robes, Banquo stood before the pyre. He had painted his face with woad, trimmed his hair with leaves. He stood barefoot, a torch in his hands. The Christian priests who were part of Fife's entourage were not in attendance, but the Thane and the household staff had come. The Thane of Fife stood on the other side of Madelaine, his hand on her back in loving support. I admired his generous spirit.

"Great Mother, Father Cernunnos, I consecrate this body and return your son back to you," Banquo called. "May the flames lift his spirit to the stars. May his body replenish the earth. May he be reborn into a world full of love and life," Banquo said.

He then lowered his torch, setting the wood on fire.

Madelaine sobbed.

Banquo circled the pyre. Orange flames flickered to life. The wood crackled and popped.

Banquo came to stand at Tavis' head once more. His arms outstretched, he looked toward the sky. "Great Mother, Father God, receive his body. May his spirit ride on the winds. May the gods bless this man and provide him comfort until the day he is reborn. Tavis, long may you be remembered."

Sparks flew as orange flame leaped up into the night sky.

The scent of pine and sage filled the air.

Madelaine watched the sparks twirl upward toward the heavens. The light of the flames bounced on her face, her cheeks slick with tears. Her eyes sparkled, and a calm washed over her features, her eyes softening.

We stayed for the longest time, keeping a watchful vigil over a man we had loved. In the end, only Madelaine, Banquo, and I remained.

"I will see him again in the next life," Madelaine whispered. "We'll be reunited once more. And next time, for the better."

I kissed Madelaine on the cheek.

She took one last look, then turned and went back to the castle.

Banquo took my hand. "I will stay with him until the flame grows cold. But the fire of the dead can't warm the spirit. Why don't you go back inside?"

"I hate to leave you alone."

"I am not alone," Banquo said, motioning to the pyre.

"Come to me tonight."

"But your guards."

"Come anyway."

Banquo nodded.

I turned then and headed back to the castle. I paused just once to look behind me. Banquo stood staring at the flames. At his side, for just a flickering moment, I saw Tavis.

*L*ater that night, once he had finished with the rites and bathed, Banquo joined me in my chamber. Killian, who was keeping watch outside, gave me a puzzled expression when I answered the door. Killian looked from me to Banquo. I motioned for Banquo to go inside.

"My lady, is everything all right?" Killian asked.

"Yes. Goodnight, Killian," I told him.

"I...Goodnight, Gruoch," he said, inclining his head. I couldn't help but notice the look of jealousy that washed across his face. No doubt he had heard the rumors. Perhaps he had hoped they weren't true. Of course, if he had affection for me, he had no doubt wished they were untrue. But jealousy was a tricky thing. When I returned to Moray, Killian might need to stay behind.

I closed and bolted the door behind me.

"I would offer you wine..." Banquo said, pouring himself a glass. "But..."

I chuckled. "Alas, no wine for me. And it's all your doing."

"I would say I'm sorry, but I'm not," he said then polished off his cup.

I slipped into bed, motioning for Banquo to join me.

Setting his drink aside, he slipped under the blankets with me and pulled me close. He kissed the back of my head then breathed in the scent of my hair.

"How I miss you when we are apart," he whispered. "And now—" he set his hand on my stomach—"what are we going to do?"

"I don't know. Once she is old enough, we could send her to fostering."

"I cannot," Banquo whispered. "I'd rather quit the court life."

His words stung my heart. Banquo still didn't know about Crearwy. I planned to tell him when he came to the coven, but now I wasn't sure I'd ever find the right time.

"Lochaber is quiet. I have a small but loyal staff there. If you come to Lochaber, it's possible we can hide the truth. No one will ever know you bore a child."

"Perhaps. That may work. But I will need to return. I will need to rule. Otherwise, we are all in ruin."

"Yes," Banquo said, kissing my cheek.

"And you?"

"I will not be separated from my child because I have placed the wrong man on the throne."

"If Macbeth ever learns—"

"If Macbeth ever dreams of touching my child, I will murder him."

"Don't tempt the gods," I whispered, remembering the terrible vision I'd had.

"No. I won't tempt the gods," Banquo said then took my hand. He paused when he saw the gloves. "I saw you wearing these. I thought you were cold. But now that I see them under the light... Cerridwen, this is no normal stitching."

"They were a gift."

"From whom?"

"Sid brought them to me from the Unseelie Queen."

Banquo rose up on his elbow and looked at me. "Why?"

"Because...because my hands are marred."

"What do you mean?"

I swallowed hard then pulled off my gloves. When I did so, I instantly saw both hands as though they were slick with blood. "Can you see?" I whispered.

"See what? There is nothing there."

"With your druid's eyes."

There was a strange hum in the air, and a moment later, Banquo gasped.

Sighing, I pulled the gloves back on.

"What is that?" Banquo whispered.

"A curse. Blood of my blood. The gloves are bespelled. They disrupt the enchantment."

"Oh, Cerridwen. Why would the gods do such a thing to you?"

"I don't know. But no matter what, I cannot get rid of the spots."

"They set us on this path, they move us toward our fates, then they punish us for following the trenches in the road they've dug," Banquo said, a hard edge on his voice. "Sometimes, I wonder about the teachings of the White Christ. The doctrine, unpolluted by his priests, promotes love and forgiveness. Maybe—"

"Oh, my love, don't even speak the words."

"Yes. You're right. But your hands. And the Unseelie Queen... such a dangerous creature. She must want something from you."

"Perhaps. One day."

"What could you give her?"

"Only time will tell," I said, then turned and looked at Banquo. "Let's leave off these things for now."

Banquo smiled down at me. He pushed my hair away from my face. "I've missed you terribly. Are you well?"

I grinned slyly at him. "Yes, I am well."

"Good," he said then leaned down and placed a soft kiss on my lips.

Once more, Banquo and I carved out a moment for ourselves. And like every time, I hoped it would not be the last.

· · ·

*T*he following morning, Madelaine met Banquo and me in the yard to wish us both farewell. Banquo would ride from Madelaine's castle to Lochaber. I would return with my guard to Glamis.

Dressed in black, her face pale, Madelaine was a portrait of misery. My heart broke when I saw her.

"We will leave tomorrow," Madelaine told me. "We'll return to Fife's keep. Ute is inside getting everything ready. She told me to say goodbye for her."

"Wish her well for me."

Madelaine smiled weakly. "I think she will leave me soon. She and one of Fife's men have formed an attachment. I suspect they will soon be married."

"I'm glad for her but sorry for you."

Madelaine shrugged. "I can lace a gown myself if I have to. I may need some time, but I will come to Glamis to help you when I can."

"Do not rush. I will go to Glamis to set my affairs in order then return to Moray."

"And then?"

"Nothing is decided yet."

"Oh, Corbie. I cannot stand the thought of you being separated from another child. Please, try to find another way," she whispered.

"I will. I promise. Things will be different this time. I will choose better."

"Take care, my little raven."

I pulled Madelaine into an embrace. "And you, my beloved aunt. And you."

Once I let her go, we joined Fife and Banquo.

Fife smiled gently at me. "We shall see you soon, Queen of

Scots," he said, giving me a bow. "And Thane," he said, turning to Banquo. "I wish you safe travels."

Banquo nodded.

"I hate to see you ride off alone," Madelaine told Banquo.

"I will take great care, Lady Madelaine," Banquo reassured her.

I went to Banquo and took his hand. We walked over to his horse. "Send a rider when you can."

"And you. Please, my Cerridwen, be careful and stay safe. My heart and my child go with you."

Our eyes lingered on one another for a long while. There were too many eyes on us. I squeezed Banquo's hand. After a long moment, we finally let each other go.

Leaving Banquo, I went to Swift and climbed on. I motioned to my guard that I was ready.

"Farewell," Madelaine called to me. Fife stood beside her, his arm wrapped comfortingly around her waist.

I waved to her then looked one last time at Banquo.

We exchanged a glance then both of us turned and headed on our separate paths, Banquo home to Lochaber and me to Glamis and Macbeth.

CHAPTER TWENTY-ONE

*W*e rode all day, finally arriving at Glamis as the sun was setting. The castle looked beautiful framed with the backdrop of a pink and orange sunset. It was made of reddish-colored brick and stone. The center building was tall with high watchtowers all around. Two small sections of the castle formed wings on each side. From a glance, I could see that either Banquo or Macbeth had housed the army in the south wing of the palace. The grounds around the castle were neatly kept, but forest covered much of the land nearby, which was not ideal for preventing subterfuge.

In spite of all my courage and sincere desire to rule the land, a knot formed in my stomach as I approached the edifice.

I had married Macbeth.

My fate was tied to his.

Now, I would need to find a way to make everything work.

While I was carrying Banquo's child.

We were met by guards who escorted us to the castle gate. Grooms came to fetch the horses. Killian spoke to Macbeth's men, nodding as he listened.

"Your Majesty," he said, returning to me. "We have been

housed in the northern wing of the castle, not far from your lodgings. Shall I go see to the Moray staff?"

"Yes, please."

"Do you want me to send someone along with you?"

I shook my head. "No, I'll be fine."

"Are you sure, my lady?" Killian whispered.

"Thank you. Yes. I have my steel."

Killian shook his head then turned and went with the others.

Steadying my nerves, I turned to the footman. "Please take me to Macbeth."

"Yes, Your Majesty."

The interior of Glamis Castle was like nothing I had ever seen before. The castles I had lived in were old, showing their ties to the ancient kings of the realm. Glamis was luxurious. Everywhere I looked, I saw tapestries and rugs, beautiful furniture, paintings, and other ornaments. As I followed the servant, I considered the castle. Fife's estate also had fine trappings. I'd never thought much of it. But as I considered, I wondered why all the wealth in the realm was centered in the south.

The footman led me to a chamber not far from the great hall. There, Macbeth was sitting at a table reading dispatches.

"Your Majesty," the footman called.

Macbeth waved his hands rudely as if to shoo the man away.

The servant shifted uncomfortably. Clearing his throat, he said, "Your Majesty, Queen Gruoch is here."

Macbeth looked up then flopped back in his seat.

"You're dismissed," he told the footman. When the man left, he asked, "Where is your guard, Gruoch?"

"I have guard enough here," I said, setting my hand on my sword.

Macbeth huffed a laugh. "I'm surprised you're back."

"Did you think you would rule Scotland alone?"

"Of course not. Why would I ever dream of that? My loving wife is here to help me."

"What's a loving wife without a loving husband?"

Macbeth laughed. "Will you sit?" he said, motioning to a chair.

I observed him carefully with my raven's eyes. It was safe, for the moment.

I took a seat.

Macbeth poured some wine and set the cup in front of me. "You've just returned from Fife."

"Yes. I put a friend to eternal rest."

"I'm sorry to hear it," Macbeth said. He poured himself a glass of wine then sat down.

"What have you been working on?" I asked.

"Deciding whether or not to attack England."

"Attack England?" I blurted out. He couldn't possibly be serious.

Macbeth nodded, his bottom lip jutting out as he considered it. "We have a great army. We're strong. Why not?"

"Because many of the southern lords are still against you. And Thorfinn has taken the army to back to Magnus. And, because, there are better ways to gain control. Allies, Macbeth. We need allies."

"Such as?"

"The Holy Church of Rome? The Franks? The Irish? We have many options to choose from. But first, we need to stop bleeding silver. Where is Crinian?"

"In Dunkeld."

"Summon him. While he is here, send a force to seize the treasury. We shall put someone truly loyal in charge of the realm's wealth. Crinian can return to being abbott if God still calls him, and Bethoc will join us at court."

"Now, that is a wily plan," Macbeth said with a tittering laugh. "You don't trust Crinian?"

"We just murdered his son."

"True. But I believe his love of silver outweighs his sentimentality for my dearly departed cousin."

"We shall see."

"Quite the sacrifice, Gruoch."

"Removing Crinian is no sacrifice."

"I mean bringing Bethoc to court. I suspect you'd rather gouge your eyes out than listen to her talk about the weather."

Surprising even myself, I laughed. "That is true. But it will be good to have her here for when we reacquire Donaldbane."

Macbeth raised an eyebrow. "Indeed?"

"Indeed. I'm working on it as we speak. Now, about the southern lords, who do we need to make an example of? Who is still backing Siward, making noise?"

"Menteith."

"Let's send some men to Menteith to let him know, by the sharp end of a sword, that we disapprove," I suggested.

"As you wish, Your Majesty." Macbeth grinned.

"I'm tired. It has been a very long day," I said then rose to go.

"Gruoch…" Macbeth called out to me. In his voice, I heard the tone of the man I had first met, the man I had first married, the man I had hoped to love. But knew that sound to be a lie.

I cast a glance over my shoulder at him.

"I'm glad you're here," he said with a smile.

"Goodnight, Macbeth," I said then turned and left.

Never.

Never again.

CHAPTER TWENTY-TWO

*F*or the next several days, I worked almost without stopping. Documents and ledgers had come from Edinburgh. I thanked Epona a thousand times over for teaching me to read and write as I went through the records. Everything was a mess. Aside from tracking land, wealth, and resources, I also spent considerable time considering what allies could be made abroad. I had just decided on a course with the Franks when a messenger arrived.

"Your Majesty, an envoy from Echmarcach of the Isles has arrived. King Macbeth has asked if you would join them in his conference room."

Setting my work aside, I slipped down the halls of Glamis to join Macbeth. I still hadn't gotten used to the lovely rugs on the floors, gold-trimmed sconces, and tapestries and paintings on the walls. Such opulence seemed foreign to me.

I arrived at Macbeth's chamber to hear the sounds of jovial laughter.

I entered without hesitation.

"Ah, here is my queen," Macbeth said, crossing the room, his arm outstretched in greeting.

The strangers bowed to me, their leader stepping forward. "Your Majesty, I'm Finnegan Macdrummel. I bring good greetings from my lord, Echmarcach of the Isles."

"We are grateful to hear from our friend and ally," I said.

"We come with news. Your Majesty, you sought word of Donaldbane, son of Duncan, who was taken by Ímar mac Arailt?"

"Yes," I said.

"We have confirmed he is with the Irish king. Lord Echmarcach was eager to learn when he should send a force to retrieve the boy. As I am sure you know, Ímar mac Arailt has taken our lord's lands by force. He is eager to repay the Irish king for this slight. Given the support Lord Echmarcach gave you in your efforts to win the crown, he was hoping to hear news of how you could repay his help—by men or by coin—to both our happy ends."

Macbeth poured himself a glass of wine. "Ímar mac Arailt is, undoubtedly, in the wrong here. Does Echmarcach have men at the Irish king's court?"

"Men, Your Majesty?"

"Spies. How did you confirm Donaldbane is with Ímar mac Arailt?"

"Oh. Well. I don't know for certain how such information was acquired. But the boy is there."

"Echmarcach has been a valuable ally. We shall reward him for that. Please, why don't you gentlemen take your rest? Feast with us tonight. I will consider his proposition and give you an answer tomorrow," Macbeth said then motioned to his servants to lead the men away.

"Thank you, Your Majesty," Finnegan said, the others echoing him. They bowed then left.

"You knew Ímar mac Arailt had Donaldbane?" Macbeth asked.

"Yes. I sent a messenger to the Irish king some time back."

"Any reply?"

"Not yet."

"We will support Echmarcach's bid to topple the Irish king and recapture Donaldbane," Macbeth said.

"No, we will not. We will negotiate with Ímar mac Arailt."

"What? Why?"

"Because we aren't strong enough to go to war in Ireland. We do not have the men, resources, support, or desire to wage another war. If we do, Siward will come running back."

"And what do you expect Ímar mac Arailt will do? Hand Donaldbane over because you asked nicely?"

"No. I expect him to ask for Echmarcach's lands."

Macbeth laughed. "And then what?"

"And then we will make a decision. How valuable is Donaldbane? If we leave him in Ireland, he will be used against us. At this time, the Irish king has no reason to entertain offers from Siward. At *this* time. But Siward is shrewd. He will not slink away. He will make new allies and regain his power. In time, he will be back. He will seek to take the throne from us on Malcolm's behalf. Wouldn't it be better to have Irish support over Irish enemies?"

"Are you suggesting we offer him Echmarcach's lands?"

"No. You must think ahead. Always think ahead. Echmarcach rules himself. Half of the time, he makes war on his Irish neighbors without the blessing or support of the other noble lords. He sees the isles as independent, and he lords over them as such. How presumptuous is he to send an envoy here to pressure us to make war?"

"You are right about that."

"There is a third option."

"Which is?"

"We support Echmarcach, *and* we try to strike a bargain with Ímar mac Arailt. Neither will be the wiser. And we will also send an operative to Ímar mac Arailt's court and liberate Donaldbane on our own."

Macbeth stared at me. He huffed a laugh. "Who knew…"

"Who knew?"

"Who knew that you were more like Malcolm than any of the rest of us."

It was my turn to laugh. "I am not like Malcolm."

"If you say so. So, you suggest we play both sides."

"Yes."

"How will we explain it once the boy is recovered."

"We will tell Ímar mac Arailt it was Echmarcach's doing. We will tell Echmarcach we were planning it all along because we hate Ímar mac Arailt, then we step back and let them finish out whatever game they are playing. When they are done, we make peace with the winner."

"Very well. I shall arrange to have operatives sent into Ireland."

"Good."

Macbeth nodded then stood staring at me.

The silence went on for too long.

The hairs the back of my neck rose.

"I should be going," I said.

"Gruoch, where is Lulach?"

"What difference does it make?"

"People talk. It's strange that he is not here with us."

"Is it? Let people talk. If they knew the truth, they wouldn't find it strange at all."

"The truth? And what is the truth?"

"If we are to co-exist, it is better if we let the truth lie dead and buried."

Macbeth scowled. "If Lulach plans to be king, he should be here at my side."

"No. Don't push on this topic."

Macbeth slammed his fists down on the table. "It is you who is pushing. You are forcing me into a corner. I must have an heir, don't you realize? To secure the throne, I must have an heir. You… you will produce no other child for me. Lulach must come here. I must show this land that I do have an heir, even if he is just my step-son."

I exhaled lightly, trying not to let Macbeth's words unnerve me. There was a grain of truth to what he said. The only problem was I would never let Macbeth near Lulach again. "We shall see."

"You will do as I ask. You will bring that boy here, or I must make other arrangements."

"Other arrangements? Like what? Divorce me? I would like to see you try."

"There are other things that can be done."

"I suppose you could try to kill me. *Try*, of course, being key there. What else could you possibly do to harm me that you haven't already done?"

"Gruoch," he said, his voice dark.

I sighed wearily. "I'll leave for Moray soon. You can make your *other* arrangements then," I said then turned and left the chamber.

"Gruoch?" Macbeth called.

I kept walking.

To my surprise, he rushed down the hall after me, grabbing my arm. "What do you mean you're returning to Moray?"

"I think I was perfectly clear. I will return to Moray."

"Lulach is not there."

"I am well aware of that."

"Lady Gruoch," Killian called. He rushed down the hall toward me, pulling his blade as he went. "Your Majesty, I strongly suggest you let go of Lady Gruoch."

"Or what?" Macbeth spat at him.

Killian's gaze darkened, answering Macbeth's threat.

"You see that? See how he disrespects me? I should have him killed," Macbeth hissed.

"It's not him you should be worried about. Leave it to you to miss the obvious," I said, pressing the tip of Scáthach against Macbeth's neck. "Now, let go of me, or I'll plunge this dagger in an inch deep."

Realizing the danger, Macbeth pushed me away from him.

I caught myself before I crashed against the wall.

"One day, I'll melt that dagger down to nothing or maybe... maybe I'll plunge it in your damned chest," Macbeth said then turned and headed back into his chamber, slamming the door behind him.

I stared at the closed door. Had Macbeth just threatened to kill me?

"Gruoch, are you all right?" Killian asked, rushing to me.

In the hall around us, the servants had stopped to stare.

I nodded then slipped Scáthach back into her sheath. "Yes. I'm fine."

"Bastard," Killian spat, glaring at the chamber door. "I always heard rumors that Macbeth was unkind to you. I couldn't believe it."

"Well, now you see."

"You would do well to return to Moray."

"Yes."

"In the meantime, you must have a guard on you at all time. No arguments."

"If you insist."

"I insist. Though I have to say, even I missed that move with the dagger. Who taught you that?"

"Uald."

"Uald? That *lady*?"

I laughed. "Yes, that *lady*."

"Secrets again?"

I nodded.

"Your secrets are safe with me, my lady."

"And for that, I am grateful," I said then cast a glance back at the conference room door. My heart was beating hard in my chest. I knew Macbeth. His ravings often amounted to nothing. But he was also a dangerous man. It had never occurred to me that he might actually kill me. Was it possible?

No. Not if Scáthach had anything to say about it.

CHAPTER TWENTY-THREE

*I*n the days that followed, I did my best to avoid Macbeth. Instead, I made plans to return north. I could still do good for Scotland. I could still make my country strong, but I couldn't do it at Macbeth's side. Not only was such a condition miserable, but it was dangerous.

Midafternoon three days later, there was a knock on my door. My guard, Magnus, opened it to reveal one of Macbeth's messengers.

"Your Majesty," he said. "Crinian, the Abbott of Dunkeld, is here, but King Macbeth is…indisposed. Will you see the Abbott?"

"Where is Macbeth?"

"He's unable to attend to state matters at this time."

I stepped closer to the boy who looked so unnerved that his spirit was about to jump out of its skin.

"What is your name?" I asked the footman.

"Aed, Your Majesty."

"Aed, please take me to the king."

The boy nodded then motioned for me to follow him.

Without another word, Magnus fell in line behind us.

The boy led me down the halls of Glamis to the chapel. Inside,

I spotted Macbeth before the altar. He was wearing a simple white robe and lying prostrate on the floor.

I suppressed a gasp, but then anger washed up in me.

Now what?

By all the gods, now what?

I entered the chapel, Magnus just behind me. I motioned for him to stay by the door. Moving carefully, I approached Macbeth.

He was lying there, his eyes open wide as he gazed off toward some faraway place. The back of his dressing gown was wet with blood. The fabric had been torn. He had flagellated himself.

"And what are we doing, Macbeth?" I asked.

"Praying," he whispered.

"Prayer is important, but there is an element of timing to the matter. Crinian is here."

"You see to him," Macbeth said absently.

"Very well," I said then turned to go.

"Gruoch," Macbeth called weakly.

"What?"

"I'm sorry for what I did."

I huffed a laugh. "Which thing, Macbeth? Which thing?" I said then stalked away. Leaving the chapel, I entered Macbeth's meeting chamber located not far away. "Bring Crinian here," I told Aed.

The boy nodded then rushed off.

I took a seat at Macbeth's desk. All around the table were notes, most of which I couldn't read, mad scribbles. Amongst the incomprehensible papers were dispatches with important news. As I waited, I started sorting. From what I could see, Macbeth had left many important matters unattended.

Chains rattled, and a moment later, soldiers led Crinian into the room. I frowned when I saw that he had been roughed up, his lip bloody.

"Unchain him," I said.

The men removed the bindings.

"Your Majesty. Thank you," Crinian said, rubbing his wrists.

I inclined my head to him then crossed the room and poured him some water. I handed him the glass. He drank greedily.

"You may sit," I said, motioning to a chair by the meeting table. I signaled to a servant at the back of the room. "Bring food."

She bobbed a curtsey then disappeared.

"My lady, your cousin, Bethoc... What have they done with my wife?" Crinian asked.

"Bethoc will be brought to court. There is no reason for her to live in fear or discomfort. We are, after all, kin. She need not fear me."

He sighed in relief. "Thank you, Your Majesty."

"So," I said, taking a seat across from him. I relaxed back into my chair. "What are we going to do now?"

"Do, Your Majesty?"

"Yes. What are we going to do with you? You've been funneling silver to Siward and lining the pockets of the lords in the south—presumably to buy their support. I see you have been unequally distributing coin to the church, which, of course, has made your life very comfortable. So, I am in a conundrum on what to do with you. I'm inclined to have you killed. Can you think of any reason why I shouldn't?"

"I...I only did as my son asked."

"Duncan ordered you to rob the country?"

"Duncan ordered me to rob the north."

"I'm sorry, but I met your son. He lacked the imagination."

"No, Your Majesty. You're right. Forgive me. I'd forgotten how *astute* you are. I did what I could to safeguard my son's realm."

"At your own devising."

"Yes. At my own devising."

"I see. You have been a man of the world for many years. Perhaps it's best we return you to holy things. After all, you are the Abbot of Dunkeld. The monastery needs its master. You should turn your mind to less worldly things. Yes. That will be good. A return to the spiritual life might just be what you need. Perhaps some time spent in prayer, illuminating manuscripts, seeing to the holy brothers at the monastery will feed your soul."

"Your Majesty," Crinian said, the look of relief plain on his face.

"And, of course, you can guide the holy brothers on how to run self-sufficiently, without the support of the crown."

"You…You're going to cut off support to the monasteries?"

"They should have plenty saved from your years of generous patronage."

"But Scotland is a Christian nation. We must be supported by the monarch."

"Must we? Half of Scotland is a Christian nation. Considering the years we have spent money to support the Christian faith, it's only fair we send some wealth to provide backing to those who follow the old gods. And you should be feeling lucky to be alive."

"Lady Gruoch, you will take the country backward."

"If you're disinclined to accept my offer, that's fine. I accept your decision either way."

"What is the alternative to returning to my position as Abbot of Dunkeld?"

"Oh. Sorry I wasn't clear about that. The second option is death. Really, it's your choice."

"And my wife…she will come to court?"

"As I said."

"And the king, is he in agreement?"

"No. Not at all. He wanted to murder you, but we'll handle things my way today."

"Then I am grateful for your mercy and the chance at life you've offered. I accept."

"Very good."

The serving maid returned then with a platter heaped with meat, bread, cheese, fish, and potted fruits and vegetables. She set the tray in front of the abbot.

"Funny," I said, leaning forward to snatch a tender morsel from his plate, popping it into my mouth. "Gillacoemgain used to hunt to feed us. I remember how happy we all were when he returned with a stag or wild hog. We would make tarts from berries I found in the field. There we were in Moray, foraging for food like villagers, while you saw to it that the monks ate better than the lords in the north," I said then rose. "Eat well, abbot. We'll see you returned to the monastery as soon as you're done."

I motioned to my guard who stepped in to keep an eye on Crinian.

Just outside, however, I found Macbeth's soldiers still waiting.

"When the abbot is done eating, put him back in chains and have him taken to the monastery of Dunkeld. He won't need his fine clothes and jewels. A simple shift should do."

"Yes, Your Majesty."

"And the treasury?" I asked.

The man motioned for me to follow him. We headed back outside. There, I found three wagons waiting. They were surrounded by a ring of guards. The soldier lifted the tarp on one of the wagons to reveal chest upon chest within.

"Have it all secured in Glamis' armory. Put men on it at all times."

"Yes, Your Majesty. As King Macbeth ordered, we have sent men to secure the silver mines," he said, handing some scrolls to me.

I nodded. "Very good. I will see to the rest. And Lady Bethoc?"

The man sighed heavily, exasperation filling in his voice. "Another battalion was sent to the castle to retrieve her ladyship. She should arrive soon. I understand that removing her was more difficult than displacing the abbot."

"Well, the abbot can always be smacked about the head and neck if he fails to comply. Her ladyship is quite another matter."

The man chuckled.

"When she arrives, she can be taken to a family chamber. Surely there's a maid or two around here who are hard of hearing."

At that, he laughed aloud. "Very good, Your Highness."

"And well done, sir…"

"Wallace, Your Majesty."

"Well done, Wallace."

He bowed. "I shall see to the rest now, Your Majesty."

"Thank you."

I tapped the scrolls in my hand then headed back inside. Getting the crown's coin in hand was a critical step. But more importantly, I needed to get the ladies' chambers ready for Bethoc. It was of the utmost importance to my sanity that she was housed far, far away from me before I started seeing blood spots everywhere.

CHAPTER TWENTY-FOUR

*O*nce Crinian was dealt with and on his way back to his monastery, I returned to Macbeth's chamber and began sorting through the mess. As I went through the papers on his desk, I could see his slip from competent to his current position on the chapel floor. There was so much work to be done. There was no time for madness. No time for anything. The state of the realm was one of upheaval. I hardly knew where to start.

But I did start.

One item at a time, I answered every letter, sent messengers, ordered supplies, redistributed troops, and plotted a way forward.

Wordlessly, servants brought in food and drink for me, but the day passed so fast that I was surprised when it was nightfall once more.

I rose, pulling up my gloves, then headed back to the chapel.

There, I found Macbeth sitting cross-legged in front of the altar.

He stared at the crucifix hanging there.

"Go to bed, Macbeth. You need rest."

"I am tired," Macbeth said.

"Yes, I'm sure you are."

Macbeth rose on unsteady feet. I gestured for his man to take his arm. "Think nothing of this. He'll be well in a few days," I told the servant.

"Of course, Queen Gruoch."

"And say nothing."

"Of course not, Your Majesty."

I nodded then watched the two depart.

I stood in the chapel for a few moments. It was a small, congested space with wooden walls, floor, and a low ceiling. A breeze blew in from the open window. On the breeze, I caught the slightest scent of spring tinged with wood smoke.

Moonlight shone in from the window, casting its rays on the effigy of Jesus hanging above the altar.

"If he is your son, as your priests say we all are, then heal his mind," I whispered to the effigy.

There was no reply.

I had not expected one.

The White Christ had never spoken to me.

As I crossed the room to leave, however, there was an odd commotion behind me. A bird had come to roost on the open windowsill. It was a dove. It turned and looked at me, it's dark eye glimmering in the moonlight. It cooed softly.

I sucked in a breath, remembering the vision Scotia had given me.

Perhaps there was a way to put the pieces of Macbeth together after all.

CHAPTER TWENTY-FIVE

I worked tirelessly over the coming weeks as Macbeth lay in his bedchamber staring at the wall. It was long past time when I had hoped to return to Moray. I eyed my growing belly skeptically, knowing that I would soon have to think of a solution to my problem. Aside from fleeing and letting everything fall into disrepair, my options were limited. I needed to get Macbeth on his feet if I had any hope of making my way north before anyone knew I was with child.

Of course, hiding such knowledge from my maids was impossible.

"I'll select dresses with more fabric at the front. They will conceal your state better," Tira told me. "And I'll loosen the laces where I can."

Rhona studied me carefully then shook her head. "You know there will be talk."

"And Macbeth... Would be best if we move back to Moray," Tira said, echoing my thoughts.

I nodded. "I agree. But there is much to be done."

"Yes. But I worry, my lady."

She didn't have to tell me. I, too, worried. I needed to leave, and soon.

*R*ising early one morning, I took out my box of medicines and went to Macbeth's chamber.

"Queen Gruoch," his servant said, bowing when I approached. Remembering Macbeth's whoring at Inverness, I hesitated.

"Is His Majesty within?"

The man nodded then went inside, motioning for me to follow.

The room was dank and dark. Incense burned, making the air stifling.

"Has he left the chamber at all?" I whispered.

"No. But the priest comes three times a day."

I nodded to the man then motioned for him to leave.

Crossing the room, I pulled back the heavy drapes and flung open the windows.

"Who is there?" Macbeth called from his bed.

"Your wife."

"My wife," he repeated.

I pushed open every window then eyed the room. Macbeth had drawn the drapes on his bed closed. Feeling unreasonably furious, I snatched the fabric back.

"What—what are you doing?" Macbeth asked, wincing at the bright sunlight.

"Airing out this sty."

Macbeth sat up in bed. He had grown a scraggly beard. His bedclothes smelled sour.

I went to the door. Macbeth's man came to attention. "Have fresh linens brought. I need a maid to come tidy the room."

The servant nodded then rushed off.

Turning, I headed back inside. Opening my box, I pulled out

one herb at a time, carefully selecting those I thought might ease his mind and balance him. I ground the herbs into a fine powder then mixed them into a glass of water.

"Get up," I told Macbeth, pulling out the chair at his table.

"What is that?"

"Medicine. I made you a similar tonic in Thurso...many moons ago."

Macbeth rose slowly then slumped into the chair.

I pushed the cup toward him.

"Your Majesties?" a voice called from the door.

I turned to find the maid there.

"Strip everything," I told the maid, motioning to the bed. Macbeth's servant stood at the door. "And you, sir. Set out fresh clothes for the king. Get his washing tub. And a shave..." I said then paused. "Well...the beard suits you," I told Macbeth.

"I'll leave it," he said absently.

I nodded. "It needs to be trimmed, as does your hair."

I turned to Macbeth's servant who nodded.

Just outside the chamber, I spotted another footman. "You there," I called to the boy. "Bring a breakfast for His Majesty. Tell the cook I want whatever fresh fruits and cheese there is to be had. Fish, if there is any. Honey cakes."

I looked back at Macbeth who was staring at me, his eyes wide and fixed.

"What are you doing?" he whispered.

"What needs to be done."

One obstacle at a time, I would make my way to my fate.

I glanced at Macbeth's cup. "Drink. Finish it."

He did as I asked then slid the cup toward me. I took it from him, rinsing it in the basin. I cleaned my tools then packed my bag back up.

"After you are dressed, you will go outside, walk the grounds, and check on the soldiers."

"Gruoch, I—"

"I don't want to hear anything. You need fresh air and exercise. I will be in your council chamber when you are finished," I said then latched my box closed once more.

Satisfied I'd made a start forward, I left Macbeth's chamber.

*I*t was some time after lunch when Macbeth arrived. He looked pale and gaunt. There were dark rings under his eyes and an odd gleam within them. He sat down in a chair in front of the fire.

"Gruoch," he said, but then he said nothing else.

"I've had an idea," I told Macbeth.

"What idea?" Macbeth asked absently.

"That you should take a pilgrimage to Rome."

Macbeth turned and looked at me. "To Rome? Me?"

"Many rulers do so. We need to strengthen our ties abroad, and you need to strengthen yourself."

"I don't understand."

"Yes, you do. I have never fully agreed with the priests of the White Christ nor do I embrace your faith. But I believe that if you embrace your faith, you may find a way back to that man I met at Lumphanan."

"That man is a stranger to me."

I laughed. "And to me."

Macbeth smiled slightly. He looked at his worktable where I had neatly stacked all the correspondence. I'd had shelves moved into the chamber where I kept ledgers and essential missives. Ruling Scotland, it turned out, was not much different from ruling Moray. Scale was the only factor. After the initial shock at the confused state of things, I was beginning to make progress.

Macbeth exhaled a heavy sigh. "You have been doing everything."

"Someone has to."

"And things are…"

"Settling down. You'll be delighted to know that cousin Bethoc is here. If you wanted any greater motivation to walk to Rome, I can't think of another."

To my surprise, he chuckled. "I'll consider it. And Crinian?"

"He's revisiting his dedication to his vocation. He is Abbott of Dunkeld once more. The mines and treasury are secure. Now that I've choked off the money we've been bleeding south, the southern lords are suddenly very eager to ally with us."

"Thank you, Gruoch. These days have been very strange for me."

I bit the inside of my cheek but said nothing. How many strange days had Macbeth caused me?

When I looked up, I realized Macbeth was studying me carefully. "Are your hands cold?"

"Yes."

"Oh." He eyed the papers on the table once more. "What can I do?"

I looked across the desk, selecting the messages I'd received from Thorfinn. I handed them to Macbeth. "Get well."

He took the parchments from my hands. "Gruoch, I don't deserve—"

"No, you don't. So do us all a favor and come back to yourself. For now, I have to send some messages," I said then strode out of the room.

CHAPTER TWENTY-SIX

I was both sad and relieved when Madelaine arrived with a small party the following day. She looked very pale and weary, but she smiled when she saw me.

"Corbie," she said, kissing me on my cheeks.

"My dear, sweet aunt. How are you?"

She shrugged. "As well as I can be."

"Perhaps you should not have come. If it will be too much burden—"

"No. I need to stay busy, to distract myself."

"Good, because I have a dozen letters from noble lords, thanes, and clansmen who want to send their wives and daughters to me. I need your help."

Madelaine smiled. "Of course."

"And Bethoc is here. I haven't actually seen her, but they tell me she is here."

"Ahh," Madelaine said then nodded. "Very well. Let me rest for a time then I'll get to work."

"Whatever would I do without you?"

"I love you too, my dear."

Motioning to the servants, I directed them to come help Madelaine. As I watched her go, I thought about Crearwy. If she had stayed with me, she would have honestly been a princess. She would have had beautiful clothes, jewelry, a fine chamber, tutors, and more. It would have been a very different life. Clearly, she had imagined a life like that. She wasn't wrong to want those things. The idea of her being here with Madelaine and me would have been good, happy. But at what risk? Everything could change in a moment.

My hand drifted to my stomach.

Very soon, I would have to make the same choice again. Was there a different way, a better way?"

"Gruoch?" Macbeth called from behind me.

I turned to see him standing alongside a gentleman who was holding a large piece of rolled parchment and wearing a square builder's cap.

I swallowed hard, hoping Macbeth had not seen my hand on my stomach. "Yes?"

"Is that Madelaine who has arrived?"

I nodded.

"Very good. This is Kirk. He has been working on Dunsinane."

"How nice to meet you, sir. I've been reading over your updates. It seems as if the work is coming along very well," I told the man.

"It is. In fact, I've just convinced His Majesty to come to have a look," Kirk replied.

"I thought you might like to come along," Macbeth said tepidly. He still looked terrible. He was pale and gaunt, his eyes sunken. If I hadn't despised him, I might have felt sorry for him.

"You will have to stay the night," Kirk said. "You won't be able to ride back in time."

"Is the castle suitable for the queen?" Macbeth asked.

"We can make it so," Kirk assured Macbeth.

My curiosity piqued, I nodded. "Yes, I will come. I'll need a few moments to get ready. And I need to let Madelaine know."

Macbeth nodded. "I'll have your horse saddled."

While I had no interest in going anywhere with Macbeth, I really wanted to see the fortress. I headed back to my chambers to dress in my riding clothes.

"Where are you going?" Tira asked.

"To Dunsinane."

"I heard it's a craggy old thing, not at all like Glamis," Rhona said.

"Glamis is small and insecure," I said.

"And, no doubt, too fancy for your liking," Rhona added.

I chuckled. "How did you know?" I asked.

"Because it's too fancy for me," she replied.

We all laughed.

"Can the two of you please check in with Madelaine? She's just arrived. She'll need your help getting settled in the coming weeks."

"Of course," Tira said.

After I slipped my riding clothes on, I collected Magnus and two other guards then went to find Madelaine. She was busy settling into her chamber.

"Madelaine, if you don't mind, I will ride to Dunsinane and return in the morning."

"Of course, dear."

"I've asked Tira and Rhona to look in on you."

Madelaine nodded mutely. "They'll have to find me a maid. Ute didn't want to come."

Of course, she didn't. "That won't be a problem."

"Are you up for such a long ride?" Madelaine asked, keeping her words as guarded as possible. But I hadn't missed her meaning.

"It will be fine."

"All right. Be careful, love," she said, kissing my cheek.

"Take your rest," I told Madelaine. "There is no rush."

She smiled softly, but there was a dullness to her eyes I hadn't seen before. All that mirth that used to live inside her had gone dim.

I let her go then returned to the courtyard. There, I found Macbeth. He was already mounted, a dozen of his own men in attendance. I also spotted Killian mounted and ready.

"Sir," Magnus said then went to him.

I mounted Swift then watched as the two Moray men exchanged words. Magnus nodded to me then headed back into the castle.

Killian reined his horse in alongside mine. "I will come with you. Just to be safe," he said, eyeing Macbeth warily.

I was glad. While I trusted all the men who had come with me from Moray, I had faith in Killian.

"Ready?" Macbeth asked, glancing quickly at Killian.

I nodded, and then our party set out.

The ride to Dunsinane was, to my surprise, enjoyable. A road had been cut through the winding, hilly path between the old fortress and Glamis. We rode through a thick forest filled with ancient trees. The old oaks swayed in the wind, their limbs rubbing against one another.

"Listen to how they speak," I told Killian.

"And do you understand their words, or are they secret?"

"Anyone can understand. Just close your eyes and listen."

Killian closed his eyes. "You're right. Squeak, squeak, squeak."

I laughed, which made Macbeth glance over his shoulder at me. For a moment, a storm cloud rolled over his visage, but he hid it behind a smile and turned back around.

I frowned. There was no settling the man. No matter how

much I secretly hoped he could be recovered, there was no hope. I had to remind myself of that fact again, and again, and again.

"Now, one such as you, who knows the old gods, should know better," I told Killian.

"Oh, I know the trees speak, just not to me. Yet I feel the presence of the gods in the deep woods all the same. Squeaking and all. For instance, the trees near that old camp I visited felt like they had a lot to say."

"Did they?"

"I must say, I was rather glad when those ladies arrived. I was beginning to worry dryads were about. And I don't spook, Lady Gruoch."

"I certainly hope not, or you'd make a terrible guard."

Killian chuckled. "Well, you're still alive. I must be doing something right."

"I'm glad for it," I said with a laugh.

It took most of the day to cross the countryside to the old hilltop fortress. As we rode, I gazed into the woods. Part of me wanted to jump off Swift and go back where I belonged. In the woods. Among my own people. With my druid under the limbs of an old oak. With my son and daughter. And soon, with my baby. My hand drifted to my stomach. I needed to get north very soon.

Stopping only to rest and water the horses, we reached the path that led up to the winding hilltop fortress of Dunsinane just as the sun was setting. To my surprise, the edifice was massive. The castle was made of large grey stone and built in three tiers, ramparts on all three levels. Long ago, a mighty king must have ruled in this place.

"Whose castle was this?" I called to Kirk.

"You are in the land of the Parisi, my queen," he replied, referring to the ancient Celtic tribe who were once near neighbors to the Iceni, Boudicca's people.

"Such an ancient place," I said.

"With deep foundations and strong walls."

"Revived, thanks to your help," Macbeth told the man.

"Ah, Your Majesty, I'm only touching up the work of masters."

Even as we approached the hilltop, I could see the construction going on inside. Everywhere I looked, I saw masons, stone workers, and carpenters.

Macbeth turned in his saddle and smiled at me. "Your castle, Queen Gruoch," he said, flourishing his hand.

Kirk laughed. "What a fine gift for a king to give his queen."

I studied Macbeth's face. He wore an honest, open, even hopeful expression.

"It's a wonderful, strong place," I said.

"A new home, a new start," Macbeth said with a smile then turned around.

Killian gave me a sidelong glance, but I didn't look at him. I didn't need to. I wanted Macbeth to be well, but not for my sake. I wanted him to be well, so he would rule well. As for the man, I wanted nothing from him. If he ever thought we would reconcile after all the harm he wrought, he was sadly mistaken.

We rode to the gate which was securely locked with a heavy steel grate. The men within worked the levers, and a moment later, the gate lifted.

Swift huffed and snorted.

"It's all right," I told the horse, patting him gently.

We rode through the entrance into a yard where men worked and soldiers patrolled the grounds. Grooms met us to take the horses. An attendant came from the castle.

"Please arrange some spaces for King and Queen Macbeth and their escort. They will be here tonight. The second level on the western side should work," Kirk said.

The man nodded then headed within.

"Come," Kirk called to us. "We will still have time to get a look before the sun sets." He motioned to us to follow behind him as he headed across the yard. We climbed the stairs to the first rampart. Walking apace, we then climbed another flight of steps to the uppermost section of the castle. Kirk waved for us to join him as he walked toward the western wall. I could see then why he was so eager.

While it was windy on the uppermost rampart, the view was spectacular. All around, I saw the vast, ancient forest. The sunset painted a vista of red, orange, gold, and deep, dark blue at the horizon. It was beautiful. I closed my eyes and swayed in the wind. I could feel the energy of the forest all around me. But beyond that, I heard a deep whispering voice. I couldn't quite make out the words, but an ancient song echoed all around me, and the castle itself seemed to speak.

"What is the name of this forest, sir?" Killian asked.

"Birnam Wood," Kirk said. "It stretches on for miles and miles. It is said that a great battle happened in that forest long ago. The bard Taliesin tells of how Gwydion fought with the Celtic gods against the Lord of the Underworld. Gwydion used his magic, calling the trees of Birnam Wood to life. They did his bidding, fighting at his side until the battle was won."

"*Cad Goddeu*," I said. "*The Battle of the Trees*."

"Yes, Your Majesty. That's right."

I stared out at the forest.

"That explains the voices," Killian whispered to me.

While I knew he thought he was jesting, Killian was right. This place was full of magic. The trees had been touched by the Otherworld. The ancient oaks and ash, once living warriors, carried on. No wonder all my senses were on edge, my breath quick, and the wings of the raven were thundering in my heart. Macbeth had chosen a castle in the seat of magic.

"What a strong edifice. No one can defeat this castle," Macbeth said proudly.

"Macbeth shall never be vanquished until Birnam Wood comes again to high Dunsinane Hill," I said in a voice that was mine and not mine. I gazed out at the trees, watching in my mind's eye as they rose, pulling their roots from the ground. They moved toward the castle. Their weapons glinted in the moonlight. In my mind's eye, I saw the trees scale the walls and overtake the castle. Macbeth fell amongst the tangle of limbs and roots. They pulled him down until the very breath was choked from him.

I swooned.

Killian reached out to catch me before I fell.

"My Queen," Kirk said.

"Gruoch," Macbeth called, reaching out to grab me.

I shied away from Macbeth, nearly causing Killian and myself to tumble in the process.

"I'm all right. I'm all right," I reassured them.

Killian, handling me gently, helped me back on my feet.

"Must be careful, Your Majesty. Such heights make many people dizzy. Why don't we get you back inside and find something to drink? It was a very long ride," Kirk suggested.

I inhaled deeply then slowly exhaled, shaking off the remnants of the vision. "Yes, you're right," I said. "The height got the better of me. It's a beautiful view though. Thank you for bringing us."

Motioning for us to follow, Kirk led us within the castle. As I went, I turned the vision around and around in my mind, puzzled by the sight. But most of all, I felt troubled by my reaction to the dream. When Macbeth's eyes had closed, when death had finally taken him, a deep sense of relief had washed over me. I had been glad.

CHAPTER TWENTY-SEVEN

*W*hile the castle was still under construction, Kirk saw that a small meal was prepared for Macbeth and me and our guard. We kept the conversation pleasant and light, Macbeth mainly asking about the construction of the castle and me keeping quiet as I mulled over my vision and fought off fatigue. The ride had taken more out of me than I had expected. I really needed to go north soon.

"Sir," I said to Kirk, "has a chamber been prepared for me? I'm a bit weary."

Kirk motioned for a servant to come forward. "No ladies' maids on hand, Your Majesty. We could ask one of the cooks or serving girls—"

"No. I know well enough how to dress myself," I said with a smile. "Thank you."

Killian motioned for the other men to stay and eat while he joined the servant and me.

"This way, Your Majesty," the servant said.

"Goodnight, Gruoch," Macbeth called.

"Goodnight, Macbeth."

The servant led me down the halls to a room on the second tier of the castle. Some of the rooms were still having masonry work completed, but the chambers on this end of the castle seemed to be in good condition.

"Here you are," the servant said, opening the door. The room was simply adorned with a huge but old wooden bed. I could smell the scent of new straw therein. Skins lined the floors. There were no windows in the space.

Killian inspected the room, nodding when he found everything in order.

"I'll have two guards on the door all night," he told me.

"Thank you," I told him. "And please, don't forget to rest."

He smiled.

"Do you need anything, Your Majesty?" the servant asked.

I looked around the room. Both water and wine had already been set out.

I shook my head. "No. Thank you."

At that, they left me. I closed the door behind them then went and sat down on the bed. I sighed heavily, feeling overcome by weariness. I set my hand on my stomach.

"What do you think, little one? Do you like this old, magical place?"

I could sense my tiny babe there but heard nothing more.

I lay back and looked up at the stone ceiling. The land of the Parisi. Well, at least I was in the home of my allies once more. Closing my eyes, I soon drifted off to sleep.

*I*t was the caw of a raven that woke me late that night. Sitting up, I listened intently. It sounded like the raven was in the castle, not outside.

Rising, I grabbed a taper and went to the door.

I was surprised to see that there was no guard stationed there.

"Killian? Camden?"

No one answered, but from deep within the castle, I heard the call of a raven once more. How strange.

Taking my candle with me, I followed the raven's cries. I had nearly reached the feasting hall—and I had still not seen anyone else in the castle—when I heard the raven caw once more.

I looked all around, realizing that the sound was coming from the lower level of the castle. Maybe someone had a pet raven. They were smart birds. Some said they made good pets.

Panning my candle all around, I looked for any sign of the servants.

"Hello?" I called.

While the wall sconces were lit and there was a fire burning in the great hall, no one answered.

It was very late, and the castle was not fully staffed. Perhaps everyone was asleep.

Again, the raven called.

Grabbing my skirts, I went downstairs. It was only then that I realized I had left my gloves behind. They must have slipped off in my sleep. As before, my hands were covered in slick, red blood.

I frowned and told myself to ignore the sight.

I followed the winding castle down to the first level. Here, I caught the scent of the woods outside. Having not yet toured this level of the castle, I felt easily turned around. I looked about for a servant or soldier, but everything was quiet.

"Hello?"

Again, the raven cawed.

I passed through another elaborate hall and down a narrow hallway. Here, the castle stones were a different color. The rocks were darker. The candlelight woke the sparkles in the stones. They shimmered. The masonry was shaped differently here as well. When I studied the walls, I noticed someone had made carvings around the doorways.

I realized then that I was in the original section of the fortress.

These stones were the first stones. These walls were the first walls. I reached out to touch them.

When my bloody fingertips grazed the stones, the entire castle seemed to shudder.

The raven cawed once more. It was somewhere inside. Somewhere still ahead. I shifted my taper and moved deeper into the castle. This part of the fortress had not yet been touched. It was full of dust and cobwebs. I followed a narrow hallway that led into a wide, open room. Old, broken furniture littered the place. As I gazed across the room, a sense of wonderment filled me. This was the hall of some forgotten king or queen. A cold hearth trimmed with finely chiseled masonry work was on one wall. A raised dais, where the throne must have once sat, was on the other side of the room.

I jumped when a fire sprang to life in the hearth.

A raven shrieked sharply.

I followed the sound.

I spotted a stairwell that I hadn't seen before in one corner.

The raven cawed, its voice echoing up from below. Had the creature gotten trapped inside?

Moving carefully around the broken stones, I followed the sound of the raven, winding down the stairs.

The air chilled. I smelled the thick scents of loam and lime. I was moving underground. This part of the castle had been dug into the very mountain. When I reached the bottom of the stairs, I realized I was standing in a cave. Torches on the cave walls had been lit. A raven sat on a perch. When it saw me, it cawed then flew into one of the connecting tunnels.

My hands shaking, I followed the bird.

The gods were at work.

I walked down the dark passage. I heard the call of the raven ahead of me. A dim, blue light shined. I moved toward it. All the hairs on the back of my neck had risen. To my surprise, the amethyst gems on my raven torcs and amulet began to glow. I could feel the buzz of magic in the air. The scents of heady white sage perfumed the place. Under them, I smelled loamy earth and mud. Water trickled down the cave walls. The ground below me was wet.

As I walked, I noticed the cave walls were lined with tombs. The empty eye sockets of skeletons looked out at me. An arch trimmed with skulls led into an open space that was illuminated blue.

I crossed the threshold only to find myself standing in the chamber of the Lord of the Hollow Hills on Ynes Verleath. It was just as I had left it. The place was full of skeletons, the lord still seated on his throne. Blue flames shimmered in the sconces. And in the center of the space stood Andraste who was leaning against her staff.

The raven landed on the back of the throne of the Lord of the Hollow Hills. It cawed at Andraste then it turned and flew off down another tunnel.

"Well, now I know what all the screeching was about," she said, her eyes following the bird. She looked back at me.

"Tell me the truth," I said, glaring at Andraste. "You cannot hide from me now. The Goddess has brought both of us here. Tell me the truth about Lulach and Crearwy."

"I moved you where you needed to go. I did as I was charged. I protected the land, and I moved you as the visions told me to."

"And you lied to me."

"Yes."

"Lulach and Crearwy are Gillacoemgain's children."

"Yes."

"And that night, you pushed me back into the world, then and there, knowing I would meet Duncan on the road."

"Yes."

"How could you do that to me?"

"I did what I must. We are all the tools of the gods. I moved you so that a thousand other seeds would grow. I moved you as I foresaw. I moved you as I had to."

"Have you no pity? No love?"

"Love?" Andraste said, scoffing. "What is love to a creature like me? You cannot escape your fate. Good and bad comes to us all. Do you think I wanted to live on after everything I *loved* crumbled to nothing, after everyone I *loved* was killed?" she said, motioning around her. "Do you think I wanted to take on the heavy burden given to me? We cannot escape our destinies. The Goddess has her ways. Her eyes see farther than ours. And we must move as she decrees."

"But the cost."

"There is no cost; there is only destiny."

"No. I would have made different choices."

"But you were not given a chance, as fate decreed."

"Don't riddle with me, Andraste. You turned my life into a lie. You took everything from me."

"And yet," she said, motioning to my stomach, "something has come back to you. Don't hate me, Cerridwen. I only do as the Goddess bids. One day you will too."

"Never," I spat.

Andraste crossed the room and stood before me. The lines on her ancient face were deep and grooved. I remembered what Epona said, that Andraste herself had become a Goddess. Once, she had been a mortal girl like me. Was that the fate the Goddess had laid out for me—for Cerridwen—that I would become like Andraste? I couldn't think of a destiny any less appealing.

"I *am* sorry, Cerridwen. Now, go from this place," she said then reached toward me. "Out, out brief candle," she whispered, then snubbed the light on my wick.

I shuddered then found myself standing in complete darkness.

My heart was beating hard in my chest.

I stilled and listened. It was so silent. Reaching out, I felt for the wall. I touched cut stone. Patting the wall, I moved slowly across the room, nearly stumbling when my foot found the stairs leading upward. Moving carefully, I made my way up the steps. As I neared the top, a dim light shone. I was in the ancient throne room of the castle.

Retracing my steps, I wound my way down the hall on the first floor of the castle. A few moments later, I heard voices.

"Here, let's go down here," someone called, panic in their voice.

Following the sound, I made my way forward. I exited a hallway to find myself face to face with one of Macbeth's soldiers.

His eyes went wide. "She's here. She's here. I've found her," the man screamed.

Behind him, I heard a flood of footsteps.

Killian appeared at the end of the hall. He rushed toward me. "Gruoch," he called.

Macbeth's soldier raised an eyebrow but said nothing.

I looked out the window. To my surprise, the sun was rising. The horizon was lit bright pink and yellow. It was morning once more.

There was shouting all around the castle.

"Gruoch, where were you?" Killian asked.

I shook my head.

A moment later, Macbeth turned the corner. His sword was drawn. He had a look of panic on his face.

What in the world was happening?

"Gruoch," Macbeth called, crossing the hall toward me as he slipped his sword back in its sheath. "Thank god. Are you all right?"

"I'm fine. Please, there is no cause for alarm. I'm fine. I think I...I got turned around in the castle."

Macbeth turned on Killian, rage in his eyes. "How did you let this happen?"

"Your Majesty," Killian said, his voice stiff. "We didn't even know she was out of the room until this morning."

"How is that possible?" Macbeth spat.

"We…we don't know. We had a guard on her door all night."

Both men turned and looked at me.

"I think I was walking in my sleep," I said, knowing then how ridiculous the excuse sounded.

"But how did you get out of the room without your guard noticing?" Macbeth asked.

"When the watch changed, maybe," I said, meeting Killian's dark blue eyes. I begged his help.

"Yes. Yes, I forgot about that. When the watch changed, there may have been enough time," Killian said, his gaze on me.

"Change your procedures, soldier," Macbeth said roughly. He reached out to take my arm, but I moved away from him. "Please, Gruoch," he said. "We were afraid someone had abducted you. We turned the castle inside out searching for you."

"I'm so sorry."

"Please come. Let's have some of your sweet herbs and settle all our nerves," he said. It was then I realized how pale he looked, his eyes wild.

I nodded. "All right." I set my hand on Kilian's arm. "I'm all right," I said, reassuring him. I then turned and went with Macbeth.

"Gruoch, are you sure you're unharmed?" Macbeth asked.

"Yes. I'm sorry I frightened everyone."

Macbeth nodded. "I was…I *was* frightened," he said in a soft voice. "If something ever happened to you, I would never have the chance to win your forgiveness."

I felt my heart harden. I would hear nothing from him. Nothing. "Well, we wouldn't want that."

Macbeth sighed.

I ignored him, my mind turning to what I had seen.

Despite how strange and horrible Andraste's truth was, the truth was revealed at last. Andraste had deceived and lied to me.

But in the end—in the end—Lulach and Crearwy belonged to Gillacoemgain. Knowing that gave me a piece of my husband back, something I thought had been lost forever. And no matter how angry I was at Andraste, I also blessed her.

No one had ever told me a better lie.

CHAPTER TWENTY-EIGHT

*C*alm returned to Dunsinane once more. We lingered over breakfast, and I tried to soothe everyone's rattled nerves.

"I was so eager to see the castle, I walked in my sleep," I told Kirk.

Killian, who was sitting down the table from me, looked skeptically at me. He knew very well I had not sleepwalked. He knew I was lying. Luckily, *I* knew he would keep my secret.

"They said you were discovered in the oldest part of the castle, my queen," Kirk told me. "If you and the king are done with your morning meal, I would love to show it to you in the light of day."

I nodded.

"Yes, let's have a look," Macbeth said.

The three of us rose, Killian coming to attention. He motioned for Magnus to join us.

"Now, the original castle dates much older than even the Parisi," Kirk told me. "The section of that castle you discovered was the very first castle. It was molded from the land itself.

"And who ruled that place?"

Kirk shook his head. "I cannot say, my queen. There are some markings in the walls, but there are no records left from those days."

Taking torches, we wound down the narrow halls to the part of the castle where the stones shimmered.

"You see here," Kirk said, his fingers touching the carvings. "Like the marks on the standing stones that dot this great land."

"Such an ancient hall," Macbeth said, a wistful sound in his voice.

Kirk nodded. "The Parisi built upon this place, and then up and up over the years," Kirk said, awe in his voice. "But below. That is where the roots of the castle lie."

"What is below?" Macbeth asked.

"A cave network."

Macbeth frowned. "Is it safe?"

"Oh, I suppose, if one knows their way around," Kirk said.

"But can the castle be breached through the caves?" Macbeth asked.

Kirk shook his head. "No. The caves wind from chamber to chamber, but there is no outlet. I believe the old lords used it as living and storage space. Rudimentary, but secure."

Macbeth nodded. "Please be certain."

"Of course, Your Majesty. Shall we have a proper look at the rest of the castle?" he asked then led us away from the old throne room. Kirk guided us through the rest of Dunsinane. He spoke excitedly, gesturing as a man does when he's passionate about his craft. And I could see why. The improvements he made to the castle were magnificent. And the structure itself...I had not expected to, but how could I not help but love Dunsinane. Its very roots led to Ynes Verleath. And the trees surrounding the castle whispered.

Once we were done overseeing Kirk's work, we got ready to ride back to Glamis.

"Thank you, Kirk," I told the man. "Your castle enchanted me," I said with a laugh.

He chuckled. "I'm pleased to hear you say so, Your Majesty."

I nodded to the man then mounted Swift once more. Our party ready, we turned and rode from Dunsinane.

"Did you like the castle?" Macbeth asked, reining in his horse beside me.

I nodded. "Yes. It's an ancient thing."

Macbeth smiled. "I remembered the place. We stopped there when we were hunting…my father, Gillacoemgain, and me. I never forgot the castle. I had never seen a more amazing place, greater in my eyes than even Inverness."

A bubble of fury sparked up in me to hear Macbeth toss around Gillacoemgain's name so freely, a name he had cursed far too often to have any right to use it in fondness.

I said nothing, simply kept my face blank then rode ahead.

Noting the tension, Macbeth reined his horse away from me. He trotted forward to speak with his men.

My gaze drifted to the forest as we rode, remembering the poem *Cad Goddeu* and *The Battle of the Trees*. It didn't take much imagination to envision the massive old oaks coming to life.

But as we wound deeper into the forest, I felt eyes on me.

I scanned the woods.

Were there spies on the road? Enemies? I frowned and studied the green. As I did, my raven's eyes sharpened. There, well-hidden amongst the trees, stood a girl. She was wearing breeches and a tunic, a bow strapped over her shoulder. For a moment, I thought it was Uald. But this girl was far younger, her hair very dark.

She stilled when she realized I had picked her out, then she raised her fingers to her brow and then bowed to me.

My gods, she was from a coven.

There was a coven near here.

She turned and slipped unseen back into the forest.

"Lady Gruoch, is anything the matter?" Killian asked, reining in beside me.

"No. Nothing at all."

"How filled to the brim you are with secrets," he said with a laugh.

"Am I? Doesn't that make me interesting?"

"You are far too interesting for my own good, Lady Gruoch. I am very sure Lord Banquo would not appreciate the depth of my interest," he said, his voice low so no one else could hear.

I smiled at him. He really was a very handsome man, and more, I liked the spirit within him. "I appreciate the thought, but as you have already gleaned, my life is…complicated. Perhaps in another life. But let's keep that a secret," I said softly.

He smirked. "As I assumed. Though, a man can always hope. Yet, there is one secret I am particularly interested in," he said. And I could see from the expression on his face that he was trying to turn the conversation away from his confession. I followed where he led, never wanting him to feel uncomfortable around me.

"Oh? What is that?"

"When did you learn to walk through walls?"

"Well now, *that* is very secret."

"It's a very neat trick. Perhaps you'll teach me sometime."

"If the right time ever presents itself."

At that, he chuckled lightly. I joined him in his laughter.

Once again, Macbeth looked back at us. Jealously flickered across his face. What did he expect from me? As it was, he was getting far more from me than he deserved. I had stayed in Glamis for Scotland, not for Macbeth. I had worked to heal Macbeth for Scotland, not for any love I had for the man.

And I still had work to do.

If there was a coven near Dunsinane, I needed to know. I would need to talk to Balor. If there was anything I could do to help the practitioners of my faith, I would do so.

But even as I thought it, a voice whispered within me: *Then do it soon, before great Birnam Wood to high Dunsinane hill comes again.*

CHAPTER TWENTY-NINE

I returned to Glamis and set about my work once more. As I did so, I watched Macbeth with a wary eye. He was recovering. And so far, he seemed far steadier than he had in the past. Perhaps he had finally found the bottom of his ailment and was slowly rising again. Either way, I did my work and steered clear of him. Macbeth busied himself with the building of Dunsinane, spending more time at the old fortress than at Glamis, a fact about which I was eternally grateful.

As the weeks passed, spring came, and the forest around Glamis came alive once more. The weather grew warm, and the land came back to life. I was at my desk working one morning when my back started aching. I rose and stretched, pressing my fists into my back.

Madelaine, who was hiding from Bethoc, had come to join me. She'd been working on her embroidery. When I rose, she looked up. She watched me arch my back.

"Corbie," she said, setting down her work. "Your belly… There will be no hiding it soon. You need to make plans to depart."

"There is so much work here," I said.

"Take a secretary with you," she told me then rose and came behind me. With a mother's care, she worked the knots on my back. "Macbeth may be steady now, but I see that spark in his eyes still. Trust me, I know it very well. You need to leave."

I nodded. She was right. "I'll make preparations today. Will you be all right alone here with him? Are you sure you don't want to come?"

"I wish I could, my love. But you need me here, so here I shall stay. And alone? I'm not alone. I have Bethoc," she said with a laugh.

"And how is the weather today?"

"Ripe for causing gout. But more, she hasn't stopped talking about the fact that she has neither seen nor heard from Crinian since she arrived."

"Perhaps he's happy to be rid of her," I said.

"Perhaps," Madelaine considered. "But if I were you, I would send someone to ensure he is where you left him."

I nodded. Madelaine was right. "Yes. I'll do so. Right after I send a rider to Cawdor to let them know I'm coming home. Would you like Rhona to stay with you? I know Tira is pining for her family."

"No," Madelaine said then shook her head. "Let them go home. I'm training one of the kitchen maids. She's working out very well. Smart girl. Too smart for the kitchens. And Bethoc brought four or five maids. I'm sure she'll let me borrow one, if needed."

I smiled at Madelaine. In the months that had passed, she had started coming back to herself again. Part of me worried that Tavis' death might break her. In a way, it had. I saw that there were pieces of her that were still injured. I understood the feeling. The death of a loved one is a wound that never heals. Their absence lives on with you.

"Very well," I said. I kissed Madelaine's hands, thanking her for her care, then went back to my desk. Given my condition, I didn't want to send a casting to Banquo, but I was thrilled to share the news. I would return north very soon.

*O*ver the next two days, I made ready to depart. It wasn't until the third day, on the morning I planned to leave, that Macbeth appeared at the door of my bedchamber.

"Gruoch, may I have a word?" he asked.

Tira and Rhona looked at me.

"Please finish taking our things to the wagons. I'll meet you below," I told them.

I closed the door behind them.

"I wish we had discussed your return to Moray," he said simply.

"I was waiting until the weather cleared. I will tour the north while I am there, make sure things are as strong as we left them."

"When will you return?"

"I'm not sure."

"Dunsinane should be ready by winter. Will you be back then?"

"I don't know yet." The truth was, I didn't know when I would return. With my child due in the winter, even if I wanted to return, it wouldn't be feasible for me to come back until spring.

Macbeth ran his hand through his hair and took a slow, deep breath. He still looked far too gaunt, his eyes ringed black. He stared at my cold hearth, his eyes vacant. "Are you running from me?"

"I'm done running. We are king and queen. We will rule this land together as best we can. I am going north and will see to the northern provinces while I am there. You must retain a tight grip on the south while I am gone. Madelaine is here to see to the ladies, and you have your advisors. Listen to them, to Fife, and send word if you need to."

"Will Lulach be in Moray?"

I stiffened. "Perhaps."

Macbeth nodded glumly. "All right. I wish you safe travels," he said. Without another word, he rose and exited the room.

I raised an eyebrow and watched him go.

I could only pray to the Goddess that he did not undo the progress I'd made.

Glancing around the chamber, I saw that everything was ready. I pulled up my gloves then grabbed my cloak. I was ready to go home.

*A*fter I said farewell to Madelaine, our party headed north. The Moray guard and a dozen of Macbeth's men, men of Inverness who wanted to go home, rode with us.

At Rhona and Tira's urging, I rode in the cart with them. Swift was decidedly unhappy about walking behind the cart. When we stopped to water the horses, Killian came to me.

"My Queen, shall I exercise your horse? He looks like he's taking being tied to the wagon personally."

"I'd consider it a favor," I said.

Killian nodded then untied Swift.

"Do you remember his father and brother?" Rhona whispered to Tira, motioning to Killian as he walked away.

Tira nodded. "I remember his brother. He was a handsome one."

"That he was. And his father was a great clansman, a good leader."

I furrowed my brow, looking from Killian to the maids. "What happened to them?" I asked.

Tira and Rhona turned to me, both looking surprised to find me listening.

"Oh," Rhona said. "His father and brother were with the Mormaer when…when they all perished."

I looked at Killian. He was chatting with Swift, calming the animal. "They were with Gillacoemgain?"

Rhona nodded.

"Who leads their clan now?" I asked.

"Killian's uncle. Killian was the youngest son, too young to rule. He came to the castle to serve. Standish is connected to that somehow," Rhona said.

Tira chuckled. "Standish is related to everyone."

I stared at Killian. It moved my heart to know that he too had lost something that terrible day. But it was also a poignant reminder. Macbeth was the one who had ordered that fire. Macbeth. May the Gods reward me for my patience in dealing with such a man. Given all his treachery, I wondered why his hands weren't covered in blood. But then a realization struck me. Macbeth's hands might not be stained, but his mind was. He had always been unsteady, but it seemed to me, he was teetering very close to being undone. I could only hope he held the pieces of himself intact while I was away.

We rode throughout the day, camping that night. When the sun rose, we took to the trail once more. I was relieved when the ramparts of Cawdor appeared on the horizon. The sound of trumpets lit up the night, heralding our arrival. Finally, I was home. I exhaled deeply. All this time, I'd felt like I was carrying a weight on my shoulders. In Moray, I could let go.

Even before I got to the gate, I spotted a black shadow rushing across the grass to meet us. She barked loudly as she raced toward the wagon.

"Thora!" I called. I set my hand on the wagon driver's arm, motioning for him to stop.

I slipped out of the wagon.

"Come here, bad girl," I called to her.

Thora ran to me, more waddling than running, but her eyes glimmered with excitement. I couldn't help but notice how stiff her legs were and how round she'd become.

"Just look at you," I told her. "My gods, did you eat all the winter stores yourself?"

Thora barked lightly then licked my face. I ruffled her ears then pressed my head against hers. "I'm glad to see you too."

Stretching my back, I walked through the gates, following the others into the yard.

"My lady," Standish called, crossing the lawn to meet me.

I smiled happily. "Standish."

Standish kissed me on both cheeks. "How well you look, Lady Gruoch. Red in your cheeks and all."

"I am very well. And you?"

"We've managed quite well. I dare say, we appreciated the financial support you sent to Cawdor. I could finally afford to get some repairs to the castle done. And we made some improvements in Nairn, as you requested."

"It's about time Moray received some support from the crown."

"Indeed. Now, your old chamber is ready—Morag saw to that —and we've prepared a feast for your homecoming."

I watched as the grooms led the horses to the stables. "Thank you, Standish," I said, patting his arm.

Standish smiled then looked down at Thora. "Finally got up, did you? She's been lying by the fire since you left. I think she's finally feeling her age, my lady."

"Aren't we all?" I said with a laugh that Standish joined.

Motioning to Thora, I left Standish and went in the direction of the stables. The grooms bowed to me as I passed. Thora trotted ahead to Kelpie's stable.

"What, are you sleeping, old man?" I called to Kelpie who didn't seem to notice I had come. Usually, he kicked and whinnied the moment he caught my scent.

Drowsily, Kelpie turned and looked at me. He whinnied softly.

"Oh, my dear, how are you?" I asked, patting his ears.

"Lady Gruoch," a voice called.

I turned to see the groom who had treated Kelpie after the war.

"How is my boy?" I asked.

"Well, my lady. Well, but tired. He sleeps a lot."

"Ah, so everyone is lying around in my absence," I said, patting Thora on the head. But the truth was, both Kelpie and Thora were well beyond their prime. The war, it seemed, had taken a lot out of them. "And his wound?"

"Healed, but he limps on the leg and favors the others instead."

I patted Kelpie on his nose then pressed my forehead against his. Sorrow filled my heart. "My old friend," I whispered then turned to the groom. "Thank you for taking good care of him. I'll be back again soon," I told Kelpie then motioned to Thora. We headed back toward the castle. As I crossed the yard, I was greeted with bows, curtsies, smiles, and wishes of welcome. I exhaled deeply then gazed up at the castle.

"Gillacoemgain, I'm home."

CHAPTER THIRTY

That night, for the first time in months, I truly slept. Something about lying in the bed I had shared with Gillacoemgain made my heart feel safe. I was behind the walls of my own castle and surrounded by my own people. No harm could come to me or my unborn child here. I set my hand on my stomach. The little one inside jiggled, the fluttering feeling making my heart stir with joy.

I sighed contentedly.

"Ah, are you awake?" a familiar voice called.

"Good morning, Morag."

"Afternoon, actually," she said. I heard her chair scrape as she rose. "I have some food here for you. No doubt, you are hungry."

"Famished."

Morag chuckled. "That's the way it is after the morning sicknesses pass. You look about that far along."

I sat up. "Morag!"

"Oh, don't worry. I doubt many other eyes would notice. They probably all thought you were getting round off the rich, southern food. Now, does my Thane know he's going to have a wee babe?"

"He does."

"Good. Otherwise, he was about to get a big surprise," she said then grinned at me.

A moment later, there was a knock on the door. Morag went to answer. I heard low voices, then a moment later, Banquo walked into the room.

"Gruoch," he said, rushing to me.

"Call me if you need me, lady," Morag said then pulled the door closed behind her.

Thora, who was lying by the fire, lifted her head and whined at Banquo, her tail thumping.

"Banquo! What are you doing here?" I asked.

"I didn't want to be apart from you a moment more. Oh, my Cerridwen, look at you," he said, taking my belly into his hands. He kissed my stomach then leaned in and kissed me. "How are you feeling?"

"Very well. She's started moving about."

"Any problems, issues?"

"None."

Banquo exhaled deeply. "May the gods be praised," he said then flopped down onto the bed with me.

I laced my hand in his then lay my head on his chest. "How I've missed you."

"And I you," he said, then kissed my forehead.

I closed my eyes, feeling a deep sense of bliss.

I passed the summer in Moray, continuing to guide the country as best I could, and ruling the north. My work felt good, right. Perhaps this separation between Macbeth and me was for the best. The north was at peace and prospering. The south was quiet. Dispatches came regularly from Macbeth. He kept me abreast on what was happening and the progress on Dunsinane. Madelaine wrote as well. Macbeth was holding steady, though he seemed greatly distracted. Again, I thought about suggesting Macbeth pursue his pilgrimage to Rome, but the timing was not right. Winter would come soon enough. And with it would come my daughter. As much as I hated to admit it, I needed Macbeth.

"Before the weather turns and you get much larger, we should remove to Lochaber," Banquo told me as we sat beside the fire in my chamber late one night. "It is three days' journey. I don't want you to make the trip in the cold."

"When do you want to go?"

"When can you leave?"

"Tomorrow."

Banquo laughed. "I'll make arrangements. Morag should come with us."

"Yes. If she's willing to travel so far. I will work with Standish. He can tell any riders I am traveling to the north."

Banquo slid his chair toward mine and set his hand on my belly. "What will we do after she's born? I'm plagued by the question."

As was I. "I don't know."

"I don't want you to give up being queen. And for Lulach's sake, you cannot. But she's our child. You won't be able to acknowledge her. Will that be too hard for you?"

I bit my lip. My hands shook as I braced myself. "It won't be the first time."

"The first time for what?"

"For...for me to have a child I could not acknowledge."

Banquo sat back, a look of surprise on his face.

"Do you remember when we first came to Moray. They asked me about my twins. I...I lied. I told them my other child had died. She didn't. She is alive and well."

"What? Where is she?"

"With Epona."

"Why?"

"The gods decreed that she would be the next leader of our coven. Epona and Andraste urged me to leave her to the gods. And Madelaine and I...we had our own reasons for not wanting her to join court life. I wanted to save my child from the treachery of this world and give her the life I was denied."

Banquo sat back in his chair. He stroked his chin as he thought.

Out of the corner of my eye, I saw a flicker as Gillacoemgain's shade appeared. He watched Banquo.

"Why didn't you tell me?" Banquo asked.

"No one knew. I planned to tell you, in time. I did not mean to deceive you. Everything was in shambles when I first arrived. Time slipped away, and... Banquo?"

Banquo stilled. He straightened in his seat then turned and glanced around his room, his eyes resting on Gillacoemgain's shade. I looked up at Gillacoemgain who stood with his arms folded across his chest.

The two men stared at one another a moment then Gillacoemgain faded.

Banquo shook his head then turned back to me. "I won't speak against your choices. Your daughter was Gillacoemgain's, and you did what you could to protect her. Her father seems to stand by your decision," he said, smiling softly. "And I have already made the wrong decision in my allegiance to Moray. I won't make that mistake a second time. My Cerridwen...how difficult it must have been for you. Such a painful choice."

"It was."

"With Gillacoemgain dead, you had no one."

"That's right. He was dead, and I was on my way to marry his killer. I did not want my daughter to suffer my choices. Lulach, I knew, could endure. But my daughter..."

Banquo nodded. "I am sorry you have carried this secret burden. I love you, Cerridwen. Nothing will ever change that."

I reached out and stroked his cheek with my gloved hand.

"What is your daughter's name?" Banquo asked.

"Crearwy, after her aunt, Gillacoemgain's sister."

Banquo smiled. "One day, we will go together and see her."

"She's a very smart girl, very strong. She has the stuff of MacAlpin in her." In truth, Crearwy showed herself to be made of stronger fiber—the kind of steel needed to rule—than Lulach. While my son was destined for the throne, he always had an Otherworldly sense about him. Crearwy was a far different matter.

"We will find a way for our child. When Merna died, I didn't know what I was going to do. But because of you, I found a path forward."

"Do you think Balor would bring the boys to Lochaber? I ache for Lulach."

Banquo nodded. "I will ask. Shall we make our plans to depart?" Banquo asked.

"On one condition."

"Which is?"

"You get to ask Morag."

He laughed. "Fine."

I looked at Thora who lay sleeping. As for me, I had something else to do.

CHAPTER THIRTY-ONE

I waited patiently for Thora at the top of the steps leading to the second floor of the unused part of the castle. She dawdled along slowly, finally reaching the top step. She was panting hard. Lighting a taper, we headed down the hall to the door that led to Crearwy's chamber…and beyond. Today, I needed to find the beyond.

I knelt and pet Thora's head.

"I think you know where we are going," I told her.

She licked my hand and pawed at me.

I gazed into her brown eyes. "How little you were when I found you on that hill. No bigger than a tiny babe. But your feet were half the size of my hands. Did the fey really send you to me as the priest complained?"

Thora's eyes sparkled, and she wagged her tail.

"Willful, magical dog. Let's see what we can do to draw things out a bit more for you," I said then set my hand on the latch. I closed my eyes. Gathering magic around me, I opened the door.

Waving for Thora to follow, we entered to find ourselves standing on the cauldron terrace at Ynes Verleath.

Nimue, who had been reading, looked up. Andraste's eyes, however, were on her cauldron.

"Cerridwen," Nimue said, standing.

"Sister, I've come to ask a favor."

Nimue looked at Andraste who had not looked away from the cauldron.

"Of course," Nimue said, frowning at Andraste's lack of engagement. "What is it?"

"It's Thora," I said, motioning to my dog. "The war wearied her. I know her time is coming. She is moving so slowly. I hoped maybe…"

Nimue knelt and clapped her hands, calling Thora to her. "What do you think, Graymalkin? Will you stay with me? Very soon, your mistress will join us. Stay with Andraste and me, and it will seem as if no time has passed at all."

Thora wagged her tail then went to Nimue.

I stared at Nimue. "What do you mean, I will join you soon enough?"

At that, Andraste finally looked up. "We will look after her. Now go. Stay no more for the sake of Aelith," she said, eyeing my growing belly, then she waved her hand in front of her.

I pitched sideways as I suddenly found myself standing in Crearwy's chamber once more.

"Andraste, you old crone. You didn't even let me say good-bye," I complained loudly to Andraste who, I knew, could still hear me.

My hands drifted to my stomach. "Aelith," I whispered. "A lovely name, isn't it, my rose?"

I turned to go but spotted the shade of Gillacoemgain's sister standing by her bed.

How much she and my Crearwy looked alike. It moved my heart to no end to know, for certain, it was no mere coincidence. I was angry with Andraste for her deception, angry beyond measure. But the truth was far sweeter.

Crearwy motioned for me to come close to her. With ghostly hands, she touched the small wooden box at her bedside.

Following her gesture, I opened the box. Therein lay small trinkets, rings, and necklaces, ladies' things.

Crearwy touched a small silver pin lying in the box. On it was the same flower that trimmed Gillacoemgain's dagger, broach, and even his seal. She motioned for me to take it.

I picked it up and looked it over.

Crearwy moved to touch my hands, to press the item toward me, but she hesitated. Even her spirit would not touch my cursed fingers.

"I will give it to Crearwy," I told her.

She nodded then looked back in her box once more. This time, she touched a small ring. It was a dainty silver thing with a piece of amber at its center.

I lifted the ring from the box.

Crearwy smiled once more, this time setting her ghostly hands on my stomach. She inclined her head, then gave me the softest of smiles. Meeting my eyes once more, she slowly disappeared.

I closed my eyes, feeling hot tears burning behind my lids. Poor girl. Poor spirit. Poor lost sister. How everything would have been different if evil had not lodged itself in the hearts of foul men. Crearwy was the sister I never had, and in her countenance, I saw that same soft spirit that had lived in Gillacoemgain. I felt like I had missed my entire life, like a version of myself existed in a different reality where they both had endured, me along with them.

But it was not so.

And because it was not so, I was carrying the child of the man I loved.

What a bittersweet irony.

. . .

"*M*y lady, I hate to see you leave," Standish said as he helped me into the wagon. He had fluttered about me all morning as we got ready to depart for Lochaber.

"I hope to be back in the spring. We shall see what the season holds for us all."

Standish nodded. "Stay safe, Lady Gruoch. And give the young mormaer my greetings. We are looking forward to seeing him again."

I smiled. "Thank you, Standish."

I nodded to Banquo who was mounted on his own stead. He had come to Moray with a contingent of his own loyal soldiers. We were more than protected, but Killian and a small group of Moray men had insisted on coming along to Lochaber. I decided not to dissuade them. Remembering Rhona and Tira's words, I pitied Killian. He had lost everything in the war trying to protect Moray and Gillacoemgain—and he was still doing that job. How could I stop him?

*T*he journey took three days, but the ride was not hard. The countryside, dotted with rivers and lochs, was beautiful. The summer sun shone down on us. I missed being in the forest. I missed the smells of pine, loam, and flowers. I knew my daughter was angry with me for settling her in a life of service, but it was a peaceful life. In many ways, I envied Crearwy as much as I knew she envied me. I only hoped that in the future, she would come to understand my reasons. Given she had not had to endure the same struggles as Madelaine and me, such a realization might not come easy for her. But my daughter was intelligent. Even if she didn't feel it, perhaps knowing would be enough. I hoped so.

Soon, the River Lochy came into view.

"Tor Castle sits on a hill above the river. Look there," Banquo said, pointing in the distance.

Following his gesture, I spotted a castle tower looming high above the trees not far from the water.

I smiled at Banquo. While he had always been a part of my life, I had not been privy to this part of his world. I remembered him telling me that his father had been a cruel man. When I was married to Gillacoemgain, his father had passed, his mother died while I had been at Ynes Verleath. Banquo had lived the life of a druid, a wanderer. As chief of Macbeth's generals and loyal to Thorfinn, he'd spent most of his time in the field and little time in his ancestral halls. Now, however, he had a reason to go home.

The wagon slipped through the castle gate. The tall castle had high walls, the inner yard safely hidden behind the stone. Banquo dismounted and began directing his servants. Morag, who'd been riding with me, slowly slipped out of the wagon.

"Come along, Lady Gruoch. Let's see what the thane has prepared for you and how much I have to fix to make it right."

Banquo grinned. "Morag, I did my best. I swear. But I will leave Gruoch in your capable hands while I see the men settled in and attend to affairs."

I gave Banquo's hand a squeeze. Turning, I caught Killian's eye. I inclined my head toward the castle, letting him know I was going inside.

He nodded to me.

I followed Morag into the castle. I was surprised to find that the ceiling was very high. Stairs twisted up the wall to the second-floor balcony that overlooked the massive, open great room. There was an enormous hearth at one end of the room. Light shone in through the embrasures on the walls. A huge chandelier made of deer horn hung over the central open space.

"Kitchens and meeting rooms on the first floor," Morag said, gesturing to the hallways leading from the great hall. "On the second floor, some private rooms," she added, pointing to the doors that looked over the balcony. "The hallway leads to chambers and the stairs to the third floor. It's really a small place, once you get used to it."

"Morag?" a voice called.

Morag and I turned to find an elderly gentleman crossing the room toward us. He was a slight thing who looked like he could be blown over in a sharp breeze. He had wispy white hair on his head. He was dressed in the tartan of Lochaber.

"Lewis," Morag said warmly. Surprisingly, very warmly.

"What a welcome return this is. And is this Her Majesty?"

"Yes, this is Lady Gruoch."

"So very, very pleased to meet you," the man said, bowing to me. I reached out to stop him, afraid he might not be able to righten himself if he bowed too low.

"Lewis, where has the thane asked for Lady Gruoch to be lodged?"

The man shifted. "He's taken the chambers in the southern end of the castle. He...his lodgings—and hers—are there. Though I've also readied an adjoining room," the man said, flicking an eye at me.

"Don't worry, Lady Gruoch," Morag said, taking my arm. "You are in Lochaber. Not a soul in this castle will speak a word about anything they see here."

"No, Your Majesty, we certainly will not," Lewis agreed.

"We are all loyal to this house. Lewis has been here longer than me. But don't let our old bones worry you. There are plenty of young, strapping boys and girls about to get things done. And, of course, your Moray men. She has her own guard," Morag told Lewis.

"Oh! Very good. I will make arrangements for their comfort."

"Thank you," I told the man.

"Come along, my lady," Morag said, leading me upstairs.

"Now, there is one thing you must know about Tor Castle."

"What is that?"

"Despite all our love and loyalty, we have the worst cooks in the realm."

"All things considered, that is terrible news," I said, my hand resting on my stomach. I laughed.

Morag laughed. "Don't worry, Lady Gruoch. Don't worry. I'll look after you as best I can. And I'll send for my niece to help me."

"You have a niece?"

She nodded. "Smart girl. She always wanted to come to the castle. She'll help me look after you since Rhona and Tira were too lazy to come this far."

"I think they missed their families."

"They are lady's maids, and their lady is with child. Well, no matter. Come along. I'll have you settled in no time."

Morag led me upstairs to the second floor. We followed a narrow hallway which led to yet another set of steps to the third floor.

"This is the family wing. The southern end has the best view of the river," Morag told me.

She led me to a chamber at the end of the hall. She pushed open a wide door to reveal a beautifully bedecked room.

"Well, look at that," she said, her hands on her hips. "It's all new."

"All new?"

"The bed, the linens, the rugs, the tapestries. This was the old thane's chamber. Banquo closed it. But look at this place, like life has been breathed in once more," she said then chuckled. "My thane is acting like a newly married man."

Stepping inside, I turned around to look at the room. Red and blue silk drapes covered the bed. The room was made of fine furnishings, the tapestries on the walls depicting forest and farm scenes.

"Lovely," I said, turning about.

"Why don't you take a little rest, my lady? I doubt they expected you to be such a worker. I'll see to it that you have a conference chamber ready," Morag said then left me alone.

I went to the window. The room had a good view of the river. I could see the mountains and fields all around. Lochaber was beautiful. Wind blew in the open casement, carrying with it a warm summer breeze. I closed my eyes and let the wind caress my cheek.

"Well, my little one, what do you think of this place?" I whispered, setting my hand on my stomach.

The baby moved and kicked.

I laughed. "I agree."

I left the chamber and explored the other rooms in the hallway. Beside our bedchamber, another room had been prepared. There were other chambers all along the hall, many of them recently refreshed. At the other end of the hallway, however, I found a second large bedchamber. This one looked out on the forest. The place had not been used of late, but I noticed there were ladies' things—a spinning wheel, dresses, and a tray with a comb and mirror sitting at the bedside. I looked at the small ladies' items, spotting a familiar comb amongst them. The adornment was made of ivory, a merwoman carved on it. It was Merna's. This must have been the room she and Banquo had once shared.

I glanced around the room.

I didn't feel Merna's presence there, but all the same, I felt like I was intruding. I exited the space. Retracing my steps, I found the stairs leading to the second floor. I worked my way down the hall, looking here and there, familiarizing myself with the castle. Morag was right. It was a small citadel, but it was warm and cheerful.

I had just arrived on the balcony overlooking the second floor when Banquo entered.

In that single moment, my breath caught in my throat. If we had gotten married from the start, would I have been lady here? How many times would I have come to this balcony to welcome my husband? Lochaber, rather than Moray, would have become my home. It was a beautiful country with tall mountains, dense forests, and lochs.

I smiled at Banquo.

He returned the gesture. His expression told me he shared my thoughts.

Maybe everything had been delayed.

Maybe a life with Banquo had seemed impossible.

But here I was.

At last.

At last.

Banquo.

CHAPTER THIRTY-TWO

Summer passed peacefully, and soon, autumn came to Lochaber. The forest vista outside Tor Castle changed to ruby red, burnt orange, and vibrant yellow. The landscape was lovely, and I felt very much at home there. While Lochaber proved quiet, my work continued to be challenging. I'd finally received correspondence from the Irish king. He was willing to negotiate a release of Donaldbane, provided I came to talk in person. While I knew there were risks involved, I agreed. Being Emir's daughter, I wanted to see my mother's lands and maybe even meet my own flesh and blood. I promised the Irish king I would come in the spring.

I wasn't surprised to see Banquo was a caring and thoughtful thane. Much like Gillacoemgain, he rode out to ensure his people's harvests were coming along well. Many of the local families fished the lochs and rivers, Banquo often joining them for a day trip onto the water. Since arriving, I had eaten more fish than I had my entire life—most of which was terribly seasoned and often burnt, but Aelith never complained. In fact, I'd grown very round and fat-cheeked. When I was pregnant with Lulach and

Crearwy, I often felt ill and tired. Aelith was proving to be considerably kinder to her mother.

I was resting in our chamber when Banquo returned home early one evening. He was tapping a scroll in his hand, a pensive look on his face.

"What is it?" I asked, setting down the letter I was writing.

"From Macbeth. He's making some plans and would like me to come to Dunsinane in the spring."

"What kind of plans?"

Banquo shook his head. "I don't know, but he says he could use the help of his most trusted general."

"I don't like the sound of that. He has said nothing to me."

Banquo nodded. "That's what worried me as well."

We were not yet sure if Macbeth had learned that I was in Lochaber. Thus far, his letters to me had been delivered to Cawdor —Standish sending them along to me on a weekly basis. It was only a matter of time before someone said something. Yet Madelaine assured me all seemed well. Macbeth stayed busy moving the court to Dunsinane, which was nearly ready. And she applauded Macbeth's tact in dealing with the southern lords. Part of me wondered if Macbeth's invitation to Banquo was nothing more than bait.

"I do have other news, good news," Banquo said with a smile. "Our sons are coming home."

"You've had word from Balor?"

Banquo nodded. "He sent a casting."

"Thank the gods."

"I knew you would be happy. And, my Cerridwen, there is a fresh delivery of honey in the kitchens. Morag promised me she'd make something special for you and my little one," he said then got down on his knees before me. Wrapping his hands around my waist, Banquo pressed his cheek against my stomach. "How are you, my wee babe?"

"Rolling and kicking," I replied.

Banquo laughed then kissed my stomach. "We cannot wait to meet you. Will you look like your mother or me?"

"Or both."

Banquo gazed up me, a look of love on his face. But I also saw the lines around his mouth tremble.

"What is it?" I asked.

"It's just…it should have always been like this."

"Yes. You're right. But in spite of it all, we have won this moment," I said, taking his hand in mine.

Banquo nodded then embraced me again. "How true. How very true. Don't tell her I said so, but your mother is the wisest woman I've ever known," Banquo whispered to my stomach.

"Is that so? There are *none* wiser?" I asked playfully.

"Well, there is Sid. She's wise in her own way."

I chuckled. "That makes me wonder what she's said to you when I wasn't around."

Banquo laughed. "You wouldn't believe your ears."

"I can only imagine."

a month later, a horn sounded as riders approached the castle. I had been sitting in the great hall by the fire, trying to warm my perpetually cold feet when I heard the noise. I set down the letter I was reading.

All at once, I was overcome with thoughts of Lulach.

"Lulach," I whispered then rose. Grabbing a fur, I rushed outside.

Balor, Calean, Beric, and raven-tattooed Diarmad arrived, Fleance and Lulach along with them. My heart skipped a beat when I set eyes on my child, a deep feeling of relief washing over me. I looked then to Fleance whose eyes were fixed on me. He smiled.

Swift hoofbeats raced toward the castle. Banquo rode into the yard behind them.

Tears welled in my eyes, a deep sense of relief washing over me.

Killian appeared from within the castle. He eyed the party.

"Is that the mormaer?" he asked, his voice full of surprise. He stared at Lulach who was smiling at me.

"Yes." I grinned when I realized that two dogs also traveled with the party, a white dog with red ears, and a massive black brute who looked just like his dam.

"Who are those men?" Killian asked.

"Druids," I replied.

Killian shook his head. "Lady Gruoch and her secrets."

I winked at him then went to Balor.

"Fair greetings, Father," I called. I took the reins of Balor's horse.

Smiling, Balor dismounted. He bowed to me. "Your Majesty."

I took his hands, kissing them both. "You are welcome in Lochaber."

"We are pleased to find you here, my lady," he said then eyed me over. Smiling, he set his hands on my stomach. "A girl."

I nodded.

"May the Goddess bless her and keep her from harm," he said then turned to Banquo, leaving me to wonder about the druid's words. Surely, he meant nothing ominous by them. A blessing was a blessing. Leaving a mother's worries behind, I inclined my head to my druid brothers who returned the gesture then made my way to Lulach and Fleance.

"Mother," Lulach called, passing off the reins of his horse to a groom.

Only a year had passed, but I could already see that Lulach had changed. He was at least a hand taller, and his baby-soft features had started to lose their roundness, his chin taking on the

217

same square shape of Gillacoemgain's features. How much like Gillacoemgain he looked.

"Son," I said, pulling him into an embrace.

"Mother, how big you are."

"Very soon, you will have a sister."

"*Another* sister," Lulach corrected. I caught an edge on his voice that surprised me.

"Yes, *another* sister."

Lulach smiled at me. "We've just come from visiting Epona. They all send their greetings, and Crearwy sends her love."

Ah. So, they had been together again. I was dying to know what conversations had transpired between Lulach and Crearwy, but Lulach's correction told me he and his sister had bonded, for better or worse. In the end, what more could I ask for?

"Corbie," Fleance called, coming to greet me. Thor, his dog, followed along behind him.

Fleance, a few years older than Lulach, had taken a leap into manhood in the year that had passed. He was taller, his voice deeper. He looked much like his father.

I embraced him.

"How do you like Tor Castle?" Fleance asked.

"You have a fine home," I said.

Fleance eyed my belly. "Corbie?"

"You and Lulach will soon share a sister," I said, measuring my words carefully.

Fleance looked at Lulach, a glimmer of excitement in his eyes. "We will truly be brothers then."

I touched Fleance's cheek then smoothed his hair. "Come, let's go inside."

"We'll see to the horses," Mackintosh, Banquo's sentinel, told me.

I motioned to Killian, encouraging him to come along.

Banquo draped his arm over Fleance's shoulder. "Son," he

said, smiling at his boy. "And the Mormaer of Moray. It is good to see you again, Lulach," Banquo told him.

"And you, Thane," he said, an awkward smile on his lips.

Lulach slipped his hand into mine. He lifted our joined hands and looked at the gloves, studying them carefully.

"Are your hands cold, Mother?"

"No," I replied.

Lulach raised an eyebrow but said nothing more.

Banquo and Fleance joined Balor and led the druids into the great hall.

"Lulach," I said, pausing to wait for Killian. "Lulach, I want you to meet Sir Killian. He is a loyal man of Moray and my guard."

"Sir," Lulach said, inclining his head to Killian.

"My Mormaer, I am pleased to see you again."

Lulach smiled.

"Killian's father and brother served Gillacoemgain—and they were lost alongside your father at the very end," I told Lulach.

Killian looked at me, an expression of surprise on his face.

Lulach turned to Killian. "Is that so?"

"Yes, my lord," Killian said.

Lulach set his hand on Killian's arm. "Then tonight, we shall toast them together."

I swallowed hard, feeling proud of my son. He nodded to Killian then went to join the druids.

"Lady Gruoch," Killian whispered.

When I met his gaze, I saw his eyes were wet with unshed tears. I patted his arm gently then went to join the others.

The servants worked quickly, passing out mulled wines and honey mead to our guests. I caught the sweet scents of freshly baked bread and roasting meat. My stomach growled hungrily. I sat beside Lulach, listening as the druids spoke about their travels. Soon after, the servants called us to feast. I was relieved. Aelith had been rolling and kicking since I'd caught the first whiff of food. I took my seat at the head of the table, Banquo at one side, Balor on the other. It seemed strange to take precedence over Banquo in his own castle. In Lochaber, it was easy to forget I was Queen of Scotland.

As we ate, Banquo fell into conversation with Fleance and the other druids. My attention turned to Balor.

"I understand you've come from Epona," I told him. "How is she?"

Balor shook his head. "It wounds my heart to see her thus." I was sure it did. Balor and Epona had always been very close.

"When I saw her last, I asked her what I could do to help *our* people. She advised me to speak with you," I told Balor.

"We could use your aid, Queen Gruoch. Lands granted for our use, protection, coin, and acknowledgment. The south has shifted toward the White Christ. The southernmost coven is over. The last of the priestesses have gone."

"How terrible."

Balor nodded.

"I will do anything in my power to help you. It would be useful if I knew where my holy brothers and sisters resided, the locations of the other covens and holy sites."

Balor considered the matter. "We have always thought it unwise to set such information down."

"Do you read Ogham, Father?"

"Of course."

"Are many others learned in the art?"

He laughed. "As far as I know, only Epona…"

"And me."

Balor chuckled. "Very good, Your Majesty. Very good. Let's meet and discuss further before we depart."

"And Crearwy," Lulach piped up.

"Sorry, love?"

"Crearwy can also read the language you speak of."

Banquo cast a wary eye toward Lulach.

"Very good," I said, seeking to curb Lulach's tongue. It was one thing for him to be proud of his sister, but quite another to speak her name in open spaces.

Fleance, who must have had a better sense of the matter then Lulach, elbowed his old friend.

Lulach gave Fleance an annoyed look but said nothing more.

We spent a pleasant evening feasting and talking of old things. Banquo's staff moved in and out of the room as if the druid visitors were nothing of particular interest, but I watched Killian out of the corner of my eye. How closely he listened to their words and eyed the men over. It had been a long time since the druids had walked freely amongst our people. Perhaps it was time for that to change.

*L*ate in the night, after Balor and the others had gone to bed, I sought out Lulach. Though they were both older, Lulach and Fleance had asked for a room together. It was late in the night when I found them there—both still awake—talking like two old women.

"My boys," I said, entering the room quietly. I closed the door behind me.

Both dogs, Thor and Angus, looked up at me. Thor lay his head back down, deciding it was too much trouble to get up from the comfortable spot on the end of Fleance's bed to come see me. Angus, who'd been resting by the fire, came to me and licked my hand. I scratched his red ears then sat down on the corner of Lulach's bed.

"You should be asleep, Corbie," Fleance told me. "A woman should rest when she's coming to the end of her time."

"A month and a bit to go," I said, setting my hand on my belly. "Depending on how stubborn your sister is."

"How odd, isn't it?" Fleance asked Lulach. "We shall share a sister. What have you and father decided to name her?"

"Aelith."

"And are you sure it's a girl?" he asked.

I nodded. "As sure as one can be."

"It's a girl," Lulach said absently, his eyes fixed on the fire.

"Lulach," I said, touching his leg. "I love you well, my son, but you must hold your tongue when it comes to Crearwy. I have paid a heavy price to keep your sister's identity secret. If others were to learn you had a sister—"

"But who would ever guess?" Lulach asked.

"She is named after your father's sister. One doesn't need the sight to make connections. Among the holy brothers, it is one thing to speak her name. But never among servants or in common spaces."

"I told you," Fleance chided Lulach. "How like you she is, Corbie."

"You think so?" I asked.

Fleance smiled, and for a moment, I saw a strange wisp of a soft expression cross his face. "Yes. Though a bit more waspish."

"She is angry," Lulach said.

"Was she...unkind to you, Lulach?" I asked.

"No. Not to me."

"I see," I said, guessing that Crearwy had spoken harshly of me to her brother. "She doesn't understand. I can't blame her. One day, she will realize and forgive."

"May the gods let it be so," Lulach said, his voice resonating with a deep otherworldliness.

"Have you shown her?" Fleance asked Lulach.

Confused, I scrunched up my brow. "Shown me what?"

Lulach pushed his sleeve up to reveal a small tattoo on his

wrist. Inked thereon was a dog surrounded by swirling Pictish designs.

I took his hand into mine and studied the tattoo. "It's beautiful, but why did they give you such a mark?"

"I walked…beyond," he said. "Angus guided me."

I stared at my son. Before me sat the future King of Scotland. And before he had even reached full manhood, the gods had shown fit to take him to the Otherworld.

"And what did you see there?"

Lulach smiled at me. "You know I cannot say more."

"Then know this, my son, that the Otherworld is full of those who love us, but also many who would trick and harm us."

"Not where I went. Not who I saw," Lulach said.

"And who did you see?"

"The one who brought me my dog. Eochaid."

At that, I laughed out loud. "Fey things. Love them well, but always be cautious of fey things," I said then reached out to scratch Angus' ear. The dog tipped his head at me, giving me the impression he understood my words.

"Like these?" Lulach asked, reaching out to touch my gloved hand.

"Why are you wearing those gloves, Corbie?" Fleance asked.

"The better question is, who gave them to you?" Lulach said.

"Fey things," I said. "You know I cannot say more."

Lulach chuckled.

"But why are you wearing them?" Fleance asked again.

"My hands are…bespelled. The gloves contain the curse."

Both boys stared at me, their eyes wide.

"I'm not in any danger, I swear," I told them.

Frowning, Lulach looked back at the fire.

"As long as you're not hurt," Fleance said.

"I'm not hurt," I reassured him.

"But you should get some rest," he told me.

"Yes, you're right. Hopefully Balor lets you stay for a time."

"A fortnight," Lulach told me.

"Do you wish to continue on with him?" I asked Lulach. I wasn't sure what Lulach would make of the holy life, but I could see that it suited him as it had suited me.

"Yes. I hope you will permit me."

I nodded. "Of course. My father, Boite, once studied amongst the holy brothers."

At that, Lulach smiled. "Thank you, Mother."

"And you, Fleance? Will you stay in Lochaber?"

Fleance laughed. "Only if father makes me."

"That is unlikely."

Grinning, Fleance looked at Lulach. "Then we're for the road once more."

Lulach returned his smile.

Shaking my head, I rose. "Goodnight, my dears," I said then left, my heart brimming with joy.

CHAPTER THIRTY-THREE

*R*elishing every moment I had with Lulach and Fleance, I was very sorry when it was time for them to depart.

"We need to reach a holy site in the north before the weather becomes too harsh. We will winter in Caithness then return this way in the spring," Balor told me. "But if you need our prince, Banquo can always send word."

"Thank you, Father," I said, watching Lulach pack up his horse. Already the wind had become cold, and I could smell snow in the air. The autumn leaves had lost their luster and were starting to turn brown. "And thank you for trusting me," I said, referring to the conversation Balor and I'd had regarding the other covens in Scotland. With the southern-most coven disbanding, there were now only eight covens in the realm. Balor and I had pored over a map, Balor showing me the location of each of the other covens. As it turned out, the covens all sat upon ley lines, magic lines of energy, that crisscrossed our realm. I had made notes in Ogham, noting the location of each holy site. As I had suspected, deep within Birnam Wood was a sacred place.

"I know you will do what you can," Balor said. "After all, the

Great Mother and Father put you on the throne. How can you not?"

"I will do my best. Safe travels to you."

Balor inclined his head to me.

I left him and went to Lulach. Part of me wanted to bother him with a million questions and concerns—Did he pack enough warm clothes? Did he have enough supplies? Had he remembered all his gear?—but I held my tongue. Lulach was much changed. He was approaching manhood. He had always been a thoughtful child, but now his contemplation and reserve had more depth. In a way, he was becoming more like his father—thank the Goddess.

"Do you remember when we went to Thurso?" I asked as I tightened the ties on his saddlebag.

"Just a little. I remember Thorfinn and the seals. And…"

"And?"

"And…selkies."

I reached out and touched the birthmark on his forehead, a blessing from the faerie realm. "You have always been able to see the Otherworld, even when you were a boy."

At that, Lulach smiled. I could see he was pleased with himself, but he didn't want to bring attention to his pride.

"I'm sure I don't need to caution you to be careful," I told him, anxious to see him depart.

"Mother," he said with a smile. He turned and embraced me. "I wish you well. I'll be back in the spring to see my sister."

"We will see you then."

Lulach mounted his horse and reined in beside Fleance.

I went to Fleance and took his hand. "Do you have everything you need?"

He nodded. "Father provisioned Lulach and me. Balor and the others watch over us well."

"And what about Thor? How is he?"

Fleance laughed. "He doesn't realize he's grown, bouncing around like a big puppy. But he's a good hunting dog. His ears are sharp. He hears every sound in the forest."

"Just like Thora," I said, feeling sad for a moment. In Ynes Verleath, it would have seemed like very little time had passed, but I missed my dog.

"I'll be thinking of you. I hope all goes well with our sister."

"I'm sure it will," I said, setting my hand on my stomach.

"We'll be back in the spring. I can't wait to see you then. This visit was too short."

"Agreed. But for now, I wish you safe travels," I said, squeezing his hand.

Fleance's eyes grew watery, but he gave me a nod then let me go.

Banquo joined me, and we walked with the party to the gate of Tor Castle.

"Farewell, brothers," Banquo called to the druids.

I inclined my head to Beric, Diarmad, and Calean who rode out ahead of the party. Fleance and Lulach, their dogs following behind them, trotted out behind the druids. While Angus ran on, Thor stopped by to give my hand a lick before he raced after Fleance.

When Balor passed, both Banquo and I bowed.

Balor returned the gesture.

His arm around me, Banquo and I watched as the druids turned their horses from the road and into the forest, blending in with the trees. A moment later, they were gone.

I sighed heavily.

"They'll be back soon," Banquo reassured me.

"I know. It's just…they're so changed."

He nodded. "It's for the best. You've raised good, strong boys, my Cerridwen. Now Balor will shape them into men."

"Lulach's spirit is inclined toward the holy life. He already has his first tattoo."

Banquo nodded. "He showed me."

"He may struggle to rule this nation."

Banquo considered my words. "A mother's worry is never misplaced, but Lulach's thoughtful nature will make him a good ruler."

"He is very like his father."

Banquo stroked my hair gently. "And his mother. He will be a force to be reckoned with."

"I hope."

"Speaking of forces to be reckoned with," Banquo said, touching my belly. "When will this one arrive with all her sound and fury?"

"Very soon, from the feel of it. Every time I go up the stairs, I feel like she wants to jump out."

Banquo smiled. "I do not wish labor pains on you any sooner than needed, but I can't wait."

"Neither can I," I said.

Banquo smiled down at me then and planted a soft kiss on my lips.

Turning, we headed back into the castle. Just off the castle yard near the stables, I noticed Killian watching. He was smoking a pipe, the smoke twisting up in the air around him. The great affection between Banquo and me was no secret in Lochaber, but when I felt Killian's eyes on me, it made me remember I was a married woman. A twang of shame washed over me.

I pushed it away.

No. It wasn't like that. I had married Banquo first, in the eyes of the gods, and Macbeth had abandoned me. Besides, Killian would never judge me. My own guilt was tripping me up.

But why?

Why would I ever feel guilty over betraying Macbeth?

Pushing my thoughts away, I headed back inside.

CHAPTER THIRTY-FOUR

*A*s the weeks passed, autumn faded into winter. The first of the winter winds howled through the valley and snow fell. The River Lochy was trimmed with ice and snow. Life at Lochaber slowed. And so did I.

Every muscle in my body ached.

It pained me to move.

Somehow, I thought carrying one child would be more comfortable, but the pain in my lower back was excruciating. The terrible ache went on for days. Given how achy I was, it came as no surprise when I rose one morning to find my bedclothes were wet. I had barely slept the whole night. Cramps had wracked me. Crearwy and Lulach had been so reluctant to come into the world. Aelith, it seemed, was ready to go.

"Oh," I said lightly, touching the gown.

Thank the Goddess, there was no blood.

"What is it?" Banquo asked groggily.

"I think...I think I may have this baby today. Can you go fetch Morag?"

Banquo jumped from the bed, nearly tripping on the furs, and rushed out of the room.

I chuckled then winced as another pain wracked me. My labor had started in my sleep.

"Little sneak," I said, patting my stomach.

I breathed through the pain then poured myself some water.

"My lady," Morag said with a smile when she entered the room. "I hear you have news."

I nodded. "We'd best have a look."

"Come, Banquo, collect your clothes and get out," Morag told him. "We will be here awhile."

"Gruoch, I won't be far away," Banquo reassured me.

I moved to smile at him but cringed as another pain wracked me. That was fast.

"Morag, the pains are coming quickly."

Morag clicked her tongue at Banquo, hurrying him along. His hands full of boots and clothes, Banquo left.

Morag's niece, Greer, a pretty red-haired girl with a face full of freckles, closed the door behind Banquo.

I lay back down on the bed. Morag washed her hands then had a look.

"Well, Gruoch, we'll be at this very soon."

"What do you mean?"

Morag laughed. "It's almost time to push."

I wanted to laugh, but the pain took me once more. I lay back and closed my eyes.

Goddess, Mother, watch over us.

*I*t was not long after that the hard labor began. As Morag said, the time had nearly come. Giving birth to Lulach and Crearwy had been the hardest thing I had ever done. Aelith, on the other hand, seemed to be in a great hurry. I grunted and strained with the effort, but before lunch, our daughter arrived screaming.

Her squall echoed throughout the castle.

From the great hall below, I heard cheers.

Exhausted, I slumped back in bed while Greer and Morag tended to the baby and me.

"She looks good," Morag reassured me. "Everything looks perfect."

I closed my eyes, tears slipping down my cheeks.

After a few minutes, Morag came to me. "Here you are, my lady. A healthy baby girl."

Inhaling deeply, I opened my eyes and looked at the child. She had a mop of dark hair. Blinking like she was still trying to make out where she was, she looked at me.

"Hello, Aelith," I whispered.

Morag smiled at us then motioned to Greer. "Let the thane in."

When Greer opened the door, Banquo rushed past her to my side.

"Oh, my Cerridwen," he whispered, forgetting himself at the moment. He sat down behind me and wrapped his arm around me, gently holding on to Aelith and me with his other hand. "What a wondrous sight to behold."

"Say hello to your father," I whispered to the baby.

Aelith arched her eyebrows and puckered her lips.

We both laughed.

Beyond all hope, beyond all possibility, there we were: mother, father, and child.

"May the gods be praised," I whispered.

Banquo leaned forward and kissed our daughter. "May the gods be praised."

*T*he winter winds blew, snow fell, and Aelith filled our hearts. There was no describing the deep joy our daughter brought to Banquo and me. I recovered quickly, and

Aelith was in good health. For once, it seemed like the gods had blessed us.

The whole winter passed, Aelith growing before our very eyes. In March, the chill began to recede, and the winds calmed. The sun woke the land, and as it did, news began to flow north once more.

I was sitting by the fire with Aelith when Banquo came in holding a scroll.

"What's that?" I asked.

"From the king."

I frowned. Part of me didn't want to know what it said. Macbeth seemed so far away. It was like he had nothing to do with me.

Banquo warmed himself by the fire as he read. His countenance growing increasingly dark as his eyes scanned the page.

I handed Aelith a rattle, propping her so she could sit. She immediately stuck the toy into her mouth and started biting. I smiled at her. Her little teeth had begun coming in. She loved to bite to relieve the itch in her gums. Reluctantly, I went to Banquo.

"What is it?" I asked.

"You aren't going to like it."

"No doubt. But tell me all the same."

"Macbeth has talked Thorfinn into joining Echmarcach on a raid into Ireland to retrieve Donaldbane," he said then shook his head. "They are, no doubt, underway already."

"What?"

Banquo nodded stoically.

"But I told Macbeth I would go with a delegation this spring," I said.

"So you did."

"What does he want from you?"

"From me," Banquo said then scratched his chin. "He wants me to ride south to Dunsinane to help him prepare the army."

A chill washed over me. "What for?"

"For war."

I swallowed hard then took the parchment from Banquo. As I expected, the handwriting thereon was a barely legible mess. Macbeth had fallen to the darkness once again, and unless I acted very soon, we would all fall with him.

Turning, I looked back at my daughter. Her dark hair had softened to brown, much like Banquo's, but her eyes were a lovely mix of deep blue and brown. She didn't take after me as much as Crearwy and Lulach did, but she was clearly my daughter—mine and Banquo's. You could see her parents in her face.

Grinning, she pulled the toy out of her mouth and showed it to me. "Dah," she babbled with a grin.

I smiled at her. "Yes, I see it."

She giggled then began chewing once more.

"What are we going to do?" I asked Banquo.

"As for me, I will tell him I am unwell and cannot leave Lochaber. And I won't. Not for him. Never again."

"You'll resign your post as his general?"

"Yes. I won't leave Aelith. I have made too many mistakes over the years. I have sacrificed many things for Macbeth. At last, I have a chance to do something right. I will stay here with my daughter."

I felt ill. Banquo was right. His choice was best. But it was his choice. As for me, I felt the tug of fate. I was Queen of Scotland. Lulach was Macbeth's heir. I couldn't just let it all go, could I?

Aelith jabbered, picking up then setting back down the toys I had laid on the fur around her, biting each one in turn. Again, I was asked to leave a child behind to follow a destiny I didn't want.

"You won't have to go right away," Banquo whispered.

I nodded. I had known all along that I would not be able to stay in Lochaber forever, but knowing a thing and facing a thing were very different. What I hadn't expected was Banquo's decision. But now that it was out, I was glad. I wasn't leaving Aelith alone; I was leaving her with her father. That, at least, would give me some comfort. Once things were settled, I could return to Lochaber.

Banquo wrapped his arms around me and pulled me against his chest.

"I love you," he whispered in my ear.

"I love you too," I replied.

I waved to Aelith who giggled then waved back with both hands, one pointing backward. Our child. The gods were both cruel and kind. At that moment, I had the only thing I had ever really wanted. Yet a greater destiny called me, and there was no ignoring the call.

A rider came from Moray within the week. He carried messages from the local thanes as well as a letter from Macbeth.

While Macbeth's letter to Banquo had been less than detailed, Macbeth told me more. As it turned out, Crinian was not content to be Abbott of Dunkeld. He had fled south to join Siward and young Malcolm in Northumbria. Rumor had it the pair were plotting, planning to retake the southernmost lands as soon as the spring arrived. Macbeth pleaded for me to return south.

"Please come back," he'd written, then signed the letter with his name.

Given what I now knew, Macbeth's calls for war made sense. Crinian deserved to be punished, and Siward could not be permitted to step foot in Scotland. I could see Siward's plan unfolding. One square of land at a time, one turned or murdered lord at a time, he would make his way north.

I looked at the handwriting in Macbeth's letter to me. As with

Banquo's, the perfect courtly script Macbeth usually used had disintegrated to scratch. Crinian's treachery—and god knows what else—had unhinged Macbeth. But unlike in his letter to Banquo, Macbeth made no mention in his letter to me about Thorfinn and Echmarcach.

*T*hat night, while Aelith slept, Banquo and I composed our reply letters to Macbeth. Banquo wrote that he contracted an ailment in the winter and had not recovered. He could not come. I wrote that I would return south within the month.

I handed my letter to Banquo. He read it then set it aside.

Rising, I went to Aelith. How sweet she looked. Her brown hair, glimmering with red highlights, sparkled in the firelight. Her lips were puckered like little roses.

"She'll be all right," Banquo told me. "She's eating solid food very well now."

I nodded. Already Aelith had begun to wean herself, preferring the taste of table food to milk. Poor lamb, she had no sense of flavor at all.

"It would be better if I had more time."

"Of course," Banquo said. "But you do not."

"I don't want to leave her or you or this life. This was the life I was supposed to have. I don't want to go. All those years ago, we should have run away together."

Banquo huffed a laugh. "So we have said, time and time again, but we didn't. We had our reasons. Now, here we are."

"Do you think Macbeth will believe you? Will he believe the story of the ailment?"

"He has no reason not to. And if you confirm it to him, he will have no doubts."

"Will you regret giving up your duties?"

"No," Banquo said very matter-of-factly. "I have caused enough harm on Macbeth's behalf. Now, I will live my life. I will care for our daughter and look after our boys as best I can when I can. And I will rule the land of my fathers. I love Lochaber. I want to be home."

"I will miss Lulach and Fleance's return," I lamented.

"Yes, but one day, you will come back."

"Yes. I will."

"Yes, you will," Banquo echoed, but his voice had taken a faraway sound. When I turned and looked at him, he was staring into the fire. The look on his face was one of fear.

CHAPTER THIRTY-FIVE

I made ready to depart. I would not return to Moray but would ride straight to Dunsinane from Lochaber. Morag clicked her tongue and complained about Tira and Rhona who had—in Morag's words—abandoned me.

"I will send for them," I told Morag. "If they want to return, they can."

"And what will you do in the meantime?"

"My aunt Madelaine has maids."

Morag huffed. "No. That won't due. You will take Greer with you."

"Would she want to go?"

Morag laughed. "Lady Gruoch, I know your eyes have been on your man and your child. You've missed it completely. Wherever Sir Killian goes, Greer follows."

"Have they formed an attachment?"

"Well, she's certainly attached to him. I think he's still deciding. I suspect his heart is hung where it shouldn't be. It will take some time for him to realize it."

"Ahh," I said. His heart was still hung on me. "Well, I'll see what I can do to get it unhinged."

Morag laughed. "She's coming up to speed as a lady's maid, but it may still take her a bit of time."

"She helped bring my daughter into this world. What else could I ask for? Morag, she does know that—"

"That Aelith does not exist? As I told you when you came, your secrets are safe in Lochaber."

Killian organized my guard and some men of Lochaber to accompany me south. Word was beginning to spread about Thorfinn and Echmarcach's raid on the Irish king. Despite being opposed to the maneuver, I hoped it worked and wished them luck. Once more, Scotland's blood was boiling.

The morning we planned to depart, I rose early to find Aelith awake and talking. She lay in her bed, lifting and lowering her toys, studying each one and talking to them as she did so.

I lifted her from her bed then lay her down between Banquo and me. Banquo sighed in his sleep but slept on.

"I will leave today," I told Aelith.

She scrunched up her brow and looked at me. On some level, she understood. "But I will come home as soon as I can. Your dada will be here with you. And Morag. You won't be alone."

"Dada," she said, patting—more slapping than patting—Banquo's face, waking him in the process.

I laughed. "Yes, your dada. He will be with you always. He will always keep you safe."

Yawning, Banquo lifted Aelith's hand and kissed it.

"And your mother will keep us all safe. You see how perfect it all will work," Banquo said.

"I need to start getting ready," I whispered.

"I know," Banquo said sadly. "Well, my Aelith, let's get up and make sure everything is ready for your mum's ride south. Shall we go see if Swift is saddled?"

Aelith grinned with excitement.

Poor little dear, if she only knew my heart was breaking.

. . .

*K*illian had been hard at work making the preparations. By the time I was finally dressed, everything was ready.

Carrying Aelith, Banquo waited while I mounted Swift.

"I will write as soon as I can."

Banquo nodded. "Be careful, my Cerridwen, and not just on the road. Keep your man close," he said, motioning to Killian. "But not too close," he added with a wink.

I laughed. "Oh, my love. That is the last thing you should ever worry about."

At that, Banquo chuckled. He handed Aelith up to me so I could kiss her once more.

"Be a good girl," I said. "Listen to your father. Now, give me a kiss."

Giggling, she planted a very wet kiss on my cheek.

"I love you," I told her then I handed her back to Banquo.

Banquo gave me a soft smile. "I love you."

"I love you too," I whispered. With a heavy heart, I tapped on the reins then turned my horse south.

As I rode out of the gates of Tor Castle, I fought back my tears. This wasn't right. This wasn't the way things were supposed to be.

Instead of staying with my husband and daughter, I was headed back to Macbeth.

CHAPTER THIRTY-SIX

*T*he road was long and cold. Even though spring had come, snow still trimmed the landscape. The first spring flowers pushed through the snow. A deep sadness fell over me as we rode south. Despite the beautiful scenery, I was returning somewhere I didn't want to go to someone I didn't want to see.

It was a three-day ride to Dunsinane. As we rode through Birnam Wood, again I felt the eyes of the forest on me. Soon, the forest thinned out, and we spotted the massive old fortress sitting on its high hill.

A sense of dread washed over me.

"What a tall place," Greer said, her eyes wide.

"It's an ancient fortress, from the kingdom of the Parisi."

She stared up at the castle then turned and looked behind her, a smile on her face. I followed her gaze to see she was looking at Killian who had returned her grin. But when he saw me looking, he stiffened his expression, taking on a formal stance.

Sighing, Greer turned around in her saddle.

"I'll work on him," I whispered to her.

Greer raised an eyebrow at me but said nothing.

We rode up the winding path that led to the fortress. When we were spotted, trumpets blasted, and a fleet of servants rushed forward.

I was relieved to see a mop of red hair in the crowd.

"Corbie? Corbie," Madelaine called.

I slipped off Swift, handing him off to a groom, then rushed to my aunt.

"Oh, there you are," Madelaine said, embracing me. She eyed me over. "You look well. Is everything...is *everyone* well?"

"Very well," I told her, linking my arm in hers. "We shall talk tonight. But *she* is very well."

"Thank the Goddess," Madelaine said, patting my arm

As we headed toward the castle, Macbeth appeared at the wall of the second-story rampart. He looked down, eyeing over the party, then me.

I met his gaze.

He lifted a hand in greeting.

I returned the gesture.

"How is everyone here?" I asked Madelaine.

"Decidedly unwell," Madelaine whispered. "It's good you're back, but we need to talk."

I unlinked my arm from Madelaine's. "We shall, but for now, I should go," I said, gesturing toward Macbeth.

She nodded. "All right. I'll see to your staff. Where are Tira and Rhona?"

"At Cawdor. I have a new girl, Greer."

Madelaine nodded. "I'll take care of her," she said then patted my arm and let me go.

Taking a deep breath, I climbed the steps to the second-story rampart. Macbeth stood watching the activity in the yard. I crossed the space and joined him at the wall.

"Those are Lochaber's men," Macbeth said, eyeing the group.

"Yes."

"And where is the thane?"

"He is very ill. I went to see him before riding here."

"Will he recover?"

"Yes, but he is much weakened."

"How…unfortunate."

"And you, Macbeth. How are you?" I eyed him over. Once more, he looked sleepless and agitated. When I had first met him, he had the cut of a soldier. Now he looked thin and weak.

Macbeth frowned. "I… You will not need to go to Ireland."

"So I've heard."

"Echmarcach and Thorfinn reclaimed some of the lands stolen from Echmarcach. We have had success there."

"And Donaldbane?"

Macbeth didn't answer.

"And Donaldbane?" I asked again, my voice growing dark.

"I don't know. Our operatives never returned, and the Irish king has ceased all communication."

"Of course he has."

Macbeth blew air through his teeth then roughly ran his fingers through his hair.

"It is no matter. It's done now. What plans have you made for Crinian and Siward?" I asked.

At that, Macbeth grinned, a wild gleam in his eyes. "Many, many plans." He gripped the stone wall hard and rocked back and forth.

"We should go in and discuss," I said, motioning to the castle.

Still smiling, Macbeth stared out onto the horizon. He didn't move.

"Macbeth," I said gently. "I haven't seen the finished castle. Let's go inside. You can show me Dunsinane."

He turned to me. His eyes searched my face. "You came back."

"Yes."

"Come, let me show you," he said. Motioning for me to follow him, his footsteps hurried, we headed back inside.

I turned and looked behind me, unsurprised to find Killian there.

He nodded for me to go on. He followed just behind us.

With a heavy sigh, I trailed the mad king.

CHAPTER THIRTY-SEVEN

*A*fter Macbeth toured me through the castle, we went to his meeting room on the second floor. He went over all of his plans with me, and from what I could see, he had done well. The troops were rallying at Glamis. He had already called in a contingent of his army, enough men to keep the border secure from any incursion.

"Without Banquo, I will need to go myself," Macbeth said.

I frowned but said nothing. Unsteady as he was, it wasn't wise to have him on the field. But despite his nerves being wrought, the stratagem he shared with me was sound.

"If you must," I said carefully.

"And you're sure about Banquo? He *is* ill."

"Yes," I said, my tone dark.

Macbeth nodded.

"When will you go south?" I asked.

"Within the week. I was waiting for Ross and Mar. And you."

"Me?"

"Of course. You must be here at Dunsinane to manage things. They must understand we are not to be trifled with. I will leave for Glamis in the morning," Macbeth told me.

"Then I will begin my work here tomorrow," I said, fingering through the papers on Macbeth's desk, disturbed by what I saw.

Macbeth nodded then crossed the room, looking like he was heading somewhere in a hurry.

"Macbeth?"

"Oh. Oh, yes. Why don't you rest? I'll see you at supper," he said then headed out. As he passed Killian, who was standing just outside the conference room door, he ruffled the man's hair then turned and rushed off.

Gaping, Killian stared at Macbeth.

Completely bewildered, I shook my head then motioned for Killian to come inside.

"Your Majesty," he said, a concerned look on his face.

I nodded. "I know. I think we've returned just in time."

Killian sighed, echoing my thoughts.

*O*nce again, I spent my time working through Macbeth's mess. I was relieved when a servant came to fetch me for dinner. Feeling weary, I wandered to the massive banquet hall. It was still under construction when I'd come with Kirk all those months ago. Now, the place had been fully restored. Wide timbers lined the ceiling, and colored glass had been set into the windows. Sconces lined the walls, and new tables and chairs filled the space.

"Corbie," Madelaine said, catching up with me. "You're still in your riding clothes."

"Yes," I said blearily. "I'll take a bath and rest after supper."

"Corbie, there's something you must know," Madelaine whispered.

"Ah, here is Her Majesty," Macbeth called from the table. He rose, motioning for me to come sit.

"Corbie," Madelaine said, caution in her voice.

As I approached the table, I couldn't help but notice a teenage boy sitting at the end of the table near Macbeth and me. The boy looked up at me, his blue eyes wide. When I met his gaze, he looked away.

A servant pulled out my chair, and I settled in across from the boy, Madelaine beside me.

"Gruoch," Macbeth said with a smile, "this is Findelach," he said, motioning to the boy.

I looked at the young man. Aside from his eyes, which were a copy of Macbeth's, he looked much like his mother, Elspeth.

I inhaled slowly and deeply, well aware that the other lords and ladies present were watching me.

I turned to Findelach. "It is good to meet you, Findelach," I said. "How is your mother? Your grandfather?"

"They are both well, Your Majesty," he said, his voice little more than a whisper. He was just a slip of a boy, a thin, nervous thing. His hands shook.

"Your mother is an excellent horsewoman. Does she still look after beasts?" I asked, my eyes flicking toward Macbeth.

"She farms now. She and my step-father have a place in the north."

"Very good. I'm pleased to learn she's well," I said then looked down the table to find everyone staring at me, their eyes wide. "Cousin Bethoc," I called. "How have you been? Can you believe this cold weather so late in the spring? I worried we would catch fever riding across the countryside in such uncertain weather."

Bethoc gasped. "Oh, indeed, Gruoch, indeed," she said, clapping her hands in excitement. "You know..." she began, and then she let loose.

The other lords and ladies exhaled. Giving Bethoc partial attention, they turned back to their meals—or one another—once more.

Exhaling, I sat back in my seat. I glanced sidelong at Madelaine.

She arched an eyebrow at me.

I lifted my goblet of wine and took a sip. When I did so, I found Findelach's eyes on me. In them, I saw a desperate plea for forgiveness.

Raising my cup, I toasted the boy.

He exhaled deeply and returned the gesture, his hand trembling.

I turned to Macbeth who was gawking at the ceiling.

I followed his gaze. "What do you see?"

Macbeth tittered then leaned toward me. Having him so close made my skin crawl, but I held steady. "Angels," he whispered.

"Ahh," I replied then drank once more. "Of course."

By all the gods, I hated being there, but from what I could see, I had arrived just in time to save everything from madness.

My son's only rival sat across from me.

My husband saw angels.

And war was about to break out.

What better place was there for me to be?

CHAPTER THIRTY-EIGHT

*M*acbeth and Findelach—or Findelach the bastard as I learned he was called behind his back—rode out the next morning for Glamis. I went through all of Macbeth's papers, trying to make sense of the work he was doing. I could see from the dates on the notes that he had started to decline just after Yule. His bastard had been brought to court not long after. Whatever Macbeth had planned for young Findelach, that now appeared to be forgotten.

"Everyone is puzzled," Madelaine told me. "He brought the boy here. Everyone knew he was Macbeth's bastard, but he never formally acknowledged him. Since the boy arrived, he has ignored the child completely. And Findelach…he is a farmer's son. He's a good boy, Corbie. He seems like he's humiliated about the whole affair."

"He's not ambitious?"

Madelaine shook her head. "No. He spends most of his time in the barn helping the stablemaster."

I shook my head. Macbeth was lost.

Part of me felt very resentful that it would be left to me to put things right once again.

When they returned, I would speak to Findelach. From the look he gave me at dinner, he knew I considered him an enemy. Maybe he worried I would murder him. He wasn't wrong to fear. It had crossed my mind. But given Madelaine's observations, there was a better way. Perhaps having his own farm in Moray would entice the boy to go home.

*N*ews came that Macbeth had ridden south to engage the army spotted in the southern districts. Part of me hoped he would not return. If Macbeth was dead, Siward might try me, but I was not Suthen. I would be ready to face him. And if I ever saw Crinian again, he would find no mercy in me.

After the army rode out, we waited.

The news came from the north. Standish wrote that all was well in Moray. They had not been asked to join the army and go south. Banquo wrote as well. Lochaber was as quiet as I remembered it, and everyone was doing well. One surprise correspondence came from Thorfinn. His message had been addressed to both Macbeth and me. He wrote lamenting that he had failed in Ireland, asking forgiveness that Donaldbane had not been recovered. He also regretted to share that he and Magnus had a falling out, but Thorfinn was working to align himself with King Harald Sigurdsson. I was appalled to read that the alliances Thorfinn had worked so hard to win had crumbled to dust. But Caithness and the north were still well in hand. It was Thorfinn's dealings with Norway and Denmark that had fallen into disrepair. Despite the bad news in terms of political alliances, Thorfinn was also happy to tell us that Injibjorg had given birth to a son they had named Erlend.

Weeks passed.

Riders soon started flowing in. Macbeth's forces had met Siward's with success. Macbeth had pursued Siward's army back into Northumbria, burning and looting as he went. I frowned when I read about the destruction in Macbeth's wake. Having been on the receiving side of his cruel vengeance, I knew what hatred he would plant in the hearts of the Northumbrian people. When Siward called his forces in the years to come, brothers and sons would remember what the King of Scotland had done.

When summer returned, so did Macbeth. The king was at Glamis. Servants rushed about preparing a feast and refreshing rooms.

"I will hate to see Crinian in chains," Bethoc lamented. "Foolish man. Didn't he know the tide had turned? He should have made good on the generous offer you gave him, Your Majesty," she told me.

"I'm sorry he didn't."

Madelaine stared down the empty road as she waited. Her eyes took on a vacant, faraway look. Here we were waiting for men to return from battle. The last time this had happened, Tavis had died.

I wrapped my arm around my aunt's waist and pulled her close.

"When it is quiet, I will return to my keep—and beyond—for a time," she whispered.

"I'm glad to hear you say so. I worry for them all."

"Look, look there," Bethoc said as riders and carts approached.

I watched.

Macbeth rode at the front, his man, Wallace, beside him. Behind them were a number of other soldiers and lords. I saw the banners of Fife, Ross, Mar, and others.

"My Queen!" Macbeth called, jumping off his horse to come to greet me.

I took a step back.

Madelaine reached out and gently held me in place.

"Macbeth, congratulations on your victory," I told him, eyeing him closely. He was no better. He still had a wild look in his eyes.

"Lady Madelaine," Macbeth said, bowing to her. "The men of Fife and Lothian fought well."

"That's good to hear, Your Highness. Fife is on his way here now to celebrate with you."

"And where is Crinian, that wicked turncoat?" Bethoc asked, but I heard the catch in her voice. She may have been ashamed of her husband's actions, but she was also afraid.

"Lost in battle. I'm sorry, cousin," he told Bethoc.

"Lost? Lost how?"

"Well, I killed him. Traitor that he was."

"Macbeth," I chided.

Bethoc wailed then turned and rushed toward the castle.

Madelaine frowned at Macbeth then turned and went after Bethoc.

"Have you no care for ladies' sensibilities?" I asked, but then I laughed. "I'm sorry. How absurd. I'd forgotten who I was speaking to."

"What?" Macbeth asked, looking confused.

I scanned the men. "Where is your bastard?"

"Who?

"Findelach."

"Oh. He died."

"What?"

"Yeah, I guess he had never been in battle before. Pig farmer and all."

"He died?"

Macbeth nodded. "I need a bath. Wallace," he said, waving to his man. "I'll go in."

"Yes, Your Majesty," the man called.

Before I could step aside, Macbeth clapped me on the shoulder. "Dunsinane," he said, looking up at the castle. "What a lucky name."

He turned and headed inside.

Still in disbelief, I went to Wallace who, it appeared, had taken over Banquo's duties as Macbeth's chief general. He was barking orders when I approached.

"Sir," I called to him.

"Your Majesty," he said, giving me a quick bow.

"Is it true that Findelach has perished?"

Wallace shifted uncomfortably. "Yes, Your Majesty. He was… unready for battle."

"His body?"

"We buried him in the field."

"I see. And Crinian?"

"Also…deceased," Wallace said, not meeting my eye.

"And what does that mean?"

"Some matters regarding war are not suitable for ladies' ears."

"Well, I am not the typical lady."

"No, you are not, but the matter is unsuitable for most ears. The abbott was caught in an ambush. His treachery was rewarded with a violent end."

"I see."

"If you will excuse me, Your Majesty, I must see to the men."

"Very good. Thank you, Wallace," I said and headed inside.

Shaking my head, I went to the council chamber and sat down. I needed to send dispatches to let the others know the army had returned triumphant.

And now I—*me of all people*—was responsible for writing another letter. To Elspeth. To let her know her child was dead.

CHAPTER THIRTY-NINE

*T*hat night, the lords and ladies feasted, toasting Macbeth's great success. Bethoc was absent, and no one asked Macbeth what had happened to his bastard. I couldn't stand being in the same room with the rest of them. As pleased as I was about Macbeth's success, I couldn't swallow his complete disregard for his own child. But why did it surprise me? When our child had died, he had thought only of himself. He had most certainly not thought of me. Macbeth only thought of others in relation to himself. If he was not harmed by a loss, then there was no loss. If he was not in pain, there was no pain. There was only him and his desires. And right now, listening to him toast his wins was too much to take.

After checking on Bethoc, who had cried herself to sleep, I went to my chamber. Madelaine joined me shortly afterward.

"Fife arrived just after supper," she told me. "I will ride out with him when he leaves."

I nodded. "I'm worried for Epona. She was so frail when I saw her last. And Crearwy… Madelaine, she hates me."

Madelaine shook her head. "No. She loves you. She's just angry. It will pass."

"And if it doesn't?"

"Then you still did right by her, even if neither of us wanted it, and she never sees it."

Sighing, I nodded. I rose and went to my bureau. Therein, I found Crearwy's pin. I handed it to Madelaine. "Please, give this to her for me. Tell her it belonged to her aunt. The flower is the symbol of Gillacoemgain's mother's line.

"It's lovely. I will give it to her. How is Aelith?" Madelaine asked.

"She's doing very well, according to Banquo's letters."

"With the war done, will you return to Lochaber?"

"Not yet. Not with Macbeth in such a state. But I have an idea. An old idea. Let me see if I can make good on it again."

"Corbie, I don't know how you manage."

"I manage poorly, Aunt. My life is like a bucket full of holes. Every time I look, something important slips away from me."

Madelaine nodded sadly, that hollow look coming to her eyes once more. "Yes," she whispered, but it was all she said. She understood well. Sometimes, there was nothing to be done to fix the broken pieces.

Well, almost nothing.

*M*adelaine and Fife left within the week. Shortly after their departure, the bishop arrived at Dunsinane.

Macbeth was in the chapel praying early one morning. He was muttering to himself and picking at his head. I studied him as I approached only to realize he was pulling out locks of his own hair.

"Macbeth?"

"Aren't they beautiful?"

"Aren't what beautiful?"

"The angels," he said, motioning above him.

I sat down in the pew closest to him. "Macbeth, I have invited the bishop here."

"Why?"

"To talk to you about taking your pilgrimage."

"Oh. Very well."

"You will go?"

"Of course. It's a good idea, Gruoch. Do you want to come?"

"No."

"All right. I will send word to Thorfinn. He is going to come."

"That's highly unlikely."

"No. The angels told me he would come. You see them?" Macbeth said, pointing.

I followed his gaze. When I shifted my vision and looked with my raven's eyes, I saw *something*.

"Will you send word to Thorfinn for me?" Macbeth asked.

"Macbeth, Thorfinn is embroiled in his own troubles. And he just had a son."

"Ask him."

"All right," I said with a sigh then rose.

"And Gruoch?"

"Yes?"

"Will you write to Elspeth?"

"I already have."

"Thank you."

Saying nothing more, I left him there. What was there to say? There was no use in arguing with a madman.

*A*s requested, I sent a rider to Thorfinn. I then asked the bishop to make plans for Macbeth's pilgrimage. With those tasks done, I went back to work. With the flare-up in the south extinguished, and Siward's army defeated, Siward withdrew. My spies informed me that he had barely raised enough money and men to ride north again. Rumor was that Crinian had made promises that had come to nothing—just like Crinian himself. I didn't expect to hear from Siward again any time soon.

Macbeth stayed as he was. While preparations for his departure to the continent had been made, Macbeth refused to go until we heard from Thorfinn. While I took his words as the raving of a madman, I was surprised when riders approached one day bearing Thorfinn's standard.

I went to the yard to discover the jarl there. I could scarcely believe my eyes.

"Thorfinn?"

He laughed. "I figured there was no sense in sending a messenger. I would just come myself."

"What are you doing here?"

"I'm going to Rome, of course. My ships are ready to take us whenever Macbeth is ready. Where is my king?"

I sighed.

"Ah," Thorfinn said simply.

I motioned for him to follow me. We wound up the steps of the castle to the third level. "I say, what a grand edifice. Dunsinane is a sturdy old boat," Thorfinn said.

"And ancient to its roots."

"As is the wood around it. I'd swear I heard sprites whispering to me."

"Your guess isn't far off. But you must tell me, how is Injibjorg and your son?"

"Both are well. And you—please forgive my wife, but your secrets are safe with me—how is yours and Banquo's daughter."

I nodded. "Aelith. She is with Banquo in Lochaber."

"Macbeth wrote that Banquo was ill."

"Ill in spirit. He is unwilling to support Macbeth further."

"I'm glad to hear he is well in body. I love Banquo and

Macbeth like they were my brothers, but I have eyes. This trip to Rome is well devised. Your idea?"

"It was an inspired thought." It was, in fact, Scotia's idea, but I wasn't sure she wanted Thorfinn to know that. "And you want to go? Really?"

"My ambitions are different from Macbeth's. We will go to Saxony and meet Emperor Henry and then on to Hamburg. I have already made the arrangements."

"Then you must speak to the bishop. He, too, has made plans."

"Bah," Thorfinn said, waving his hand dismissively.

"You do know people make this pilgrimage in honor of the White Christ? You will go to Rome where they will, no doubt, ask you to be baptized."

Thorfinn shrugged. "After such a long walk, I will need a bath."

"Thorfinn!"

"I am named after the thunder god. He knows my heart. No pretty words and scented oil will change that."

When we reached the uppermost level of the castle, we found Macbeth looking out into the forest.

"Macbeth," Thorfinn called.

Macbeth turned around. He smiled widely.

"How gaunt he is," Thorfinn said with a gasp.

"He is unwell. It is a burden you are taking on. He believes he speaks to angels."

Thorfinn gave me a concerned look then crossed the space to meet Macbeth.

"I told you he would come," Macbeth shouted at me.

I nodded to him then turned to go.

He was right after all.

I only hoped that maybe his angels could guide him back to sanity.

CHAPTER FORTY

*M*acbeth, Thorfinn, and a contingent of guards and monks left Dunsinane within the week. They would ride to the River Tay then take a ship to the continent.

"Don't worry," Thorfinn told me. "I will bring him back the man he was."

"A better man, if you please, or not at all."

Thorfinn nodded but said nothing more on the matter. "Be safe," I said, kissing him on the cheek. "May Odin, Thor, and Freya guide your steps to the holy city of Rome."

At that, Thorfinn laughed. "Be well, Gruoch," he said then mounted.

I went to Macbeth. "I wish you a safe and healing journey," I told him.

"Dunsinane will be well cared for in your hands. Take care, Gruoch," he said then looked about suspiciously. "But watch the woods. They whisper."

"Indeed," I said. Macbeth was not wrong, I was just surprised he had the ears to hear such things. Once again, my vision of the moving forest came to mind. I shuddered when I thought of it.

Macbeth waved to me then reined his horse to join Thorfinn.

I watched the party depart.

Scotia, I hope you are right.

*W*hen Thorfinn and Macbeth rode off for Rome, I had my sincere doubts that anything about Macbeth would change for the better. They would be gone for months. So, in the very least, I would be able to complete my own work.

Time passed. Banquo wrote, sharing with me the details of Aelith's life. Our daughter was growing quickly, was in good health, and was a silly, happy thing. Fleance and Lulach had passed through once more on their way to tour the country. I was sorry to know I had missed them. One day, I would see my son again. I ached to see all my children, but I didn't dare leave Dunsinane. My eyes were firmly fixed on the south. From what I could learn, Siward was always on the move. He was looking for a way back north. Malcolm, Duncan's son, was coming of age. Soon, very soon, Siward would be back. I had lost all hope of ever recovering Donaldbane. The messengers I sent to the Irish king never returned. It was no use, and I would not risk another man in the effort.

Months drifted away.

One day in the autumn, very near Samhain, I was riding from Glamis to Dunsinane when I suddenly felt a strange chill. The wind whistled through the woods, and I heard whispering on the breeze. I pulled Swift to a stop.

"What is it?" Killian asked, looking around. He unsheathed his sword.

"I...I don't know."

Come. Come tonight, a voice whispered.

I glanced into the woods. The ancient oaks shifted, but I felt eyes on me.

"Squeaks," I said.

Killian nodded. "Always with these woods."

I nodded then clicked at Swift, moving forward once more.

"Gruoch…" Killian said, and I could tell by the tone of his voice that he had something important to say.

"What is it?"

"I wanted to ask you—well, tell you—or ask you— I'm not sure which," he said with a chuckle.

"What is it?"

"I would like to ask Greer to marry me."

I wasn't surprised. Morag had set me on the case, and I had done what I could to see that the two of them had the opportunity to get to know each other better. Greer was a good girl, and Killian a trusted servant.

"Of course, you have my blessing, not that you need it."

"Greer loves you well, my lady. But I think she's lonesome for Lochaber. I'd like to take her home."

Which would mean that I would lose both my guard and my maid. "I wish you the best. I only wish I could go with you. Would you take some things to Aelith for me?"

Killian nodded. "Anything, my lady. But I hate to leave you here alone."

"Wallace's men have proven reliable. I'm settled in Dunsinane for the moment. Please, don't delay on my account. You should leave before the weather turns."

"Thank you, Gruoch. I must say, you don't seem surprised."

"No. Of course not. I already knew."

"How?"

I grinned. "What did you think all that squeaking was about? The forest told me, of course."

Killian chuckled. "Of course. Do you think Lord Banquo would take me on at Tor Castle?"

"Yes. And you shall carry a letter with you that states the same. I would feel better to have trusted eyes on Aelith. And Greer will be needed at the castle as well. Aelith will need a maid."

"You're too good, Your Majesty."

"It's the least I can do."

When we returned to the castle, I sent Greer and Killian off for the night to celebrate. While I wanted them to enjoy their exciting news, I had other plans. After it grew dark, I grabbed a torch and headed to the oldest part of the castle. Slipping down the steps, I retraced my path to the caves below.

"Guide me," I whispered into the darkness.

I closed my eyes and called the raven.

I could hear the bird coming from a far distance. The sound of beating wings slowly approached me, growing louder with each passing moment. My body rocked when the raven and I became one.

Opening my eyes, I looked around.

The cave before me glowed, etchings on the walls shimmering with silver light. I followed the cave, winding through the darkness. The cave walls were covered with odd symbols and markings, things from a time long past. As I went, my torchlight revealed bowls carved from wood and jugs made out of clay. I twisted, going down and down, deeper and deeper. The air was very still. I could smell the earth. In the darkest corners, where my torchlight did not reach, I heard whispers.

The creatures of the Hollow Hills.

If they truly existed, this is where they would live.

Of course, such a place would connect to Ynes Verleath and the Lord of the Hollow Hills' chamber. This was his realm.

But the raven did not fear old things.

I wound down the path until I caught a fresh breeze. I could sense an opening to the outside world. The passage narrowed. I knelt and looked up at a small hole at the end of the cave. I could see the night's sky.

I extinguished my torch then crawled up.

Slowly, pulling and pushing, I crept up and out. I emerged through an opening at the base of an old tree. I crawled out then stepped into the night air. The massive old oak sat at the bottom of Dunsinane Hill.

I brushed off my dress and looked up at the castle.

"Not as secure as you thought," I said to the absent Kirk.

Behind me, someone cleared their throat, and I heard the jingling of rigging.

I looked back to see the girl I had spotted in the woods. She was hidden by shadows.

"I brought you a horse, Queen Gruoch."

I looked from the castle to her once more then went to her.

"Thank you," I said then mounted. "And please, call me Cerridwen."

CHAPTER FORTY-ONE

*T*he woman turned her horse and led me into the forest. She clicked at her steed. The beast picked up his pace, the horse I was riding following along. We rode through the forest at a brisk pace. As we went, I eyed the trees. Soon, a pattern emerged: nine ash, nine oak, and ahead of me, I spotted the first thorn tree.

Guiding her mount, the girl led us to a river. She clicked at her horse and soon, we forged our way across. I pulled up my feet and held on as we moved through the deepest part. Once we had crossed, she drove us toward a thick patch of woods.

My raven's eyes had not yet left me. Ahead, the trees glowed silver. Two tall monoliths stood sentinel at the entrance to the old forest. The woman guided her mount, and we rode through the stones. The air shivered. On the other side of the rocks, situated within a ring of massive old oaks, was a small village with nine houses.

At the center fire, a woman with long black hair waited. Eight other women, all of whom were robed in green, stood behind her.

"All hail," the woman with long, black hair called. "Hail the Dark Lady. Our queen has come."

. . .

$\mathcal{T}$he girl who'd brought me slipped off her horse then took my reins so I could dismount.

I climbed down and went to the leader of the coven. "Mother," I said, inclining my head to her.

"Welcome, Dark Lady, to Birnam Grove," she said. "I am Diana, leader of this coven."

"I am pleased to meet you."

"Come," she said, motioning for me to follow her. She led me to her home, a dome-shaped building made of stone and earth. Once we were inside, she motioned for me to sit by the center fire. She poured me a goblet of amber-colored liquid then sat on a stool across from me.

"Amongst our people, you are called Cerridwen."

I nodded. "Yes."

The woman nodded thoughtfully. I studied her. Her eyes were lined with coal, and like Banquo, she had tattoos on her arms and brow. "I am glad you have come."

"I spoke with Balor in the autumn," I told her. "I want to help people of our faith. I have begun drafting grants of land, so the covens are protected by the crown. And I—"

"I am not interested in such matters," she told me.

"Then why have you brought me here?"

"Because I was told to do so. Take my hand," she said, reaching across the fire to me.

I watched as the flames surrounded her arm, her gown, but they did not burn her.

She eyed my gloved hand but said nothing. I placed my hand in hers.

When I did so, I felt a sharp jolt. The world around me trembled.

I opened my eyes to find myself somewhere familiar.

I was in Epona's cabin. Before me, Epona lay on her bed. Crearwy sat beside her, holding her hand. Uald sat on a chair at Epona's bedside.

Crearwy shivered then she turned and looked at me.

"Mother," she said with a gasp.

Uald rose. "Cerridwen."

Diana had cast us to the coven.

"Epona," I said. I reached out to touch her, but in my phantom form, I could not.

Epona was so pale and shrunken. She opened her eyes just a little and looked at me.

"Cerridwen?"

"Epona, I'm here."

Epona looked behind me. "Hail, Diana," she rasped.

"Hail, Great Epona. May the Horse Mother guide your passage into the great beyond."

"Thank you, sister," she said then looked back at me. "Cerridwen," Epona whispered, motioning for me to come close.

I leaned in.

"Cerridwen, I wanted to tell you... I wanted to tell you that I'm sorry. I took from you—"

"You did what you thought was right."

"No. No. I took from you," she whispered. "I had no right."

"Your actions were guided," I said, casting a glance at Crearwy who was listening intently.

"It was wrong. For you. For her. I am sorry," Epona said, a tear slipping down her wrinkled cheek.

I choked back a sob. "No, Epona. Please. You have my forgiveness. Please. You were so good to me, like a mother. You did your best. You gave me so much."

"But I took..." she said then turned to Crearwy. "Forgive your mother. Forgive her. It was me. It was Andraste and me."

"Epona," Crearwy said, her voice cracking. She kissed Epona's hand.

"Forgive your mother," Epona pleaded of Crearwy once more.

Crearwy looked at me, her face wet with tears. She nodded. "I forgive her."

"Cerridwen," Epona whispered. "When the time comes, listen to your heart."

Epona turned to Uald. She smiled at her old friend.

Uald choked back a sob.

Epona patted Uald's arm.

She turned and looked at all of us once more, then she closed her eyes. Epona exhaled heavily then became very still.

"Epona?" Crearwy whispered.

Epona didn't answer.

Uald rose. She rushed past us and out of the house. I heard the front door slam behind her. A few minutes later, I felt others approach. I turned to see Aridmis, Druanne, Juno, Tully, and Flidas standing there.

No Sid.

Flidas looked from Epona to Diana.

"Mother," she whispered.

Diana bowed her head to the girl then turned to me. "Cerridwen, we must go," Diana told me.

I looked back at my daughter. "Crearwy?"

She looked up at me. "I love you, Mother."

"I love you too. Goodbye," I whispered.

As Diana and I withdrew, I reached out into that strange expanse of space where all the worlds touched and screamed, "Sid!"

. . .

*M*y body rocked when we returned to the forest coven in Birnam. I tumbled from my stool. It took me a moment to regain my footing.

Diana rocked, her eyes closed. She clapped her hands together then pressed her fingers against her lips.

I fidgeted, unsure what to do with myself.

I was crying. My whole body tense, I wanted to do something, anything. But there was nothing to be done.

"Breathe, Cerridwen. Breathe."

Setting my hand on my stomach, I inhaled slow and deep over and over again. Tears streamed down my cheeks. I yanked off my gloves and brushed the tears away.

I looked back at Diana who was staring at my hands.

I gazed down to see they were still covered in blood.

I sobbed.

Then, I felt it. There was a strange buzz at the back of my neck. My hands trembled.

No. Not now. Not here.

I had not had a fit in many years, and I could not have one now, here, amongst strangers—even if this was a sacred space.

I closed my eyes and breathed deeply, calming the tremors that wanted to insist themselves upon me.

"No," I whispered. "No."

Eyes closed, I pulled my gloves back on and mastered myself. Once I was steady, the shaking beaten back, I sat once more.

"How did you know?" I asked Diana.

"The moon told me," she whispered. "I am sorry to meet you at such an auspicious time, but I was guided to bring you here, so you could be with her at her last moments."

I choked back a sob then nodded.

"I will have Arden take you back now. But you and yours are welcome here. Just listen to the trees; they will guide you. In

Birnam, whenever the woods speak, listen. They always know what must be done," she said then rose.

We exited the little earthen house once more. I looked around. The place was not unlike Epona's coven, though it was smaller and more rudimentary. Like the caves below Dunsinane, it was an ancient place.

I bowed to the women collected there then mounted the horse I had rode in on.

"Be well, Dark Lady," Diana called to me then motioned to the others. "Come, daughters. Tonight, we shall pray for the spirit of a great lady who has passed."

"Coming?" Arden called to me.

I turned the horse and followed along behind her.

As we rode, I tried to wrap my head around what I had seen.

Epona was gone.

May the Great Mother help us all.

Epona was gone.

*A*rden and I took the road that led to Dunsinane. When the castle's torchlight was in sight, I dismounted and handed the horse's reins to her.

"I will walk the rest of the way. It will make for a good joke," I said absently, my heart not in it.

The girl nodded.

"Arden, isn't it?"

"Yes."

"If you should need anything, please don't hesitate to come to Dunsinane."

"And if *you* ever need anything, don't forget where we are. Just whisper to the trees," she said then gave me a soft, sympathetic smile. "Be safe, Your Majesty," she said then turned and rode back into the night.

I sighed then looked up at the castle, a terrible feeling of loss eating a hole in my heart.

Epona's words replayed again and again through my head.

I closed my eyes. "Epona, go with my love," I whispered. "I shall see you in the next life. Blessed may you be."

CHAPTER FORTY-TWO

*I*t was months before Macbeth and Thorfinn returned. When they did so, I was relieved to find Macbeth much changed.

"He is not the man we knew, before or after," Thorfinn told me. "He is a different man now. But I think…I think things will be quiet for you."

"Thank you, Thorfinn," I told him.

Before he left, Thorfinn and I stayed awake late into the night talking about everything he had seen, the other rulers they had met, and the friendships he had formed abroad, many of which would prove helpful in the years to come. Rather than staying with us, Macbeth went to the chapel to pray. I should have known from the first night that nothing would be the same. But who could guess it?

Thorfinn rode out the following morning. I stood at the castle gate and watched him go.

As I did so, a wind blew, and the trees around me swayed.

"Never again will thy eye meet. Farewell, farewell," I heard a light voice whisper on the wind.

My flesh rose in goosebumps, and I looked all around. There

was no one there, just myself and the trees. But then I remembered, in Birnam Wood, the forest always spoke.

Little did I know then, what they had whispered was true.

---

*E*verything comes in threes. Epona had taught me that. The last time I was reminded of her teachings, I had been left alone at Cawdor for six years. I should have known another such time was coming. Threes were all around me, including the number of losses I would face. Tavis's death was the first, followed by Epona's, and sadly, Standish wrote not long after Epona had gone, that Kelpie had lain down in his stall one night, and never rose again. In my mind, I imagined Epona and Kelpie together, Epona riding my warhorse bareback across the fields, both of them dizzy with joy.

Three found me once again. After three years, I returned to Lochaber to see Aelith and Banquo. My visit there was not long. While Madelaine did everything she could to care for the kingdom in my absence, I was needed at Dunsinane. Every time I rode out, I left a madman on the throne. So I saw my sweet girl, who didn't remember me at all, in the flesh for less time than a mother deserved. Aelith, who was a silly, wild thing, grew in Banquo's and my image, a miniature combination of us both. And the husband of my heart aged, silver streaks lining his hair.

Three came again, and with it, the Thane of Fife and Standish passed from this world to the next. Madelaine left Fife and Lothian to the rule of her husband's nephew and retired with me to Dunsinane.

The hardest of those three came to me in the briefest of visions. One night, as I was preparing a drink, I spied a ripple on the surface of my cauldron. The water shifted and changed, then formed a window into Ynes Verleath. I saw Andraste there.

"Andraste?" I whispered.

She inclined her head to me. "Graymalkin has gone," she said sadly. "I'm sorry," she added then slowly disappeared.

"Thora," I whispered. "Oh, Thora."

Alone in my bedchamber, I wept that night until I felt like I had no more tears in me. I knew her time would come, but I ached all the same. My beloved dog was gone.

Thereafter, another three years passed. News came that Morag had passed. I mourned her death. But it was at the end of these quiet years, a total of nine years later, that the trumpets sounded, alerting us to the approach of important riders. Not expecting any visitors, Madelaine and I looked at one another.

Perplexed, we headed outside. It was spring once again, and the forest all around the castle was trimmed with bright green leaves. The scent of fresh flowers filled the air. I closed my eyes, relishing the feel of sunlight on my face. When I did so, I went back in time to that moment in Moray when I was pregnant with Crearwy and Lulach. I remembered Gillacoemgain's laughter and the taste of summer strawberries. A soft breeze blew, and on it, I swore I could smell the deep lavender and cedar scent that clung to Gillacoemgain.

"Corbie," Madelaine exclaimed, surprise in her voice.

I opened my eyes to see a group of riders coming toward the castle, the banner of Moray flying high.

And at the front of this band was a strapping lad, a mirror of my dead husband, with long, black hair and the tattoos of a druid.

I gasped. "Lulach."

I wanted to run across the courtyard to greet him, but I restrained myself. It was then that I spotted a familiar face beside him. Looking so much like his father was Fleance.

"Corbie," Fleance called, waving to me. He grinned at Lulach, batting his friend playfully on the shoulder, then slipped off his horse.

Lulach also dismounted. He righted his doublet, and the two of them crossed the courtyard to meet us.

"My gods," Madelaine whispered. "Look at them."

I swallowed hard and tried to master my emotions.

Angus trotted along at Lulach's side, but Thor rushed ahead. Over the years, the dog had grown larger than Thora. But time had passed for him as well. He had silver hairs on his maw. Regardless, he wagged his tail in excitement.

I eyed Lulach's party. There were no druids amongst his men. The men there were all from Moray.

"Mother," Lulach said, bending to kiss me on both cheeks. "Well met."

I smiled up at him. "It is good to see you, my son. You've ridden from Moray?"

Lulach smiled. "Yes. I wanted to surprise you. And to talk."

"Of course."

"Corbie," Fleance said, embracing me. "You've shrunk."

I laughed. "I have not. Look at the two of you," I said, shaking my head as I studied them. They were both men now. "You've both shot up like trees."

"How like your father you are," Madelaine told Lulach, touching his cheek gently.

"Lady Madelaine," he said, taking her hand and placing a kiss thereon.

He smiled at her, but his brow wrinkled as he looked her over. In truth, the years that had passed had aged Madelaine as well. Her red hair had dulled to white. Lines had formed across her brow. Her croning had come upon her. I had fared little better. I was well aware that my once raven-black tresses were trimmed with silver. I sometimes wondered what Banquo would make of his aging bride. Pushing the thoughts away, I turned to Lulach and Fleance.

"Come," I said, motioning to the boys. "You will be road-weary. My servants will see to the men of Moray," I said then turned to the party. "Well met, lads," I called to them, waving brightly. "We shall feast tonight!"

At that, the men of Moray cheered.

Taking Lulach's arm, I led them to my council chamber. Madelaine sent a servant to fetch refreshments then we all sat by the fire.

Lulach eyed the room, looking at the shelves lined with scrolls and ledgers. "This is your workroom?"

I nodded. "Yes."

"Where is the king?" Lulach asked.

Madelaine and I exchanged a glance.

"We can see him later, if you wish," I told Lulach.

"We were in Lochaber before we came here," Fleance told me. "You would not believe Aelith. Jarl Thorfinn sent her a stout little Shetland pony. How wildly she rides. Like demons, the pair of them."

I chuckled. "Wildly, but safely, I hope."

"Father never lets her get too far away," Fleance reassured me.

I smiled, imagining the sight. But like always, any time I thought of Aelith, my heart broke a little.

"So, you were in Lochaber?" Madelaine said, recovering for me. "Then to Moray?"

Lulach nodded. "Fleance and I completed our service to the gods. We decided it was time to return to our duties."

"More like the gods decided, and Balor tossed us out," Fleance said with a laugh.

Lulach smiled lightly. "Yes, that's more accurate. I wanted to talk to you, Mother. I want—if it pleases you—to take up residence and begin to govern Moray from Cawdor."

"It more than pleases me, my son. My heart is full of joy to imagine you continuing your father's work."

"We saw Tira and Rhona in Moray," Fleance told me. "Rhona

is still at the castle, but Tira returned home. She came to see us. They both send their love."

I smiled when I thought of them.

"What about you, Fleance? Will you return to Lochaber?"

"Cawdor was just as much my home as Lochaber. My father has things well in hand in Lochaber. I will stay at Cawdor with Lulach. For now. Unless the wind blows me south again."

Lulach gave Fleance a look that I didn't understand.

"The gods and Balor have chosen the time very well. There are rumblings in the south. Very soon, we may be at war again."

Lulach nodded. "Malcolm's star is rising."

I raised an eyebrow at Lulach.

He inclined his head to me. "Thus, I must be ready. And where better to begin than Moray?"

*T*hat night, we dined. Everyone was delighted to meet their prince. The lords and ladies in attendance tripped over themselves to introduce their daughters to Lulach. The young ladies eyed my son. He was every bit as handsome as his father, but an otherworldliness clung to Lulach. Add to that the tattoos that covered his arms and brow, Lulach was very different from the lords. While all the pretty girls wanted Lulach to notice them, they were also wary.

"And what about you?" I asked Fleance, elbowing him as if to push him toward the crowd. "Don't you want to meet the fair ladies?"

"No, Corbie."

"What, have you given your heart elsewhere already?" I said in jest, but Fleance shifted uncomfortably. I had tripped upon the truth. "Fleance?"

"I suspect Lulach's heart is a puzzle even to him," Fleance said, diverting the topic.

"What about you?"

He patted his chest above his heart but said no more.

I didn't press. When he was ready, he would tell me.

As I watched Lulach, I was impressed with his skill handling the lords and ladies. His quiet way made them eager to talk. Too eager. Lulach listened, smiled only a little, and left the great thanes wondering what else to say or do to please their prince. I realized then the power Lulach had. Long ago, Banquo told me Lulach's reserved ways might serve him well. He was right.

It was late in the night, after the others retired, that Lulach turned to me and said, "Shall we see him now?"

I nodded.

Taking a torch, Lulach and I headed to the old part of the castle. Winding down the narrow halls, we passed the unused chambers until we found ourselves standing in the great hall of the Parisi. Long ago, I had the room cleaned and the center fire pit rebuilt. A throne had been installed on the wall once more. Here, Lulach and I found Macbeth holding court to phantoms.

"Macbeth?" I called.

Jabbering on about something, Macbeth stopped mid-sentence and looked at me. He narrowed his eyes, looking confused for just a moment. "Who is that beside you?" Macbeth asked then he rose, his face flashing with rage. "Damned, murderous uncle."

I pulled Uald's Gift and lifted it protectively in front of Lulach.

"Fool, it is Lulach you see before you. Gillacoemgain is long dead. You should remember it well. You murdered him."

"Lulach?" Macbeth asked, dropping his sword. It clattered to the floor.

"Your Majesty," Lulach said stiffly.

Turning, Macbeth gestured to the empty room. "They tell me Siward's army is growing. They tell me my cousin's son wants to kill us. They tell me I need to wake again and rejoin you. Is that right, Gruoch?"

"Their intelligence on the matter is as good as my own."

"Should I rejoin you?"

"That depends on the manner of man who will rejoin me. You know you cannot speak to *them* in the presence of others."

"They tell me they will go away so I can rule again."

"Then tell them to go."

"All right. Tomorrow. I will ask them to go tomorrow."

"Very well."

Macbeth studied Lulach. "How like your father you look. I loved him once. I loved him more than my own father, in fact. I never understood why he did it."

"He had a good reason," I said, instantly regretting saying anything.

"Did he?" Macbeth asked.

"Yes."

"Oh. All right."

"Then we shall see you soon?" I asked Macbeth.

He nodded. "Yes."

Motioning to Lulach, we left the place.

Behind us, I heard Macbeth whispering once more.

"Mother," Lulach began.

I didn't know what to say. Macbeth had been mad in fits and starts over the years. Mostly, he kept to himself. It unnerved me to think he wanted to rejoin court life. As it was, it was impossible to dispel the rumors about him. No doubt Siward had already learned that Macbeth was not at the helm in Scotland. Perhaps that is why he was plotting once more. "Lulach, Macbeth is—"

Lulach raised a hand to stop me. "No. I don't care about him. What you said about my father… Did Gillacoemgain have a good reason for killing Findelach?"

I stared at Lulach. Torchlight bounced off his face, accentuating the tattoos thereon. Of course, he would be curious. Of course, he would want to know the truth. "Yes, he did."

"Can you tell me?"

I shook my head. "Long ago, I promised I would never speak of it."

Lulach scrunched up his brow as he considered my words. "Crearwy—my aunt, Crearwy. It had something to do with her."

I stared at Lulach but said nothing.

Lulach's eyes took on a faraway gaze. "It's all right," Lulach said. "You keep your promise," he said then took my hand. He studied the glove thereon. "Still? After all these years?"

"Yes."

"I am sorry for it. I am sorry for all of it," Lulach said then kissed my gloved hand and led me away.

*L*ulach and Fleance stayed for several days before returning north once more to Moray. I made sure every lord, lady, thane, mormaer, and clansmen knew that the prince had returned and was ruling in Moray. Maybe Siward thought Macbeth weak, but with Lulach stepping into his place, it might dissuade—or at least give pause to—any action Siward might take.

I had hoped Siward would change his mind.

But that would not come to pass.

What did come to pass was the return of Macbeth. Having left behind his court of shadows, Macbeth returned to rule alongside me once more.

And our first act was to declare war.

CHAPTER FORTY-THREE

wice, Siward would rise only to be beaten back by the forces of Scotland. Twice. And on each occasion, it was the Mormaer of Moray and the younger Thane of Lochaber who rode into battle to deter the Earl of Northumbria and Malcolm, son of Duncan, who sought to reclaim his father's throne.

In the meantime, I ruled Scotland with a steady hand and guided Macbeth as best I could. The man I knew had returned somewhat, but the same darkness lurked within him. Old jealousies, those I thought long-forgotten, resurfaced one evening when I announced I would ride to Lochaber.

"Why are you going there?" Macbeth asked, a hard tone in his voice.

"To see Banquo."

"I think Banquo has lied to me all these years. I think he quit me because of you," Macbeth said.

"Banquo was ill. You, too, have been ill. This kingdom has been ruled in peace all these years while you brooded. What more could you want?"

"The truth," Macbeth replied. "I want the truth."

"About what? That I don't love you? I do not. That I love

Banquo? I do. What have you done to deserve my love? What have you done to earn anything I gave to you? Nothing. Yet here I am, your wife, and I have tended to you these many years. Me. Is there anyone else around? No. It's me who has cared for you."

"Without love."

"That's right, without love, but I tended to you all the same."

"Ride off to Banquo if you want, but don't come back. I don't need you. I shall rule this land with Lulach at my side. Already there is talk that Siward is gathering forces once more."

"So he is, which is why Fleance and Lulach are rallying the north and readying for war once again."

"I am king here."

"You are a king of shadows. A king of nothing. I have ruled this land, not you. Now, if you please, stay in Dunsinane and do not interfere in Lulach's work. I will return within the month," I said then headed outside to where my horse and guard were waiting.

To my great relief, Macbeth didn't follow.

Part of me worried. With Macbeth so unsteady, I should stay. But if war was coming again, it would be too long to wait to see Aelith. And I had not seen Crearwy in years. I could no longer cast, the skill having left me in the many years that had passed. If I wanted to see my child, I needed to ride out.

Lulach held the country safely in his hand. For a moment, just for a moment, I wanted to be with my family once more. I rode away from Dunsinane feeling swells of anger. Why now, of all times, would Macbeth revisit such nonsense? What did he hope to gain? Did he seriously think that we would ever reconcile? That would never happen. Surely, he knew that by now. And if he didn't, then he was truly mad.

It was three days' ride to Lochaber. A great sense of relief washed over me when I saw the towers of Tor Castle appear on the horizon.

I rode through the gate only to be met by an excited scream.

A girl, followed by a dozen puppies, rushed from the stable to meet us. She was a wild thing with tousled brown hair, which looked like it hadn't been brushed in days. Her gown was dirty at the knees, her hands a match.

"Dada," she screamed toward the castle. "Riders!"

Soldiers appeared to greet us, including a man wearing the badge of the castle sentinel. Killian.

"Your Majesty," Killian called.

The girl, who had been jumping and clapping her hands, froze.

She turned and stared at me, her blue eyes meeting mine. Her eyes went wide, and a second later, she turned and ran.

"Aelith?" I called after her.

Killian came and helped me off my horse. "How good to see you, Lady Gruoch. We were not expecting you."

"Didn't my messenger arrive?"

"No, Your Majesty."

"I see. I am sorry to surprise you. Will you please see to my men?"

"Of course."

"And are you well?"

"I am. I've become a father, Lady Gruoch. Greer had a boy this winter. We named him Standish."

At that, I hugged Killian. "I'm so glad for you both."

A moment later, Banquo appeared. "Gruoch?" he called.

As he made his way toward me, I noticed he was walking with a limp. When I'd seen him last, his hair had been peppered with gray. Now, much of his locks had changed color, his curly hair thinning at the front.

As he made his way toward me, he adjusted his clothes, straightening them and re-lacing his ties.

"Gruoch," he said as he neared me. "I… We didn't know you were coming."

"So Killian told me, but I sent a messenger."

"There was no one."

"That's disconcerting," I said.

Banquo nodded then looked around. "Where has Aelith gone?"

"There, Thane," Killian said, pointing to a path that led around the castle.

"She was taken by surprise as well," I told Banquo.

"Come," he told me, linking his arm in mine. My heart melted to feel the warmth of his body beside mine. We had been apart so many years. I loved him still and dreamt of him often. But nine years was a very long time.

"My Cerridwen, you must forgive me. I'm a mess," Banquo said, stroking the scraggly grey beard on his chin.

"My love, you could be covered from head to toe in mud, and I would love you no less."

"I am covered from head to toe in grey hair and wrinkles," he said with a laugh.

"And? You are always perfect in my eyes," I said.

We rounded the side of the castle. This section of Tor Castle faced the river. There, out of the eyes of the others, we paused.

I reached out and touched Banquo's cheek.

"I've been eating fish with garlic," Banquo said with a chuckle.

"I don't care," I said then set my lips on his.

Banquo pulled me close. I fell into his embrace, feeling his warmth, and loving being close to him again—garlic be damned.

When we pulled away, he smiled at me. "Come, let's see where our pixie has gone."

"She looked like she was frightened of me."

Banquo shook his head. "You are her mother. But we don't get many strangers here, and I am sure she was shocked."

I nodded.

Banquo led me down a path that led to a rocky peninsula that jutted out into the river. There, Aelith and her brood were playing. The puppies splashed in the water, chasing one another, nosing through the grass at the shoreline, snapping at fish or flipping rocks.

Aelith eyed us over her shoulder then threw a stick into the water.

The largest of her puppies raced after it.

"What a fine pack, my lady," I called to her. "Where did you come by them?"

"Found 'em in the woods," she answered in reply.

"All of them?"

"Yes. Their dam ran off, I guess. Couldn't find her anywhere, so I brought them all back with me."

"Aelith has been their surrogate mother," Banquo said. "They've been sleeping in her bed with her. Poor Greer has been beside herself for fear of fleas."

"They don't have fleas," Aelith said, sounding exasperated.

"Aelith," I called. I slowly approached her. Part of me thought she would run. But she stilled like a wild thing, watching and waiting. "I have something for you."

At that, she brightened. "What?"

I dug into the pocket of my dress and pulled out a small ring I had been carrying with me for years. It was a tiny silver band trimmed with an amber stone. "This," I said, showing it to her. "It belonged to Lady Crearwy of Moray."

The girl hopped across the stones and came to look at the ring. Taking it from my hand, she slipped it on her still-dirty finger.

"Does it fit?"

She gave her hand a shake, making my heart clench with worry as I imagined the ring flying off into the river. "It fits well. It was very kind of Lady Crearwy to give it to me. Now, is she the same person as my sister Crearwy or is she a different Crearwy?"

"Your sister is named after the late Lady Crearwy of Moray, sister of Gillacoemgain."

"Two Crearwys. How funny," Aelith said then laughed very loud. "Watch this," she told me, picking up a stone. Aiming it as best she could, she skipped the rock across the surface of the water. "See that?"

"I did."

"Nine times. Can you do better?"

"I cannot."

"You should try."

I lifted a rock and gave it a go.

"Three," Aelith said with a sigh. She patted my arm. "You need practice, Mother."

"Yes, it's been many years."

Without another word, Aelith wrapped her arms around my waist and hugged me tightly. "Don't worry. I will teach you to be good at it again."

I kissed the top of her head. "Bless you, my daughter. Bless you for your patience with me."

She laughed lightly then let me go, hopping away once more to hunt for sticks for her pack to chase.

Banquo crossed the rocks and came to stand behind me. He wrapped his arms around my waist.

"She is so wonderful," I whispered. "Thank you, my love."

He laughed. "She's wild, dirty, and odd. I'm not sure how well I've done."

I looked up at him. "You've done perfectly."

· · ·

*T*hat night, I lay in Banquo's arms for the first time in many years.

"How long can you stay?" he asked.

"I don't know. Lulach has things in hand, but Macbeth is awake once more and is agitated."

"There are rumors of war once again."

"Yes. We've found spies everywhere. I don't know what Siward is planning, but he is planning something. They say Malcolm, Duncan's son, is as shrewd. I fear for what they are planning."

"Then stay with me."

"I cannot."

"Are you sure? Cerridwen, are you *really* sure? If Lulach is ready to take his place, maybe it is time."

"Madelaine—"

"Can come here and live with us. She is old now, my Cerridwen. She would enjoy spending her final days in peace at Lochaber with Aelith."

As I lay there in Banquo's arms, I considered his words. Macbeth had told me not to return. Maybe I shouldn't. Maybe Banquo was right. Was I really needed?

"I'll have to discuss it with Lulach. And something will have to be done with Macbeth."

"Yes, but maybe, for once, not by you."

"You're right."

I crawled onto Banquo, bending to kiss his neck.

"Cerridwen," he whispered, stroking my hair.

"It has been a very long time," I murmured in his ear.

"All the more reason not to delay," he replied, his hands stroking my back.

"Then we'd better get to work," I said, setting the first of many kisses on his lips.

CHAPTER FORTY-FOUR

a few weeks later, Banquo, Aelith, and I lounged before the great fire after our morning meal.

"What happened to your leg?" I asked Banquo, watching as he crossed the hall. He was limping badly. Aelith sat pretending to do some work Banquo had given her. She was supposed to be reading. Mostly, she was just listening to us. I was just relieved that Aelith had warmed up to me after her initial surprise. But I understood how she felt. I remembered how it was for me when Boite would suddenly appear. It was like a star had fallen from the heavens.

"I was thrown, if you can believe it," Banquo said. "A deer startled in the woods, and my horse shied. I found myself lying on my arse looking up at the clouds. It's taken several months to get the leg this loose. The injury happened right before the winter. The cold weather has prolonged the recovery."

"Why didn't you send for a healer?"

Banquo smiled at me. "I did learn a few things under Balor. Now I'm teaching Aelith. She loves to stay inside and read and write. Especially when it's bright and sunny outside. She hates being outside."

"Oh, aye," Aelith said, tilting her head back and forth as she grinned.

Banquo winked at me.

I smiled at him. How sweet it was to be together like this. Banquo had proven himself a loving father. I expected no less. He had been a devoted lover. As I studied Aelith, my heart filled with joy.

If Lulach agreed, I could step back from ruling the country. I could return to Lochaber and stay there. For once, I would be able to have my child by my side.

"And what are you reading this morning?" I asked Aelith, fully aware that she wasn't reading anything. If she had, she might have missed the conversation.

"Words," she replied pertly.

"Words," I told Banquo.

He chuckled. "Words."

"Is it an interesting story?"

Aelith frowned. "No. I hate it. Just when everyone is happy, the worst thing you can imagine happens to them."

"What's the name of your tale?" I asked, but her answer was interrupted by the sound of a horn. A long, forlorn call echoed across the valley. A visitor had arrived.

I looked at Banquo.

"Lulach, maybe?" he suggested.

"No, I would sense…" I said then reached beyond me, feeling for whoever was there. I gasped. "Oh no."

Banquo rose. He looked at the castle door, his eyes going wide. He turned and gazed back at me. "Cerridwen," he whispered.

I heard the castle doors bang open and the sound of footsteps.

"Wait. Please, Your Majesty," Killian protested.

A moment later, Macbeth rounded the corner.

. . .

*W*e all froze.

Macbeth stood looking at the three of us, his eyes going from Banquo, to me, to Aelith. I moved protectively toward my daughter, my hand on my dagger.

"Ah, so here you are," Macbeth said with a smile. "I came to see you, old friend," he told Banquo.

How strange Macbeth looked. He was in full armor, even wearing his crown, but he lacked any boots or stockings whatsoever. He looked haggard, his skin pale as milk, his eyes bulging.

"Killian, will you see to the king's men?" I said.

"Lady Gruoch, he—"

"I rode alone," Macbeth told us. "I wanted to see if I remembered the way."

"Perhaps a drink," Banquo said, motioning to his servant. "A wine, for His Majesty."

The servant nodded then rushed off.

Behind Macbeth, Killian had drawn his sword. His eyes met mine. I motioned for him to hold.

"I keep seeing you at supper, Banquo," Macbeth said as he pulled off his gloves. He tossed them into the fire. "All week, you were there in the chair beside me, but you were covered in blood. I asked the others. No one else saw you. Not even Madelaine. She told me I have scorpions in my mind. But every night, you came and sat beside me. You never spoke, you just sat there, staring at me, a dagger sticking out of your chest. Isn't that strange?"

"Very strange," Banquo agreed.

"Very strange," Macbeth repeated. "So, of course, I had to come and see for myself if you were among the living," he said then hit the side of his head. "Scorpions. They scurry."

Beside me, Aelith whimpered.

Macbeth turned and looked at her. His gaze lingered far too long.

"She's very like you, Gruoch," Macbeth said. "And you too, Banquo. I see you both in her eyes."

"What do you want, Macbeth?" Banquo asked, his voice hard.

"Wine. Where is your servant?"

"Here, Your Majesty," the girl called. She carried a tray with wine goblets.

Macbeth lifted a goblet and drained it. He took another cup from the tray. He crossed the room and pushed the goblet toward Banquo.

"Drink, Thane," Macbeth said, forcing the drink at him.

"I'm well enough without it," Banquo said.

I watched Macbeth. There was a mad gleam in his eyes. I pulled Scáthach from my belt.

"I said drink," Macbeth told Banquo. "Let's drink, old friend. Look at your daughter. How beautiful she is. I never had a daughter. I had a son, but they tell me he died in battle. And then there is the child Gruoch lost. Two dead sons. But look at your daughter. Your daughter…with my wife. How beautiful she is," he said, stepping toward Aelith.

Banquo moved between us. "Macbeth," he said, his voice full of warning.

"Look at her. How like an angel," he said then exhaled loudly. "Stars, hide your fires. Let not your light see my black and deep desires." Moving quickly, Macbeth pulled his dagger and lunged at Aelith.

Aelith screamed.

Brandishing Scáthach, I readied myself, but then the unthinkable happened.

Banquo moved to protect us. He stepped between Macbeth and us. But he was unarmed. Using only his body, he blocked Macbeth's blow.

There was a terrible thud.

Banquo groaned then staggered backward.

Macbeth stepped back, his hands wet with blood.

Banquo turned to face us, a dagger protruding from his chest.

"Cerridwen," Banquo whispered.

Aelith shrieked then fled, Greer racing after her.

Banquo fell into my arms.

Killian rushed across the room. He slashed at Macbeth. Turning fast, Macbeth blocked Killian's attack. Dodging around Killian, Macbeth raced out of the hall.

"Stop him! Stop the king! Stop the king! The thane has been murdered," Killian screamed as he raced after Macbeth.

"Cerridwen," Banquo whispered. With shaking hands, he touched the dagger protruding from his chest. "Murder most foul."

Quickly sheathing Scáthach, I gently lowered Banquo to the floor.

Blood seeped through his shirt. Macbeth's dagger stuck out of his chest.

"No, no, no, no. This can't be happening," I whispered.

I pressed my hands against Banquo's chest, trying to stop the flow of blood, but it was no use.

"Cerridwen," Banquo whispered, reaching up to touch my face. "Look at me, my love."

"No, no, no."

"Cerridwen."

"No," I screamed. But this time, it was not me who spoke but the raven. Summoning the full force of that dark power, I let it overtake me. I flung Gruoch away like a tattered rag and looked down at Banquo.

He stared at me.

I lifted my hands into the air, pulled magic from the aether, and tore a hole in the world. There, on the other side, I saw Ynes Verleath. Andraste and Nimue looked up. Nimue gasped. Andraste rose, a look of astonishment on her face.

Reaching down, I pulled Banquo away from the great hall, away from Lochaber, and into Ynes Verleath. Nimue stared out at the world beyond.

"Nimue. Get my daughter. Now."

Without another word, Nimue stepped into the world to fetch Aelith.

I turned to Andraste.

"Come, you ancient, black, and midnight crone. Fix this," I commanded.

"I cannot."

"You will. Now," I ordered her, my voice booming through the hollow space.

"Foul, strange, and unnatural," she muttered as she dipped a ladle into her cauldron, filling it with silver liquid. "This was not foreseen," Andraste whispered as she knelt. "This cannot be. A price must be paid."

"I will pay *any* price."

"Hold him still," Andraste said.

I held Banquo's body firmly against the ground. His eyes fluttered open just a little. "My Cerridwen," he whispered. "I will see you again in the next world."

Andraste grabbed Macbeth's dagger and tugged it from Banquo's body. It came out with a spray of blood. She ripped the fabric on his shirt. Drawing arcane runes in the air, she began chanting in a language I did not know. She poured the liquid from the cauldron onto Banquo's wound. Still, she chanted, moving her hands in front of her. I watched with my raven's eyes as swirling blue designs formed in the air then sank into Banquo's body. Again, Andraste poured her liquid on his wound. Before my eyes, the deep cut healed.

Banquo sucked in a breath and opened his eyes.

"Cerridwen," he said, staring up at me.

I turned and looked at Andraste.

She inclined her head to me, a soft smile on her lips. "For all that I have done, *I* will pay the price," she said then fell over dead.

I gasped.

A moment later, I felt a rush of air. Nimue appeared with Aelith at her side.

"Father," Aelith cried, rushing to Banquo.

Disbelieving and in shock, Banquo stared at me.

"May all the gods be silent," Nimue whispered, her hands covering her mouth. She stared at Andraste.

I swallowed hard then closed my eyes. I tried to push away the raven, to send it back from whence it had come. But when I did so, I was met with resistance. There was no separation between it and me. There was only we.

Aelith let out a little whimper.

"It's all right, my girl," Banquo told her, reaching out to touch her cheek. "It's all right. We're safe now," he said.

"Say a prayer for this lady. Give your sorrow words," I said, motioning to Andraste. "She has sacrificed herself to save your father's life. May she be reborn into a better world." I reached out and closed Andraste's eyes.

Aelith nodded and began whispering.

A tear trickled down her cheek.

I reached out to wipe it off then hesitated.

Pulling off my gloves, I stared at my hands.

There was nothing there. The spots were gone.

I wiped away my daughter's tear with one hand then took Banquo's hand into the other.

"Cerridwen?" Banquo whispered.

"What's done cannot be undone," I said then gazed at Andraste's still form.

Thank you, Andraste.

CHAPTER FORTY-FIVE

"*H*elp me get him up," I told Nimue who appeared to be in shock. "Nimue!"

"Yes. Yes, all right," she said.

Working together, Nimue and I lifted Banquo to his feet.

"We'll take him to my chamber," I told her.

"Mother," Aelith said, worry in her voice. She held on to the skirt of my dress.

"It's safe here, Aelith. This is a hidden place. No one can come here."

We supported Banquo as we guided him to my old bedchamber. Moving gently, we lay him down on my bed. Banquo groaned.

"Are you in pain?" I asked.

"It's a strange ache," he said.

Blood still marred his skin.

"Can you bring some water?" I asked Nimue.

She nodded then rushed away.

"I know this place," Banquo said. "I was here, once."

"This is the home of the Wyrds."

"That smell…that beautiful flower smell," he said sleepily.

"Rest, my love. You will heal now, but you must rest."

Nimue returned a few moments later carrying a bowl of water. I took it from her and cleaned the blood from Banquo's chest. Again and again, I checked the rhythm of his heart, his breathing, his temperature. He was well. He was in shock and aching, but he would live.

I removed his ripped and bloody shirt then covered him with a blanket. When I was done, I rose.

"We must see to Andraste," I told Nimue.

Nimue, who had gone terribly pale, nodded. I pitied her. She and Andraste had been together for hundreds—hundreds—of years. In a single instant, her sole companion had disappeared.

"Aelith, stay with your daddy," I told the girl.

She nodded but said nothing.

"No wandering out of the temple. I mean it."

She nodded again.

Nimue and I went back to the cauldron terrace.

"What should we do?" I asked Nimue.

"We'll take her to the temple of the Lord of the Hollow Hills."

Bending, Nimue and I gently lifted Andraste. I was amazed at how light she was. Her body was frail, most of her weight coming from her robes. It was not easy carrying her down the steps and into the city, but neither Nimue nor I spoke or complained. We did the task that needed doing.

We walked down the narrow side street and then down into the temple of the Lord of the Hollow Hills. The blue fire in the sconces flickered to light before us. We turned and looked at one another but said nothing.

When we reached the chamber, we went to one of the empty altars and lay Andraste down. Nimue gently folded Andraste's arms across her body.

"Cerridwen, what are we going to do now?" Nimue asked, but my thoughts were distracted.

In the distance, coming from one of the caves, I heard the strangest whisper. Soft voices spoke.

Cerridwen, come. The forest is awake. The forest is alive with fire.

Light flickered in one of the caves, and I recognized the silver etching on the cave walls. It was the tunnel that led to Dunsinane.

"Nimue," I whispered.

"I hear it too. Go, Cerridwen."

"But Banquo and Aelith," I said, hesitating.

"Return to us when the hurly-burly is done. We will wait for you. I will watch over them."

I headed toward the cave. Taking a torch from the wall, I stepped inside the tunnel once more and set off to return to Dunsinane.

CHAPTER FORTY-SIX

*a*s I made my way back, it occurred to me that time had passed in the real world. In the wake of Banquo's death —or, at least, what they would believe to be his death—everything would have fallen into disarray.

I needed to get to Fleance and Lulach. I needed to let them know we were still alive.

As I hurried through the tunnels, I heard strange sounds beyond the rocky hill. The noises confused me. I was glad when I found my way to the court of the Parisi king but struck with a chill when I realized the center brazier was lit. Someone had been here recently. Had Macbeth returned to Dunsinane? How? Surely Killian would have followed him to the ends of the earth for what he had done. Unless Macbeth killed Killian, in which case, they might not even know.

I pulled Uald's Gift and rushed down the hall. As I did so, I heard shouting and saw fire. When I emerged in the yard, I saw soldiers everywhere. Archers were on the wall, shooting flaming arrows into the night. A battalion of men stood ready at the gate as a battering ram crashed into it. Dunsinane was under attack.

"Madelaine," I whispered.

I turned and rushed up the steps toward the second floor. As I passed, the soldiers gawked at me in surprise.

"It's the queen."

"The queen!"

I grabbed a soldier by the arm. "Where is Lady Madelaine?"

"On the third tier, with the king."

Macbeth was here. He was here! That damned, murdering bastard was here.

I raced up the steps. As I did, I felt the raven within me swell in power. My blood thundered, my heart beat wildly. I heard the beat of ravens' wings. Rushing to the third level, I watched as flaming arrows were launched from Dunsinane into the night. Outside the castle walls, men cried out.

As firelight streaked the sky, I spotted Macbeth standing at the wall. He was all alone. He stood, staring down at the forest.

I went to the wall and looked out.

There, I saw something strange.

The woods were moving. Branches and leaves made their way toward the castle.

"Loose," a soldier called from below.

Flaming arrows shot into the night sky once more. As they flew, they illuminated the hill below Dunsinane. The trees were not moving. Those were men. Siward had disguised his army. He had bedecked the soldiers with tree limbs and leaves. Under the flash of firelight, I spotted the colors of Northumbria under the disguise. Siward had used the forest itself to creep in on Dunsinane.

Birnam Wood had come to Dunsinane Hill once more.

I turned and looked at Macbeth. To my great surprise, he had turned and was staring at me.

He wore a white dressing gown and his crown. He held a sword in front of him.

"Are you real?" he asked.

"You're about to find out how real," I answered. Brandishing Uald's Gift, I rushed at him.

Macbeth blocked my attack and spun away.

I swung again. Uald's Gift glimmered in the firelight. Our swords met, and we dueled one another, moving across the stones. My heart beat hard in my chest. I would kill Macbeth. I would kill him, or I would die trying.

"Gruoch," he said, his voice pleading.

Feeling even angrier at the mere thought that he would try to talk to me, try to appease me, I attacked once more, screaming as I advanced on him.

Macbeth fell back, defending himself from my blows.

"Gruoch, I'm sorry," he whispered.

"I am sick to death of everyone's regrets," I said, launching an attack once more.

Macbeth backed toward the wall. Unable to retreat further, he blocked my moves, but he was out of space.

"Loose," a soldier called again, fire illuminating the sky.

In a final effort to save himself, Macbeth swung his blade hard.

To my shock, Uald's Gift flew from my hands and clattered across the flagstones.

Macbeth lowered his blade. "Gruoch," he began, but I rushed him.

I punched him hard in the face, hearing his nose crack, then I wrenched his sword from his hand, throwing it over the wall behind him.

From deep within the castle, there was a terrible commotion. Something crashed.

"The gate is down. The castle is breached," someone screamed.

"Gruoch," Macbeth whispered.

I grabbed the collar of his nightshirt and stared him in the eyes.

With my free hand, I pulled Scáthach from my belt. I sneered at Macbeth then said, "Join your father."

Macbeth's eyes went wide when he eyed the dagger.

With a slash, I opened Macbeth's neck.

Blood splashed all over me as his head lolled, his eyes rolling back into his head.

With a hard shove, I pushed him over the wall. Gripping the stones, I watched as Macbeth fell into the tangle of men, stones, and trees below. The forest swallowed him.

From the castle yard, I heard screaming and the sounds of metal clashing.

"Madelaine," I whispered. I grabbed my sword then raced into the castle. Everywhere I looked, people were fleeing in terror. I ran to Madelaine's chamber and flung open the door.

To my surprise, she was standing by the window, gazing out placidly at her impending doom.

"Madelaine," I called.

Gasping, she turned and looked at me. "Corbie?"

I took her hand. "Come on," I said, then pulled her from the room.

"You're covered in blood," Madelaine said. "Are you hurt?"

"Not yet, but we better move quickly."

We raced down a back stairwell to the second floor. At the other end of the hall, I spotted Siward's men. They were already in the castle.

"This way," I said, pushing aside a tapestry to reveal an opening that led down a flight of stairs to the first level of the castle. When we reached the bottom of the steps, I peered out. Everywhere I looked, I saw soldiers. Luckily, most of them were so engaged that Madelaine and I had a chance to pass through unseen.

I nodded to Madelaine, and we slipped out.

"We need to get to the old part of the castle. Quickly," I told her. We rushed down the corridor. Turning, I spotted one of Siward's men in the hallway ahead of me.

"You there, stop!" he yelled at me.

I grabbed Scáthach by the handle and lobbed her at the man. She hit her mark, knocking the man off his feet as he fell to the floor.

Bending, Madelaine grabbed a sword off a fallen soldier, and we raced down the hallway. I stopped only long enough to grab Scáthach, and we rushed on. The corridors in this part of the castle were dark, winding, and confusing to strangers. I heard the sound of metal as soldiers rushed about the place. I turned a corner, but Madelaine let out a yelp.

"Stop," a soldier called, grabbing Madelaine by the arm.

But he hadn't seen the sword.

Madelaine thrust the weapon in the man's gut.

He groaned and fell.

Pulling out her weapon, she nodded to me.

We passed the ancient hall then followed the steps down to the caves once more. Again, my raven eyes led me.

"Corbie, I can't see anything," Madelaine whispered.

"We will walk between the worlds. Take my hand," I told her then we stepped into the deep, dark passages. We wound through the twisting halls. The sound of men and fighting receded. The air grew cold. I could smell minerals and loam. Not long after, I spotted blue fire ahead of me. Leading Madelaine, we stepped into Ynes Verleath.

CHAPTER FORTY-SEVEN

Madelaine stared wide-eyed as we made our way through the ancient city. I led her up the stairs of the temple. When we reached the top, she stopped and looked out over the city.

"I know this place," she whispered.

"This is the realm of the Wyrds."

"But I know this place."

"Once, long ago, we were all here together. In an ancient life, a forgotten life."

Madelaine turned and looked at me. She eyed my clothes then looked down at her own hands. "Corbie."

"Come," I said, leading her into the temple.

She walked slowly, gazing at the broken statue of the Goddess, past the eternal flame, then to the cauldron terrace.

Guiding Madelaine, I led her to my chamber. There, Banquo slept, his arm around Aelith who was curled up at his side. Nimue rose when we entered.

"Nimue. How is he?" I asked.

She nodded. "He is well. Aching but well. Your little one just fell asleep."

"What happened?" Madelaine asked.

"Macbeth came to Lochaber. He tried to kill Aelith, but Banquo saved her. He was injured," I said, eyeing Nimue. We needed to say no more.

"Aelith," Madelaine said softly. "Oh, Corbie. How beautiful she is."

"Nimue, this is—"

"Elaine. Yes, I know. Welcome, sister. I am Nimue."

Madelaine gave Nimue a weary smile then turned and looked at me. "Corbie, there were dispatches before the attack. Macbeth sent a rider to Lulach. I don't know if word reached him in time."

"I will look," I said.

"And Macbeth?" Madelaine asked.

"He has paid for his treachery."

Madelanie breathed a sigh of relief then nodded.

"Come with me, Elaine," Nimue told my aunt. "There is water and fresh linens here."

Madelaine turned and left with Nimue.

I gazed down at Banquo and Aelith.

Macbeth was gone.

Finally, we were free.

But now what? And at what cost?

I went to the cauldron terrace. When I arrived, however, I found I was not alone.

The red-robed Morrigu waited for me.

We stared at one another.

"Come," she said. "Come and see." Her hand danced over the cauldron.

Reluctantly, I came and stood beside her. I looked into the cauldron then watched events unfold at great speed. I saw Lulach and Fleance on the field, overtaking Siward's army. The Northumbrian forces retreated after the attack on Dunsinane. Lulach and Fleance won the day, repelling the invaders once more.

I saw Macbeth laid to rest on the Isle of Iona.

Gripping the side of the cauldron, I watched Lulach go to Scone, the ancient crown of Moray placed on his head as he sat on the stone of destiny and was declared King of Scotland.

The Morrigu waved her hand over the surface of the cauldron. I saw the coven. There, under the limbs of a tall oak, I saw Fleance lean in and place a soft kiss on Crearwy's lips. Blood dripped from their entwined hands where they had made their hand-fasting cuts.

Again, the Red Lady touched the surface of the cauldron. I saw Lulach at Dunsinane, but shadows surrounded him. Dark, evil things whispered in the corners. In the hallways, in the stairwells, I saw men talk behind my son. I saw coin change hand. Men rode away from Dunsinane to Northumbria where a fair-haired man who looked much like my father stared out the window, his angry blue eyes bent on the north.

"Prince Malcolm," one of the shadowy men whispered. "It is arranged."

The Morrigu touched the surface of the cauldron, and the images disappeared. "You once told me that Lulach was not beholden to me or anyone else. That his fate was his own. But is it? Has Lulach carved out his own destiny as he willed it, as he wishes?" the Morrigu asked.

I glared at her. "Of course he has."

She touched the surface of the cauldron once more, revealing Lulach. He was alone in Birnam Wood. He had come to a ring of standing stones. He wove through them, touching each stone as he passed.

"A different world. A different life. I would give it all away in service of you."

I covered my mouth with my hand.

"Lulach," I whispered, reaching out to touch his reflection.

He paused. "Mother?"

I looked at the Morrigu.

With a wave of her hand, the boundaries between the worlds faded. I saw Lulach before me, standing amongst the stones. He stared at the Morrigu and me.

"My lady," he said, inclining his head to her. He looked at me. "Mother...are you alive?"

"Yes, my son."

"I am king now."

I could feel the Morrigu turn and look at me. I didn't give her the satisfaction of returning her gaze.

"Lulach, you are in great danger," I told him.

He nodded. "I know. They will try to murder me. But isn't it a beautiful day?" he said, motioning to the forest around him.

"Lulach..."

My heart beat hard in my chest. I could hear Lulach's thoughts, I could read his heart. He didn't want any of this. He didn't want to be king. He wanted a life of service; he wanted a life with the gods. *I* had guided his fate. *I* had led him down a path of my choosing. *I* had picked Lulach to be king. I had not hidden him as I had Crearwy. *I* had forced this gentle soul into the world of men. *I* had seen to it that there was a crown placed on his head. For what? I had sacrificed everything; I had given up everything to secure a destiny for Lulach that he didn't want.

I turned to the Morrigu.

"It is not an easy thing to guide people to their fate," she told me. "But you will learn," she said. Much to my surprise, she handed me the crown of Moray.

Taking the crown, I stepped through the gateway into the world.

The warm summer sun shone down on my face. I heard the birds call, and a soft wind swept across the forest, carrying with it the perfume of flowers, ferns, and leaves.

I closed my eyes. "I need you now," I whispered.

The wind blew, the leaves of the trees rustling. I could hear soft whispers on the breeze.

Taking Lulach's hand in mine, I led him to the center of the ring where there was an ancient stone altar. Moss and lichen grew on the sacred stone, nearly covering the faces that had been carved thereon. I handed the crown of Moray to Lulach.

"From this day forth, you shall be the master of your own fate. Choose, my son. Choose what life you will. You are free."

"But...but how?"

"Walk away," I said. "Listen to the trees, if that is your wish. Listen, and you will find the way.

Lulach looked at the crown. "If I leave, I have failed Scotland."

"That is what I told myself too. But there are other ways to serve."

Lulach set the crown of Moray on the altar stone.

"Mother, what about you? What will you do?"

"I am for the Wyrds, as was always intended. And Banquo is with me."

"The Thane of Lochaber lives?"

"He does."

"I must tell Fleance."

"Please do," I said then slipped off the raven torcs on my wrists. "And give these to Crearwy. Tell her they are a bridal gift from her mother," I said, handing them to Lulach. "Tell her and Fleance to follow their hearts. That they are beholden only to one another. I free her from any obligation I ever laid upon her. I love her, and I set her free."

Lulach flexed his brow, a move he had made a thousand times since he was born, then he nodded. "And Aelith?"

"You will see her soon."

Lulach nodded. "Thank you, Mother."

A horse whinnied. Lulach and I turned to see Arden, the priestess from Birnam grove, there.

"Go, my son. The green calls you."

Lulach looked at Arden, a curious expression on his face. He turned back to me. "I love you, Mother."

"I love you too," I whispered, then closed my eyes and willed my spirit onward.

A moment later, I found myself standing beside a brook. Water fell gently into a pool at its base. The surface of the water rippled as a fey thing bobbed on the frothy waves. Grinning mischievously, Sid splashed water at me. She laughed when the droplets passed through me.

"Well, finally did it, eh?" she said.

"Did what?"

"Became the raven."

"Yes."

She nodded then dunked under the water. After a moment, she broke the surface once more, gasping for breath. She pushed her hair away from her face. "I hate that city of yours. It's too dark," she said with a frown. "But I suppose I'll come anyway."

"Good. Otherwise, I'd have to force you there. But, Sid, I need your help. I must bring—"

"Mad Elaine. I know. We've been waiting for her. Our ninth will return to us once more but this time as the crone. Tell her to come when she is ready."

"I will. I don't know yet what we will do about Aelith."

Sid shrugged. "The answer will come to you in time, raven beak."

"Sid," I said with a shake of my head. She could make light of the most serious matters.

She grinned wickedly at me. "Now go away, and no spying on me through that cauldron of yours."

I laughed. "I love you, Sid."

"I love you too. Now, go run away with Banquo," Sid called then disappeared under the water once more.

Laughing, I closed my eyes.

*M*y body swooned, and once again, I found myself standing at the cauldron terrace. I breathed in the heavy scent of wisteria. A strange sense of peace came over me.

"Cerridwen?" Banquo called.

"Coming. I'm coming," I said then turned and left it all behind.

AUTHOR'S NOTE

Thank you for reading *The Celtic Blood Series*. This series has been an important part of my life for more than a decade. I am so pleased to bring you Gruoch's final chapter. As you know, I started writing this series many, many years ago. When I started revising *Highland Queen*, I realized the book needed a complete overhaul. Gruoch has become a part of me, and the first draft of this novel did not give her, or many of the other characters, the endings they deserved. Just to give you an idea, in the first draft of *Highland Queen*, Banquo, Sid, Madelaine, and Lulach were all violently murdered. Sid's death was the worst. I shudder to think of it. When it came time to complete this series, I realized the story I'd written in the first draft was no longer the story I wanted to tell. Killing Sid would have been like killing *Harry Potter's* Hagrid. You just don't do that! I hope you enjoyed the way the story ended. I loved that Madelaine finally showed her MacAlpin blood in those last moments—she surprised me with that one. And Macbeth got what he deserved. He knew Scáthach was after him.

I am sure you are wondering what happens next for Crearwy, Lulach, Fleance, Aelith, and the others. One day, I will write an epilogue for you. But for now, please know they go on to have happy-enough lives. Not perfect, but Gruoch sacrificed for them. Those sacrifices will not have been in vain.

As for the historical elements of this final book, I found myself at a crossroads. The purpose of this novel was to tell Gruoch's tale, snatching her back from William Shakespeare and giving her life context and meaning. In order to stay in line with Shakespeare's story, I bent a few historical details here and there. The real Macbeths ruled peacefully a bit longer than in this novel. The real Macbeth was eventually killed by Malcolm, son of Duncan, at Lumphanan. To this day, there is a stone in Lumphanan called Macbeth's stone, which marks where Macbeth was beheaded. This stone is in my series. Macbeth and Gruoch meet for the first time beside this stone in *Highland Vengeance*. Lulach did become King of Scotland following Macbeth's death. He ruled for a year, and it is recorded that he was killed by deceit (aka, assassinated). Malcolm, son of Duncan, takes the throne after Lulach. Research yielded other fun details that found their way into the book. Once upon a time, there was a Stone Age fortress on Dunsinane Hill. Only the foundation remains now. But in the 11th century, there would have been a castle on the hill. I enjoyed imagining what that castle might have looked like. Thorfinn and Macbeth did go on pilgrimages to Rome. It's unclear if they went together or separately. In the end, Shakespeare maligned Lady Macbeth. The real Macbeths were good, peaceful rulers.

As for Ynes Verleath, I'll leave it up to you and your raven eyes to determine if that is fact or fiction.

Thank you for taking this journey with me.

Much love,
    Melanie

THE ROAD TO VALHALLA

SHIELD MAIDEN
Under The
Howling Moon

NEW YORK TIMES BESTSELLING AUTHOR
MELANIE KARSAK

WHAT TO READ NEXT

Ready to dive into a new historical fantasy world? I invite you to meet Hervor, the legendary shield-maiden in my *Road to Valhalla* series. This series, like the *Celtic Blood* series, dives into a mystical, pre-Christian world—this time, the Norse gods and Scandinavia — while following the life of an amazing woman.

SHIELD-MAIDEN: UNDER THE HOWLING MOON

CHOSEN BY ODIN. DESTINED FOR VALHALLA.

In my dreams, Odin whispers to me.
He tells me I'm destined to wield a legendary sword.
He tells me my road will bring me to Valhalla.
But when wake, I'm only Hervor. Fatherless. Unloved. Unwanted.
Jarl Bjartmar, my grandfather, despises me. My mother has forgotten me. Everyone tells me I should have been left in the forest for the wolves. But no one will tell me why.

None but Eydis, a thrall with völva magic, seems to believe I'm meant for a greater destiny. Yet who can believe a devotee of Loki?

When the king and his son arrive for the holy b*lót*, the runes begin to fall in my favor. A way forward may lie in the handsome Viking set on winning my heart, but only if I unravel the mystery hanging over me first.

Fans of *Vikings* and *Mists of Avalon* will relish *Shield Maiden: Under the Howling Moon*. This sweeping **Viking Historical Fantasy** retells the Norse *Hervarar Saga*, depicting the life of the shield-maiden Hervor, the inspiration for J. R. R. Tolkien's *Éowyn*.

GET SHIELD-MAIDEN: UNDER THE HOWLING MOON ON AMAZON!

ABOUT THE AUTHOR

Melanie Karsak is the author of *The Harvesting Series, The Celtic Blood Series, The Steampunk Red Riding Hood Series, Steampunk Fairy Tales,* and *The Chancellor Fairy Tales.* A steampunk connoisseur, zombie whisperer, and Shakespeare junkie, the author currently lives in Florida with her husband and two children.

facebook.com/authormelaniekarsak

twitter.com/melaniekarsak

instagram.com/karsakmelanie

pinterest.com/melaniekarsak

bookbub.com/authors/melanie-karsak

Golden Braids and Dragon Blades: Steampunk Rapunzel

Steampunk Red Riding Hood:

Wolves and Daggers

Alphas and Airships

Peppermint and Pentacles

Bitches and Brawlers

Howls and Hallows

Lycans and Legends

The Airship Racing Chronicles:

Chasing the Star Garden

Chasing the Green Fairy

The Chancellor Fairy Tales:

The Glass Mermaid

The Cupcake Witch

The Fairy Godfather

Made in the USA
Las Vegas, NV
09 August 2021